Love is Darkness

CAROLINE HANSON

Also by Caroline Hanson:

>Bewitching the Werewolf

>Love is Fear (Dec. 2011)

Copyright © Caroline Hanson 2011

Published by Host of the Hills Publishing

Cover Illustration by Phat Puppy Art.

This is a work of fiction any resemblance to persons living or dead is purely coincidental All Rights Are Reserved. No part of this book may be used or reproduced in any manner whatsoever without written permission from the author.

ACKNOWLEDGMENTS

I want to thank my husband for being supportive and inspiring. This time I'm not kidding or being sarcastic when I say—you're a great man of our time.

To my two little girls who really are the sweetest children ever. And if you tell them differently, they'll make you regret it.

Finally, to my friends—writers and non-writers both—who read the stupid thing when it was an abominable mess and still managed to look me in the eye and lie well enough to keep me plugging away.

Thank you!

PROLOGUE

PRAGUE, CZECH REPUBLIC
15 YEARS AGO

He wasn't God.

Although there had been a handful of years between his ascendancy to the throne and the killing of the Others, where he may as well have been. The world had not only responded to his whims but feared them.

He wasn't Death.

He'd created death, given death, even taken death away by making someone immortal. But Death had never come for him.

Time to rethink that one.

He supposed it was fitting that he would die like Gaius. Lucas, a 900 year old, vampire 'upstart', had walked straight up to him and cut off his head without Gaius even blinking in protest. One swing of his sword, a clearing of ash and he had taken the throne.

Gaius had sat there for weeks, staring at nothing like a mindless fool, until Lucas had decided it was enough, that faded glory and reverence only lasted for so long.

But now Death was stalking *him*, sinking claws into him slowly and sweetly so that he barely noticed. Did it matter? Did he care? If he went back into that catatonic state and never came out again, would it be so bad?

He shuffled memories like a deck of cards in his mind, turning over static pictures of his life: himself laughing, despairing, fighting, even fucking. Events that should prompt vividly colored reactions, yet all he felt was gray.

From birth he had known his death would be in battle, fighting for something with all his heart. And *that's* how he knew he wasn't Death. Because Death knew what he wanted and was able to keep it well out of reach.

The sound of wild masculine laughter floated up the stairs to his room and Lucas returned to himself quickly, his heart thundering loudly as it sped up, momentarily blotting out the sound from below. His heartbeat calmed and he blinked, thick, dark lashes shuttering his pale blue eyes. There was a rustle of silk outside the door; Marion was coming.

He'd sired her centuries ago. She knocked and he bid her to enter. Almost quivering with agitation she went down on one knee, head bowed modestly.

"My King, Roberto has returned from the New World. I would ask that you come to see him, if it pleases you."

A thread of excitement weaved through her words. She was uncommonly tall, almost six feet, and painfully thin, her features sharp and harsh. Marion's hair was a vivid auburn, her eyes forest green. She looked just as she had at eighteen, the year she had died and become a vampire. But centuries of hard living, dissipation and unhappiness had hardened her, leaving their mark upon her frailness so that her vitality was a brittle mask.

Lucas stood and went down the stairs, the vampire guards straightening as he passed with Marion at his heels like a vengeful spaniel. The New World she called it, as though she'd never heard of the United States of America.

He looked at the grandfather clock as he passed, noting that it was now the 30th and he'd been inward for... *twenty one days. Was it possible?* His hands tightened into fists and he felt a pang of worry that the episodes were getting longer.

In the entryway to the great hall, Lucas and Marion came to a halt, taking in the tableau before them. The room was almost empty and dimly lit. A vaulted ceiling was high over-head, the beams dark with age. A gigantic limestone fireplace dominated one wall, necessary to generate enough warmth for the room which could easily seat two hundred people for dinner.

Roberto was standing on a table, walking heel to toe in a careful process like he was drunk. He began singing, a soft song in Spanish.

"What did you do?" Lucas' voice was deep and deceptively calm as he eyed the vampire up and down before pulling out a chair from the dining room table and sitting, crossing his legs casually as he studied Roberto.

"I was in California, and I found a woman," he started giggling then tried to stop. "She was like...flowers, like drugs or candy—" He gave a loose shrug, like he was giving up on finding the right words.

There was a long pause and when he spoke again his voice sounded dreamy, maybe even a little regretful. "Stupid to have drunk her in one." He sighed, his red lips tilting downwards into a frown. "Her blood burned me it was so sweet. An explosion and now it's like colors racing through me."

Lucas stayed still. He didn't want to make any gesture that might betray his shock. "Everyone out."

Marion waited as though 'everyone' didn't include her. After all these centuries did she finally think she was powerful enough to challenge him? Then she bowed and left. He dismissed her from his mind. She was irrelevant.

As soon as the room was empty, Lucas began asking questions. "How many people did you kill?"

"Just the one! But her daughter was there. Saw the whole thing. Don't know if she'd taste that good."

"What is the family name?"

Roberto looked up, a cunning expression on his ferret-like face. "Why? You want some, too? I would be happy to take you. Umm, the name. Happy, no that's not it. Dee—oh wait. *Dearborn*. I think." Then he laughed again.

Roberto was behaving like he'd drunk the blood of an empath. But they were extinct. It was impossible. When was the last time he'd drunk from an empath? Four, five hundred years ago?

Lucas remembered the man clearly. The bold, intense flavor of the blood as it had coursed down his throat. Like drinking wine instead of vinegar. Afterwards, he'd gone berserk, killing humans and vampires alike until the gamut of emotion had fled and left him yearning for death.

Only Marion had risked coming to find him, his murderous rage keeping the others away. She'd found him in Austria, next to the lake he'd grown up on, crying and waiting for the dawn to kill him. Marion had held his hand and spoken to him soothingly, her maternal instincts at the fore as she convinced him it was just the blood and the empath's magic that made him so upset, he didn't really want to die. Didn't want to kill everyone he met.

When she'd tugged him up off the ground, the sky pink and yellow with the coming sun, he'd gone with her, feeling wrecked and defenseless. She'd led him to safety, finding them refuge in a cemetery. The same cemetery where he'd buried his wife and children centuries before.

Lucas had dreamed and felt, reduced to near humanity all because of that man's blood. They'd been a vampire's biggest weakness, both a curse and a balm. A drug that he'd thought long exterminated. But here was Roberto, high as a kite, reeking of magic and blood, the woman's bright scent on his clothes and skin.

Dangerous. But his fangs ached from the sudden craving that swamped him. Even after the last time, the pain he'd felt, he still wanted it. At least it was emotion, something to feel when all he'd felt for hundreds of years was empty darkness.

It would be madness to indulge; a potential nightmare instead of Roberto's drunken happiness.

But the woman was dead, wasn't she?

No revenge, no psychic connection where she could control him and manipulate his feelings. Roberto said there was a daughter, but her blood might be normal, the power an aberration. This could be the last chance to experience an empath's gifts.

Decision made, Lucas grabbed Roberto, biting into his neck before Roberto could defend himself. Blood coursed into him with a hot rush. The taste was bitter because it came from another vampire, but underneath that was a faint sweetness and spice that infected him.

Just a taste and then I'll stop.

He knew that for a lie. He'd stop only when the blood finished riding him.

Lucas drank furiously, like he'd just emerged from the desert, some unknown amount of time passing before he became aware of himself and his surroundings. Gathering himself, he forced himself to slow his drinking, feeling a physical pain as he released fangs from flesh.

He threw Roberto from him and Roberto scrambled away, his hand at his neck, holding the torn flesh together.

Lucas paced away from Roberto, hand over his mouth. *What am I doing?* His hand was frozen, blood coating his lips and now his fingers.

He wanted to lick his lips, suck his fingers clean, go back to Roberto and find more. *What a mistake.*

His hand trembled, in moments he'd be overwhelmed.

His whole body pulsed in time to his heart, the blood snaking through him, leaving each nerve, blood vessel and cell altered and waiting for the magic to strike.

He was a rod in a lightning storm.

Was there even time to dispose of Roberto before he succumbed to the blood? He had to kill him, couldn't risk anyone finding out about the daughter.

The daughter.

Swiftly, he went back to Roberto, circling behind the crying man, hiding death for a few moments longer. With one solid blow his fist punched through Roberto's back and into his chest, gripped the man's heart in his hand and tugged it free, Roberto dissolving into ash.

Lucas felt caged, the need to move, run, cry, laugh and hurt all vying in him for control.

No.

He could control himself. After almost two thousand years he was his own master. He was the oldest and the strongest. Lucas was his own law.

His hands clenched.

Emotion touched him like a cattle prod and he fell to his knees, dead heart pounding in a staccato rhythm. His hand rose to his chest like he could catch the sharp pain knifing from his heart outwards.

Then it was gone. For just a second he thought that was it, that over the last four hundred years he'd become so deadened and powerful that the magic touched him, sputtered and died.

Then there was a pulse.

It's not over.

A small kiss of sensation that was almost visible, like heat shimmering off asphalt, tickled down his spine.

This was a fatal mistake.

Emotion crashed over him. Feelings of joy filling him until he wanted to laugh like Roberto had, laugh like he was happy, carefree and mortal. But he couldn't remember how to laugh, a rough sound erupting from him instead.

The feeling changed, became a heavy pulse that left a deep throb in his sex. He was suddenly hard, full to bursting, aching painfully. Desire gripped him and he began to tremble in his need to—

No.

But the blood twisted through him, invaded every cell and molecule of his being, urging him onwards.

He'd forgotten this power. The tide of emotion that even a small amount of blood had upon him.

He'd known and forgotten.

Lucas remembered being a man, the pleasure taken and given. He could almost smell feminine heat around him, what it was like to feel a woman's thighs lock around his head in pleasure. The whimpering cries as he kissed her deeply. Once he'd become a vampire, sensations and feelings had become muted, but not now. Now he felt human again.

Desire became a fire within him, consumed him so that he was nothing but need. He fell to his knees, staring at his fisted hands. He swore, surprised to find his own hand gripping his cock. His hips rose jerkily, body demanding release even as his mind resisted.

And lost.

His whole body seized, feelings of pleasure twisting within him, the power rebounding. He shouldn't fight it, he knew that, but it went against his nature to give in, and so he tried to hold out against the blood's call.

His breath sawed out of him as he remembered the blood's rich sweetness. He squeezed himself reflexively, the memory of flavor flashing through his mind and then his body.

Like a landslide, the orgasm swept through him, his mental shields collapsing and he felt the heavy spasm of his cock as he came. He breathed heavily, unable to move as the aftershocks of pleasure gripped and released him.

An empath.

Stumbling to his feet, Lucas went to his rooms, discarding his clothes haphazardly on his way to the shower.

His mind raced and he remembered the world as it had been centuries ago. An uneasy balance of vampires, witches, werewolves, empaths and Fey. For centuries there had only been vampires, the Others gone. But an empath had escaped. Maybe the vampires were not as alone as he'd thought. Maybe the Others were scattered or hiding.

What if they could come back? Restore a balance to the world and keep vampires under control. Could he find them? Did he want to?

The thought was... intriguing.

And then he remembered the dead empath had a daughter.

Interesting.

CHAPTER 1

SAN LOARAN, CALIFORNIA
5 YEARS AGO

"Why?" Valerie's heart was hammering in her chest, a dull ringing in her ears. *If I puke, I hope it's on his shoes.* She inhaled deeply, trying to keep the nausea at bay.

She looked around the living room, at the boring furniture, the slider that led to the backyard, then to the front door, which she'd no doubt be leaving through in a few minutes. Unless she was crafty. Who was she kidding? The odds of her being crafty enough to get out of this were just about as good as a hamster seeing a shiny new wheel and choosing not to run.

I might die and I can barely drive.

Her father, Nate, looked at her disappointedly. "Valerie, I've been lenient with you. I had hoped that given a little distance, a little time to mature, you would get over your fear, but that hasn't happened. Don't you want to survive?"

This is a trick question. Val felt her palms get damp as she tried to think of the right thing to say—something that would make him leave her alone. If she said she could defend herself he'd want her to prove it. But, if she said she *couldn't* defend herself, then he'd take her out there to learn. *This is so messed up.*

Jack stood beside her father, examining the floor and trying not to draw attention to himself. He was 19, her father's apprentice, and the star of every fantasy she had. And it was always a fantasy, because in real life he didn't want her. And he certainly wasn't going to stand up for her like a fantasy man should.

Jack probably knew she'd attack him if he tried to leave her here with dad while he snuck off, so he stood there, but he wouldn't help. Jack was *too* good. He owed her father, was grateful that he'd given Jack a purpose in life.

Her father gave an impatient sigh and she tried to remember the question. Oh yeah, *don't you want to survive?* She felt the tension building, her father becoming frustrated by her silence.

She gave them an overly bright smile, hoping it would make her dad think she wasn't about to pee her pants. "I have a quiz tomorrow in science and I'm not ready. Doesn't school come first?"

Her father was a tall, thin man. His hair had been light brown but was now mostly gray. His eyes were brown and sad. In old pictures, his eyes were different.

Valerie thought grief from her mother's death had changed them, sucked the vitality right out of them. Even though her mom's death had been over a decade ago, he still hadn't recovered.

He never would.

Those sad brown eyes stared at her like he was deciding whether or not to confront her on her probable lie. She *did* have a science quiz tomorrow, but she wasn't worried about it, knew she'd get an A. But did *he* know that?

"I'm sure we will be home in time for you to study." Nate raised an eyebrow at her.

Could an eyebrow express 'gotcha'? Apparently.

"Perhaps next time you can study appropriately, during the allotted time, and then you won't find yourself with a time conflict. Life is about juggling obligations, Valerie. You need to study smarter, not harder." *Great. What did that even mean? If I could study smarter, wouldn't I be doing it already?*

"You're right! That's why I make sure to do my homework *before* cheerleading, and stay at school to do it. That's why I get to school *early* on Wednesday so that I can go to swim team." Her voice was rising and she felt some air quotes coming on, "If I have *warning* I can put it in my schedule and study "appropriately". Surprisingly, random vampire stake-outs don't fit into my schedule easily." Crossing her arms under her chest defiantly, she waited for the verdict.

He gave a small frown and turned to Jack who was being 'one' with the wall. *Yeah, you're still here, you jerk.*

"What about you Jack? You seem to make it all fit and you're in college. That's a lot harder than high school, Valerie. How do you plan on being successful if you can't schedule your days?"

"My back up plan is to drop out and get pregnant," she said.

Jack's shoulders straightened a little, pulling at the corners of his long sleeved black t-shirt. His lips thinned in disapproval, perhaps a hint of a smile, but she doubted it.

"Yes, because the one thing that will give you more time to get school work done is to have a child out of wedlock." He shook his head, "Just go get in the car."

Nate turned away from her and she heard him mutter something about pitchers, or catchers, something sports related, and Jack gave a stilted laugh.

She went to the car and sat in the backseat, waiting for them to come out. Morbidly, she began imagining all the terrible things that might happen to her tonight. She imagined her father dying, a vampire drinking Jack's blood, then discarding him and coming for her. She slapped her hands on her thighs, trying to distract herself.

Impending death requires chocolate.

Val reached into her back pack and found a pack of M and M's. By the time the guys got to the car she'd eaten all the red, orange and brown ones separating them out into little piles that rolled around the seats and occasionally vanished. She looked at her watch. *Well, that took care of five minutes.*

Her father opened the back door and threw a huge, orange duffel bag of weapons down next to her, the wood making a hollow thunking sound as the stakes bounced against each other.

The station wagon backed out of the driveway and Valerie looked longingly at her room as they drove away. She turned back to the front and saw Jack watching her in the rear-view mirror, his slate-gray eyes intense. She stuck her tongue out at him and slouched back into her seat, hoping he wouldn't see her blush.

Jack was so impossible lately. He was high on power now that her father had started taking him places. It seemed like he was always watching her in a disappointed way, looking for faults and quick to 'helpfully' criticize. Jack said it was 'helpful' because it was in her best interest.

They were both so worried about her staying alive and yet tonight they were taking her to fight a vampire. How could they not see the logical flaw? If she was the Einstein of this group then they were in deep crap.

Jack had studied martial arts since coming to America with them at the age of thirteen. Now he was nineteen and he'd been going with her father to hunt for three years. He wanted to be here, whereas she was being dragged to her doom. What would she do if a vampire tried to attack her again? Val almost moaned in fear. Where was Child Protective Services when she needed them?

She chastised herself, rubbed her hands together and thought about her 'game face'. Was that the same as a poker face? Val needed to be irritated and sarcastic, that was her fall back persona when her father was trying to get her killed. "Wax on, wax off," she mumbled.

They drove down the Garden Highway, a two lane stretch of road that was sparsely populated and next to the river. It started in San Loaran but went for miles. It was dark, the city lights far away. If she were a vampire she'd live downtown. How the hell did this guy get food when he was so far away from everything?

"So, what's the deal with this clown?" Val asked.

Her father kept looking at his map of the area, ignoring her. He'd already been out here during the day, so she didn't know why he was looking at the map anyway. They pulled off the road and onto a dirt track, bumping along for a mile or two before turning down another path, this one graveled. The car stopped in front of an old cemetery that was in the middle of nowhere. Her stomach flip flopped.

"A cemetery?" she said plaintively, "Why is he living in a cemetery? Couldn't we have come for him during the day?"

Nate turned around and gave her an irritated look. "No, we couldn't come for him during the day. We tracked him here yesterday but he disappeared. I'm not sure where he's staying. He could be underground, in a family crypt, I just couldn't tell. And before you ask, we can't wait because he's already killed someone. I won't risk him doing it again just to make our lives a little easier. If we catch him when he's just starting to rise, he'll be confused and it should be relatively easy."

She didn't like the way he said we. "Yes, *you* will. I'm sure the both of *you* will have a very easy time staking him."

Her father's voice was quiet. "You listen to me, Valerie. I think you have been sheltered quite long enough. Being lenient with you hasn't sweetened your personality either. Tonight, you are going to help. I'm not asking you to fight. You can stay near the car, but if we need weapons you will be expected to bring them, do you understand?" He had a mean stare and wasn't shy about using it.

Valerie's mouth flopped open and closed like a fish. She looked to Jack, but he was staring at the road and staying out of it. *Wuss*. She felt the anger rising up like a fist inside of her, choking her.

Nate undid his seatbelt and got out of the car, started walking towards the side where the weapons were. Jack undid his seat belt slowly and she knew he was about to say something supportive.

"Don't bother. If you knew how much I wanted to hit something right now, you'd keep your mouth shut."

Jack put up his hands, like he was surrendering to the police, and then got out of the car, slamming the door shut behind him. She heard him say something to Nate but didn't know what it was.

Val threw her door open and stuck a leg out but she'd been too aggressive and the door rebounded back on her, slamming into her shinbone. She managed to hold back a yelp of pain, but felt stupid and even angrier.

Her father took the weapons from the backseat and set them on the hood of the car. Jack was right behind him and she was relieved they hadn't noticed her klutziness. A helpful lecture about how anger 'hurts us more than anyone else' would have sent her screaming off into the woods, vampires be damned.

She limped to the front of the car, thinking she should 'shake it off', and about how the pain was 'getting better'. It was, honestly! Any moment now she wouldn't notice it and tomorrow how she'd *laugh*.

Her leg began to throb.

The sun was almost down and vampy would be stumbling out of his crypt pretty soon. Jack and her father were ready: a knife strapped to one forearm, a stake on the other, spare gun in a shoulder holster and some holy water sitting on the hood.

Her leg tickled and she looked down at her calf, blood staining the leg of her pants. Shit, she'd cut herself on the stupid door! Her father was striding off towards the crypt but Jack was looking at her leg and he looked worried. He took a step closer to her, and she could smell his woodsy cologne. Jack was taller than her father, but lean, his teenage metabolism devouring the fat from his body.

His dark, coffee colored hair was a bit tousled from running his hands through it, a five o' clock shadow visible on his jaw.

"You should get in the car. You can't be out here with a bleeding leg, it will draw them to you like...well, like vampires to blood." His tone was worried, urgent as he tracked the darkening skyline.

She wasn't sure what to do. Her dad had told her to stay out and help but man she wanted to be in the car with the doors locked. Val heard the sound of grating stone—harsh and loud. Jack swore, then ran towards Nate.

"Get into the car!" he shouted over his shoulder.

She stood indecisive for a moment and then decided Jack was right. Lord knew there would be other vampires she could help with. She watched for a moment longer, Nate and Jack with their guns drawn, ready to shoot the monster that came out.

As she reached for the door, a pale, hairy hand appeared in front of her, holding the door closed.

Her eyes jerked up, taking in the vampire who looked at her like she was a deep fried Twinkie at the state fair. He was close to her height, his eyes a glowing honey-brown.

He shoved her, knocking the wind out of her so she couldn't scream, her chin hitting the hard metal roof of the car before his cold hand clamped around her mouth, dirty nails digging into her cheeks.

She felt the drag of gravity as he leapt, forcing them upwards and away. It was different than flying, as though he'd bounded into the air, using all the power his body contained to propel them into the sky.

The ground shrank as he took them thirty feet into the air. As soon as they landed, he'd kill her, she thought frantically. Jack and her father were in the crypt and she knew they hadn't seen the vampire take her.

Val's whole body shook with fear, and the way the vampire's arms clamped tighter around her, his body pressed flush to hers as though he knew she was terrified, and liked it, made her skin crawl. He was like a python, squeezing a little tighter with each frantic exhalation. She reached for the stake in her pocket, her wrist turned at a painful angle so she could reach it.

Don't make it too easy.

The wood was warm in her hand from her tight grip. Adjusting the stake, she turned her wrist so that it was angled towards his body. His feet hit the ground and as he bent his legs to absorb the shock, the stake sunk into his stomach. She heard a startled grunt and he pushed her away, the stake sticking out of his stomach. She fell forward hard, her knees jarring painfully upon impact, even though he'd borne most of their weight.

Scrambling frantically, she tried to get to her feet and run but he recovered, grabbing her ankle and pulling her back to him.

Her fingers clawed into the ground, trying to stop her backwards slide. Her nails caught and broke; small pine needles and bits of leaves forcing their way deep into each nail bed.

I'm going to die in the damned woods. I knew it! Although it would have been nice to be wrong this time.

Then everything got worse. Another vampire appeared, landing in front of her. His movements were too quick, his landing too graceful to be anything but vampire. Her eyes swam with tears, making him a blurry image of black clothing and golden hair.

It was fully dark, and the only light came from the moon, giving his paleness an odd cast. She saw long hair, golden and straight, that fell halfway down his back, but his face was shadowed. He was a giant, towering over her and the vampire who knelt behind her. The golden vampire crouched to his knees before her, forearms resting loosely on his thighs.

His face was close to hers, the desire to scream choked in her chest by his proximity. His cold hardness slapped at her, feeling like an almost physical barrier between them. He was hard and terrifying. The most terrifying vampire she had ever seen because he was beautiful. He was death and she wanted to touch him. Then he spoke to her and it was like all the blood in her body wanted to well to the surface and spill out towards him.

"Be still Valerie. You will be well."

She heard a huff behind her and the vampire who was gripping her leg, suddenly let go. He swatted her on the butt before moving away a little. "Don't you go anywhere," her captor said, like she was a disobedient animal. He had a rough accent. Irish, maybe?

Then he ignored her, turning to the golden one who was still next to her.

"Well, that's a bit rich. She'll only be well in my stomach. What brings you out on a nice night like tonight, my Lord?"

"You do," the golden vampire said, his voice gravelly and dark.

"I don't share well, but it would be an honor to make an exception for you, my Lord. In fact, we can celebrate! What's it been now, ten years? Five? Who knows, am I right or am I not wrong?" He laughed, as if keeping track of time was a crazy concept.

Val needed to move but couldn't. Frozen like a rabbit, she trembled and tried to think about what she should do. She wasn't five anymore. She wouldn't lay here and let them kill her when they got around to it. She wouldn't be her mother. *Then run you damned fool! Run!*

"This one is forbidden. You will release her."

The man chuckled, "She's a bit young for you and scrawny to boot. I'm surprised. Not your usual style, Lucas."

Her arms jerked under her, ready to push herself up and run away. Then Lucas put his hand on her jaw, searing her like dry ice, forcing her to look into his blue eyes. And she didn't want to run away anymore.

Lucas.

King of them all. It would be worse—much worse, to die by his hand. *Because I wouldn't fight him.* His strength and emptiness, the lack of pity and kindness made promises deep inside of her. Those cerulean eyes still held her tight, and she heard herself sob, hoping it was someone else.

He compelled her with his voice. "Stay there Valerie Dearborn. Stay there and be calm."

Val blinked and tried to move, but couldn't, his words locking her limbs into place. She felt an artificial calmness come over her, her back shifting so that she could settle against the tree more comfortably and wait.

Trees surrounded them from all sides, casting long inky shadows that would, at another time, have been scary. But there was no point in being scared of what might be lurking in the shadows when the biggest bad, of all big bads, was gazing at her intently.

The calmness he told her to feel weighed on her oppressively, snaked into her thoughts, like sleep trying to claim her. She knew that if she relaxed at all it would overcome her, and she wouldn't fight but give in to it utterly. Tears coursed down her cheeks as the vampires both watched her impassively, waiting for her to succumb to Lucas' commands.

The shorter vampire crossed his arms, head tilting to the side lightly, "That's interesting, isn't it? Quite resistant to your compulsion. Think you're losing your touch?"

Lucas seemed to ignore him, his eyes fixed on Valerie. She could see him looking at her face: her mouth, hair, chin, forehead, back to her lips and settling on her eyes.

Val looked away. She took a deep breath and watched her hand, tried to make a fist, wanting her own body to obey her will. She tried to stay afraid and belong to herself despite his compulsion.

But it's so hard.

His golden hair was shining, even in the dark, and Valerie watched it with deep fascination. She lifted a hand and hit the ground hard, the pain breaking up his insidious words. His power receded and she thought she was almost free of him, but then her gaze met his, and his power coursed over her again, like a big wave knocking over a toddler wading in the shallows.

"Calm and still Valerie." His gaze hit her and she was under the waves, the fight over.

Val stopped struggling, the desire to flee, even survive, swallowed by him. *I'll wait for him.* Wait just a minute, until she recovered from the scare she'd had. That was a reasonable thing to do, wasn't it? She could leave later, after...*something*.

The vampires turned away from her, resuming their conversation. "The reason for her protection is none of your concern," Lucas said. The words were cold and flat.

Why are my hands shaking?

I'm scared.

Why?

The vampire looked shocked and surprised at Lucas' words, his features reminding her of a pale pug. "My lord, please, let's be reasonable. I came here to check on my new child, Oliver. He's having some trouble blending in, gone all homicidal. Very disappointing to be sure. This girl, Valerie you say, is with some Hunters. I have to defend myself." He spread his arms out in a 'isn't it obvious' sort of gesture.

Then he looked even more confused. "The girl even *staked* me! Look at that!" He lifted his shirt, a gray t-shirt that said, "The Pogues" on it and which now sported a bloody tear. His skin was parted nastily, the blood viscous and black. Not human.

"Did she?" Lucas said, almost sounding proud.

Valerie looked at the vampire's torn flesh, shaking harder. *I did that*. The calmness was fracturing, tendrils of fear seeping through her mind like ivy. Once the fear consumed her, she'd run.

Lucas turned to look at her, a small frown on his face, as though both disappointed and surprised by her.

"She drew my blood, tried to kill me. Not sure why you have your panties in a twist to be frank." He paused and looked at the golden vampire again. "Err...my lord."

"She is forbidden. The punishment is death." Lucas said, his gaze still fixed on Valerie.

The Irish vampire's eyes were wide in surprise and outrage, "She's not worth all *that*! What do you care about a Hunter's daughter? Tell me what to do to make it right and I'll be on my way. Even take Oliver with me." He tried to make his voice sound reasonable, but fear pitched it higher and the words ran together.

"Oliver will be dead soon."

The man frowned and spoke angrily, "You will let the Hunters take my child? Be damned to you then!" He swung forward in a smooth arc, his fist flying towards Lucas' jaw, but Lucas moved, grabbing the hand in mid-air, inches from his face, holding back the vampire with ease. A terrible smile on his lips.

"You seek to attack *me*?" There was a hint of incredulity to Lucas' words. "Perhaps Marion is correct and I should make more displays of my power." Lucas squeezed the man's hand hard and blood began to drip from his closed fist.

The vampire cried out in pain, kicking hard, wanting to break free of Lucas' grasp. Lucas blocked the kick, squeezing harder and the vampire dropped to his knees in pain. Lucas let go and the man swayed for a moment, gripping his crushed hand protectively. Lucas punched him. His fist making such solid contact that the vampire's face was instantly altered, bones shattered, half of his skull slightly depressed.

Valerie scuttled away from the tree, Lucas' compulsion suddenly falling away like unlocked chains. She stumbled to her feet but he was there in front of her, hand on her chin, wanting her to look at him, trying to take her will away.

She could feel his power directed at her—marching over her skin, waiting for her to open her eyes so she'd be his. Val kicked blindly, making contact with some unknown part of him, hearing a slight oomph in response. And then she was free. He wasn't touching her. She opened her eyes, running forward—and he was in front of her.

This time the wave of power hurt, like a wave of acid taking her under instead of sea water. Her body halted, mid-motion and she waited. The pain vanished, like he'd whipped it away from her, but still she couldn't run away.

Val breathed in and out, then a little faster, making her lungs do what she wanted instead of what he wanted. He wanted her calm, she worked to be wild.

She made her hands open wide, got her toes to curl. She turned, faced the two vampires, unable to leave but terrified of what was going on behind her. When her death came she wanted to see it. Figured the only way she'd get near a man that hot was if he was going to kill her.

Her vision cleared, and she saw that things had changed. While Lucas had been distracted, Mr. Irish had stabbed Lucas. The stake was embedded near his stomach.

Lucas pulled out the stake like removing lint from a sweater—casually, dismissively, as though it made not the slightest impact that he'd been stabbed. Then he tossed it aside and it landed at her feet.

She wanted to reach for it, but her body wouldn't move. What did it mean that he threw that to her?

His control broke again, and Valerie grabbed the stake, gripping it tightly in her right hand. When she looked up, the fight was finished. Mr. Irish was pinned to a tree, Lucas' arms keeping the other still, as he struggled pathetically, only his head thrashing from side to side.

"Goddamn you, Lucas!" her attacker shouted angrily.

"No more talking," Lucas said. Power laced his words and her ears rang from the vibration. The Irish man's eyes widened but he didn't speak, body tense with rage.

"Come to me, Valerie. Come and kill your attacker." His voice was deep and caressing, rubbing over her skin like velvet, burrowing inside of her, the feeling intimate and alien at the same time.

She stopped herself from looking up, not wanting to meet his eyes again. She felt the need to go towards Lucas and do what he bid, but her heart thundered in protest. *He's dangerous. A killer. Going to him is stupid.*

She walked forward.

Wait.

Valerie stopped and imagined her feet rooted into the ground like a tree trunk, refusing to move.

"Look to me," Lucas commanded her gently.

Val made a frustrated sound of betrayal as her body acted without her consent, meeting his flat stare. His blue eyes were pale, shining brightly, almost oddly in the dark. She knew it when their eyes locked, felt it in a real and visceral way. One that was too intimate and personal.

"I release you to yourself."

Valerie's whole body trembled and she felt fear spreading through her, all traces of calmness and restraint gone, like heavy wet clothing removed from her body.

"Kill him, Valerie. He attacked you."

Huh. That's a twist. She shook her head and dropped the stake, hands nerveless in fear. "No. I don't want to."

"Worse will come for you. You must learn to protect yourself. I cannot be here at all times. Do it now and with my protection. No harm shall come to you by my hand."

Her heart leaped. "Why?"

"Your fear is crippling."

No shit.

"Do you want me to compel you? Take your fear from you?" The words were gentle, without judgment for her cowardice but her eyes welled with tears.

"There is no shame in not wanting to be as strong as others expect you to be." His tone matched the dark night around them.

She couldn't speak, panic overwhelming her again. Val took a step backwards and heard Jack's voice calling for her in the distance.

"Valerie, look to me," he said quietly, urging her to trust him. The words were stilted and she realized he had an accent. Nothing easily identifiable, more like he'd spoken dozens of languages over the centuries, acquiring a small accent from each of them. It was lyrical, beautiful even.

And totally irrelevant.

"Why?" The question was insufficient for what she wanted to know. Why would he protect her? Why choose her over a vampire he knew? Why did he care whether she killed a vampire or not? Why did he care whether she lived or died?

"Violence has touched you. Taken from you and you need to know your own strength in return."

She felt a lump in her throat and it made it hard to talk. "What's it to you?" Val dreaded the answer, had no idea what it might be, but was afraid nonetheless.

Lucas ignored her, the quiet of the night registering during the pause.

"Shall I help you?" he said like she was a spooked horse.

She stared hard at the ground. "Compel me, you mean?"

"Yes."

"Will you...release me again?" Why was she even thinking of trusting him? *Because he hasn't killed me yet.* She wanted to freeze time so she could think it through, but she only had *this* moment, and if she didn't keep up, he'd make her fate for her.

The vampire was still struggling, but it was as futile as a moth struggling when a child has it by the wings.

Decide. Run or stay. Her heart pounded ten times louder than the words. But he was a vampire, he'd hear it anyway. "Make me then."

Val looked back to him almost aggressively, deciding to own her decision. She threw herself into his eyes like jumping off a cliff. His will surrounded her until she was floating in the warm sea of his blue eyes, watching actions that belonged to someone else.

It was someone else who gripped the stake tighter. Someone else who walked forward, eye level with the monster who had just been about to kill her. And behind him was Lucas his large presence overshadowing everything else. She smoothed the rumpled Pogues t-shirt, wanting to hit his heart on the first try.

She struck hard and fast but the stake didn't go in far enough. Val tried again, using two hands and pressing forward, all of her weight pushing forward. It was like cutting a grisly steak with a plastic knife.

"Harder," Lucas said.

Val heard a grunt—her own—and pushed, her arms burning with exertion, until the stake slid forward and the vampire paused in mid-struggle.

His skin turned ashen then disintegrated, bones falling around the stake and clunking to the ground before her, dust settling on her tennis shoes. Her momentum carried her forward, the stake still raised, about to pierce Lucas. Deftly, he turned and caught her, his strong hands gripping her arms, keeping her and the stake away from him.

"I think one vampire is sufficient for tonight," he said dryly.

Val stepped backwards and looked up into his eyes. She thought of a gas fire, the blue that surrounded the flames, the same color and heat of his eyes.

"I release you," he said softly, looking down at her.

Valerie came back to herself, the blue ocean throwing her out, cold night air biting through her clothing, her shin painful and still bleeding. She looked down at the wound, then back up but Lucas was gone.

She heard Jack calling her. Dropping the stake, she ran; calling for Jack and her father, tripping over tree roots and slipping on damp leaves as she followed Jack's voice back to the car.

Her father looked her over, disappointment, maybe even irritation, etched on his face. "See Jack, I told you she was fine. You think that's a funny game, Valerie? Run off into the woods and scare us witless? If you couldn't help, or I guess *wouldn't* help, then you should have stayed in the car. You were stupid and reckless, Valerie." Her father strode to the driver's side of the car and got in, leaving Val in the cold night air.

She supposed she should tell him what had happened. But she didn't want to.

Did she fear Lucas? Hell, yeah! She wasn't a total idiot. But would he hurt her?

No.

Her mind and body knew it, the answer resonating through her like the vibrations of a bell. Part of her wondered how she could know, wondered at the risk she was willing to take, and then that worry resolved too. Irrationally, she knew. He wouldn't hurt her.

They drove home in silence and Valerie went to bed thinking about Lucas and her decision to stay quiet. He'd known her name, protected her, and tried to help her get over her fear. Even though she hadn't been in control of her actions, she felt a little better, like she'd kind of done it, and could *maybe* protect herself in the future.

He was like Lucifer, the angel so beautiful that all others paled in comparison. Men didn't look like him, features so bold and striking, so harsh and perfect that he was frightening. When she thought about boys, she thought about Jack. She spent most of her time imagining kissing Jack, she'd even *dreamed* about it.

Lucas was not a boy.

Lucas wasn't the stuff of girlish fantasies. He was too predatory to fantasize about. It was like a kitten admiring a lion. Val pushed the uncomfortable thoughts away, and was glad she'd decided to say nothing about Lucas. She didn't want to think about him, have Nate and Jack talk about him. They couldn't do anything anyway. Lucas had crushed that other vampire with a punch. She knew who Lucas was. All the Hunters did. He was their leader. Their King. And he could kill her and her family with one careless swipe of his arm.

And if she told them about Lucas they'd have questions. Questions she didn't have the answers to and that she didn't want said aloud. She was alive tonight because of him.

Why did he come for me?
Why did he save me?
What does he want?
And worst of all...when will he come back for me?

CHAPTER 2

SAN LOARAN, CALIFORNIA
5 YEARS AGO

Jack was sitting in the kitchen, his mouth watering in hunger as he listened to his parents bicker about the Italian government.

A pot boiled on the stove, steam hissing and rolling outwards. But it wasn't just ready, it was...jumping, lightly hopping on the stove—like it had a message of life and death, if only someone would take off the lid.

He didn't want to dream this again.

He stared at the pot, its shiny silver surface and- *there it was-* a faint blue, twinkling reflection. The twinkle altered, changed shape until it was a blue form, small and distant but becoming larger.

She's close now.

The sound of birds, wings flapping, their bodies sighing, filled his ears and echoed off the kitchen walls. He could feel them beating against his eardrums.

That's not right.

There were no birds, it was the heavy swish of rustling silk, and it grated on his nerves, like biting into chalk.

Time to turn around now.

Time to see her coming.

His heart thumped and he picked up his butter knife. His father laughed. His mother smiled. They didn't know that death was hurtling down the corridor like a freight train.

And then she was there. His mother fell to the ground, neck broken, happening in between one blink and the next. His father's face was in his food, body limp, soul already gone, leaving Jack sitting at the kitchen table, a butter knife clenched pathetically tight, a useless protection against *her*.

Marion's sapphire silk skirts blotted out the rest of the world.

She walked around the little kitchen table where he'd eaten every meal of his life. She whispered to him and teased, sounding like a coquette.

Three, four times, she walked around the table. Like playing duck, duck, goose: the agony of her walking behind him, the tension of knowing she'd passed him, but was coming around again. And when she picked him, he'd be dead.

He saw her make the decision, a slight pout marring her dark smile, as she reached out, in infinite slowness, her bony hand outstretched towards him.

Move. Run. Scream. Do something!

Instead, he sat frozen, looking at his mother and then his father, memorizing their features and this moment....

The barest tip of her finger touched him, like an ice cube on burning flesh. He screamed.

"Jack! Jack! Wake up."

Both hands were on him now, the sheets her accomplices, as they tried to pull him back under. A gasp exploded from his chest.

It had been a dream. Marion wasn't here. Jack wasn't a boy anymore, but nineteen and strong. Italy was gone; he was in America now living with the people who had saved him.

I'm alright.

His hands covered his eyes and he heard Valerie's voice speaking to him softly. But it held a tremor of sadness and fear, so he tried to get himself together.

"I'm fine," he said huskily.

"You called *her* name," Valerie said quietly.

God, he hoped she meant his mother. His breath stopped in his lungs, like a dam had been built before he could exhale. "I was dreaming of my parents."

"No. You said Marion's name."

The breath oozed out of him.

"It's been almost two months since you last woke me up in the middle of the night. I guess I won't charge you for this one." A pause "That's good, right?"

What was good about it? His parents were still dead; he was still living a nightmare, so what if he hadn't woken up screaming for a month or two? So fucking what?

But he smiled at her anyway, at her overly bright smile and the false innocence she tried to project. Because she did know that things were not alright. Valerie's own mother had been murdered by vampires and it gave them a bond made of and deeper than blood.

"When was the last time you dreamed about your mother?" He sounded normal.

Her gaze shifted away. "I don't remember my dreams anymore." It was like she was confessing a dirty secret. And maybe it was, because even though he hated the dreams, each time he had them, he was with his parents again. Hearing their laughter. Watching them live. But when he woke up they were really gone.

"Do you want to remember?" he asked, holding her hand in his, as though the dark was slightly farther away if they were together.

"No. And you shouldn't either. You need to block it out. Do what you can to pretend it didn't happen."

Jack leaned over, turning on the bedside lamp to see her face. "You can't pretend our lives are...fine."

Her look was intense, like she was at the starting line of a 100 meter dash, "I used to see it every day, and now I don't. Sometimes, I'm not even sure I was there. And that's—"

"Sad," he said, cutting into her words.

"No," she said in a way that made him blink and try to pay attention, "Not remembering her death is a miracle."

Then she stood, shaking her head slightly, so that her long, dark hair curtained her face, and walked out the door. "Get some sleep, Jack. Another big day tomorrow." She sounded miserable.

CHAPTER 3

SAN LOARAN, CALIFORNIA
5 YEARS AGO

She could see Jack through the window. She turned the car off and waited for his martial arts class to end. The class broke up and he came out the door towards the car.

"Hey kid, how ya doin today?" He sounded happy. Relaxed. Must have been a good class since Jack was usually wound so tight.

"I swear to God, I will eviscerate you if you don't start calling me by my name." Her voice was a growl.

"Your perky welcome makes me think you didn't talk Nate out of his little plan for you."

"No." It was sullen.

"You know, he only wants what's best for you."

Really? He wanted to talk about this and take *Nate's* side? Her temper spiked, making her reckless. "You know what I know? I know that whenever someone tells you they are doing 'what's best for you',

you're screwed. Those are not words you want to hear. It's right up there with 'it's not you it's me'."

He laughed a little. "What's the time frame? I need a shower."

"I thought about rolling down the windows but didn't want to be rude." She gave him a smile that wasn't very nice at all.

"Yeah, well, you after tennis is no picnic either."

"Fair."

They drove the rest of the way in silence. Jack took his shower and Val went to her room. Her bed was covered with the clothes she'd wear tonight on her mission. All black with lots of velcro and pockets for hiding deadly weapons.

Jack knocked and opened the door. "Val?" He looked at her carefully, like he was trying to determine how upset she was. A sympathetic smile flashed across his face and he rubbed the back of his neck like he was tense too.

Val pointed to the bed and his smoky eyes tracked the movement. He looked at the outfit on the bed, nodding absently. "Hmm. Those are good cargoes actually. I don't know about the top."

"Can I just tell you how hot I would look in a black leather jacket?" Her eyes slid over to his and she found him studying her, imagining her in that jacket, she thought.

She blushed and leaned down so he wouldn't notice. His hand reached out to touch her dark brown hair and he pulled some of it through his fingers.

"What about this?" he said softly.

She shrugged and stood back up. "I don't know. Braid, maybe? Cut it off for the honor of my family, Mulan style."

His lips quirked. "Braid is good, but tuck it into your shirt. You don't want him to get a handhold."

She crossed her arms protectively around her. "This is such a bad idea. What if I freeze? I could be dead before you get there. Or dad, before he gets there."

"Not gonna happen. I'll be there." His voice was commanding. He shook his head at her, stormy gray eyes looking a little tortured. He was so handsome.

Sigh.

Jack had even managed to escape the Italian nose. His nose was straight, refined. Val mentally chastised herself. Nose romanticizing was for losers.

Jack would die to protect her and just thinking about it made her knees wobble in both fear and lust.

"I know that look gets you laid a lot but it doesn't really make me fear death any less," she said grumpily, irritated at her attraction to him when he was partially responsible for what would happen tonight.

His smile was genuine. "Smart ass. Maybe I will let him bite you."

"Maybe he won't even be there." Her tone was hopeful.

His eyes met hers again, "He'll be there. Prepare for that. You won't get out of it. You get the job done. No fear, no hesitation, right?"

She nodded. Why did these conversations always sound like they came from some crappy war movie?

A moment passed and she started thinking about things that could go wrong. As though he could read her mind, he tried to distract her, lightly jabbing a fist out towards her stomach which she blocked automatically.

"What's your plan?" He was trying to be positive.

"Dad and I talked about it. I'm gonna ambush him. We knocked out the streetlights around his house. It's not too obvious though. He shouldn't be suspicious. I'm going to hide behind the hydrangea bush in front of his house. I'll shoot through it, try to take him in the chest and not have any hand to hand at all. Assuming I don't get the money shot right away—"

"Different terminology please," Jack said in a strangled voice. Was he laughing or horrified? Actually, both were good.

"I like money shot. If dad is going to send me out there to die, then I'm going to make this as uncomfortable for everyone as I possibly can."

Jack scowled at her and moved on. "Okay, you shoot him, he keeps coming and then what?"

"This is clever, actually. I rigged up a bow and arrow thing so all he has to do is hit the trip wire and it will shoot him in the back. Assuming that doesn't cook his biscuits—I'm gonna knee him in the gonads and stab him through the heart!" She kneed an invisible attacker, then smiled at him.

"Well, you scared the hell out of me. Okay, good. Solid. Has contingency options. Do you have the cyanide pill?"

It wasn't really cyanide, but that's what they called it. It was basically a small ball of silver that would disintegrate into sharp pieces on impact. She'd once seen a vampire burst into flame when hit with silver.

It would be a last ditch effort to save herself. If she was counting on that to save her, she was dead. Dread rippled down her body, leaving her cold.

Jack's lips set into a firm line, his whole body suddenly tense. She held up her hand, not wanting him to say anything about her sudden fear—and its apparent obviousness.

She needed to keep the conversation light.

He understood, adjusting his stance and scrubbing a lean hand across his face, "Right. Where are you going to keep it?"

"Pocket?" she said hopefully.

"Ooh, sorry, that's a rookie mistake. How are you going to reach into your pocket when a pissed off and hungry vampire is going to rip your throat out?" His tone was playful and she appreciated the effort he was making for her.

"What does your highness suggest?"

He shrugged. "I'd keep it strapped to your wrist. Then you can just smash it against his face."

That made her heart skip a beat. She could imagine herself being trapped under a vampire and trying to smash this stupid ball into the side of his head before he killed her.

Oh God, she was gonna heave.

Jack handed her a little bracelet that had a soft suction like cup for the ball to rest in. She looked at it suspiciously. "Does this work? I don't want to be your test chump."

"Yeah, it does. I tried it two weeks ago."

She wanted to ask questions. Had he used it on an actual vampire? Had things gotten that hairy and dangerous that the fight had been hand to hand? But she didn't. He didn't tell her stuff like that and she didn't ask.

"Okay. I'm gonna get ready. Leave before the nudity starts."

Jack left quickly, giving the door an extra tug to make sure it was closed.

After getting dressed, Val laid on her bed. Nervousness made her feel nauseous, almost like she had two hearts frantically beating in her chest, instead of one.

She wondered if Lucas would be there tonight. No, why would he? She'd only seen him that one time, although it had taken her months to feel like she wasn't being watched. Sometimes, she had the feeling that he was close by. Like if she just turned around fast enough, she'd see him.

If he was there, would he help her again? He'd said he wanted to protect her. How many sleepless nights had that one line caused her?

She looked at the clock. Time to go. At the bottom of the stairs she realized the house was too quiet and that she hadn't heard her father come home.

"Where's dad?"

Jack flinched. "He can't make it."

"Well, there will be more vampires another time. Good job security, but shitty benefits in the vampire business." She turned around, ready to head back upstairs and take off her black attack-wear.

"He wants us to go anyway."

The air rushed out of her lungs, making her words a little wobbly. "He's going to send me into this alone?"

Jack walked closer to her. He was dressed in black cargo pants too. A black turtleneck with a few knife sheaths and a gun holster were on him as well. Very black ops. "I'll be there. I won't let anything happen to you."

She knew Jack would try to save her and that they might both die tonight. It would destroy him if he couldn't save her. Even though he'd been little, he blamed himself for the death of his parents.

She felt the quick anger and sadness at her father melt away, become the more familiar feelings of betrayal and bewilderment. In a way, she'd known her father wasn't going to be here. *Cancel the 'daddy of the year' award.*

They got into the car and Jack drove. He was a very cautious driver. Like a little old Italian lady. While other guys drove at a hundred miles an hour, Jack didn't want to invite more risk into his life than he had to.

They parked down the street from the vampire's lair. In this case it was a house. A house that had seen some seriously better days. It had a screen door that was hanging on for dear life and paint that had given up the fight, peeling off the walls and dropping to its death in flaky patches.

Most of the plants were dead too. But a hearty Hydrangea and some ugly shrubs were still fighting for survival.

I could totally die here.

Fuck.

The vampire who lived here was either a total loser or really liked the monster image. Really, if he couldn't be a rich vampire, then he was a moron.

Vampires had centuries to get rich. They were strong and silent. They could resort to robbery, steal from their victims, but this guy didn't seem to have made it work. Having to take out a loser vampire would make it easier...right?

Maybe he was a newbie.

"What do we know about him?"

"Not a lot. He came into town a few weeks ago. He went to a nightclub and killed a girl in the bathroom. She died of blood loss, obviously. They found him on the security tape. Gilbert sent us the info." Gilbert Arthur was a Hunter in Australia who always seemed to know what was going on.

It was odd. But the information was always good. Well, sometimes the vampire had left by the time they got there or the details were hazy but he was always right about the attack and location of where the vampire had last been.

Val sighed, "What did Gilbert have that kept the police away from arresting this guy?"

"Ah. That would be the missing security tape."

She exploded. "Gilbert is in Australia! Why is the tape with him? How did he get it, why does he know this stuff? Shouldn't *we* be the ones in the know? No, you. *You* should be the one in the know." This wasn't her fight. She was going to college.

Her future involved keggers and one-night-stands. No doubt in that order.

"I'll let the pronoun slide. No one knows where he gets his info from," Jack said it wearily, as though he'd discussed Gilbert Arthur and his mysterious information a lot.

"Anyway, this guy—" Jack gestured towards the house, "he's laid low, but today he scoped out a playground. So, game over. Your dad doesn't want to risk waiting until he gets back. And this should be easy. He's poor for Christ's sake! What kind of self-respecting vampire would live in a dump like this? Honestly." His voice was disgusted and she knew he was trying to make her laugh.

It was something they'd always done on stake outs. Even she didn't want to be left home alone all the time. So sometimes she'd go along. Especially if she knew there was just about *no chance* they would encounter a vampire. Jack would only invite her when he thought it would be safe.

She'd make hot chocolate and bring popcorn and they'd talk about school, music, TV, life. Play twenty questions. She liked those nights.

They always trash talked the vampire in question. Usually, it was amusing, but it didn't work this time, now that she was the one who was going to be doing the fighting.

Jack tried to take her hand, comfort her but she jerked away in anger. She opened the door, popped the trunk and grabbed her stuff. Scanning the trees and houses around her intently, Val looked for a flash of gold.

Looking for Lucas.

Maybe her mind had deceived her. Everything had happened so fast that she'd decided she didn't know what he looked like. He couldn't have been that beautiful.

Her memories of that night were all twisted up so that Lucas now seemed larger than life. She feared she'd romanticized him and that she would be disappointed in his actual appearance if she ever saw him again. Which, she emphatically did *not* want!

Jack got out and waited for her, the sound of his door closing interrupting her thoughts. He was going to stay hidden on the other side of the yard. Hide in the shadows, just in case.

"You know what Jack? Fuck you! You didn't *have* to do this. You *know* how messed up this is!"

He ran his hand through his hair, uncomfortable. He'd never disagree with her father. She waited but he said nothing, seemingly at a loss.

"Kiss ass." She turned and walked away.

"Use the rage, Val. Good talk." The sarcasm made her want to scream.

Then he was serious, "Okay, this jackass works and he'll be home in twenty. Guess where he works, Val? The *library*. Honestly, you could kill him with your eyes closed."

Jack disappeared into the shadows while she quickly set up her trip wire and stationed herself behind the bushes, dried up blooms falling all around her like snow.

Knives? Check. Pill? Check. Gun? Big check!

Okay. She was ready to go. Val imagined the fight over and over. Different ways it could happen and ways she could die.

Val hunkered down behind the Hydrangea and waited. *Twenty minutes is a long time to be afraid...and I really have to pee.*

Finally, there was movement. A man was walking down the dark street, appearing and disappearing as he passed under street lamps. *Could be a normal pedestrian out for a walk.*

Or not.

The guy moved very smoothly. Her stomach wobbled. Vampires didn't have limps or glitches. Tendons didn't matter and it made them unusually graceful. It wasn't something most people would notice. But to her, it was a tell.

He came towards the house and a car drove by. The lights caught his eyes and they flashed monster bright. *Yup. This was the guy.*

She felt the gun in her hand, made sure the safety was off, then breathed in and out steadily. Slowly, quietly. Except for the desire to run away screaming she was still, calm. He turned in the gate.

Three steps, you bastard.

He walked forward and she pointed the gun. She was good, very accurate for all the days she'd spent at the range and all the hunting trips her dad had taken her on, but this was different.

She could screw this up so badly that even Jack's life might be in danger. Her hand started to waiver at the thought, but he was getting close to the trip wire now. He was tall. Why had she thought he'd be shorter? He looked kind of shy and like he could work in a library.

Vampires should be scary. It should be required. Looking normal was an unfair advantage.

Val forced herself to calm, re-imagining what it had felt like when Lucas had made her feel so eerily and thoroughly emotionless.

The vampire stepped on the tripwire, a silver-tipped arrow slicing through the air and lodging into his ribs. He spun around to find the source of the weapon, simultaneously pulling the arrow out of his body. The head of the arrow detached inside him, just as it was supposed to, and a curl of smoke rose from his chest where the silver burned him.

But he wasn't going to die from it.

Shit! Flesh wound. If only he'd been three inches shorter.

Val sighted the gun and pulled the trigger. The bullets were made of wood and the gun had a silencer. The plant shook as the bullet passed through. It pierced him in the back and he jerked around again, facing her.

He coughed, black blood arcing from his mouth like vomit. She'd hit a lung.

She fired again and he fell to his knees. She shot him again, knowing this would be the one to finish him off, but the gun jammed. *Of course! Put that on my tombstone, "Would have made it but for Smith and Wesson."*

She withdrew her knife and ran for him—acting on instinct, not wanting to give him any time to regenerate.

A wet growl gurgled from his throat as he reached for her.

Val ducked and tried to come in under his grasping arms to stab him in the chest but he was quick. Val tried to adjust and go for his thigh instead. The femoral artery was harder to get to but she was getting confused, panic rising and she felt like she was running out of options, had to end this now! No time for patience or thinking.

He grabbed her, held onto her shirt, yanking her up like a rag doll, before tossing her several feet away.

Close to the front door. *The easier to snack on you, my dear.*

Flecks of paint and dust rose around her in a clogging breeze.

Val was paralyzed, her faux-calmness gone, replaced by panic and violent memories, stunned from the painful landing.

Her lungs needed air but she couldn't breathe yet. She needed the knife, but her muscles were jerky and slow to respond.

Where is Jack?

The vampire lunged at her, throwing his weight on top of her, banging her head against the ground. It felt like a firework exploded in her head.

Her wrist!

She slammed her arm into his face and the ball exploded. His skin sizzled, shards of silver embedded in his skin.

He screamed and rolled off of her, hands cupping his face. She grabbed the stake from her waistband and threw herself forward, holding the stake steady with two hands, stabbing him in the chest with all her strength.

It wasn't deep enough.

She remembered the last time she'd done this, with Lucas holding the other vampire. Val had thought it would be easier, that she'd be stronger now that she was older, but she was still too weak.

The wood clung to his flesh, not pulling clean freely but like it had melded into his body. Blood pumped out of him, gushing in time to his heartbeat, oozing up from around the stake.

So close!

Val went for the same hole again, slamming down with all of her strength, screaming in fury. He exploded.

She closed her eyes and tried not to breathe vampire ash into her lungs.

Everything was gone except for a few bone fragments. He'd been older than they'd thought. The really old ones left nothing behind. In their natural state they wouldn't even be dust anymore.

She held the stake in her hand, still clutching it tightly.

Jack ran towards her, dropping to his knees beside her and said something she didn't understand. She'd been so scared. This was so awful! She kept reliving those final moments again and again. Hearing the echo of stake pulling free from flesh. The displacement of air when he'd disintegrated.

Furious, she lashed out at Jack. Screamed and pushed him. He fell backwards, allowing her to push him onto the ground. She followed, straddling his chest as she tried to slap him.

"Damn you! Damn you, you *know* what this is like! Why would you do this to me? He wouldn't have known!" Val paused to take a breath, the anger lessening with her violent outburst, instantly replaced by a sad tiredness.

She didn't know how to explain to him how betrayed she felt. "I thought you were on my side. That if you could protect me, you would. Wasn't that the deal? But, this was your chance and you didn't. You threw me into this, just like my father would." She felt like she was babbling and stopped talking.

Jack hadn't let her hit him but had grabbed her wrists in his hands, holding her as loosely as he could as she thrashed against him and tried to rail at him. He listened to her torrent of words and didn't know if she was right. Didn't know if this had damaged their friendship.

Would it change her? Make her more cold and distant than she already was? She threw herself into life like she had mere moments to live, but it was so frantic that he never knew if she even enjoyed it. That was how she protected herself. No one could get a hold of her because she was always moving so quickly through life.

She was all speed and fire, walls and prickliness to keep people away.

Her attention and affection were weapons. At least they were for him.

Jack cleared his throat, unable to speak the first time he tried. He still held her hands, didn't think about letting go.

Did she really need to have a kill under her belt to live her life?

Val tried to move off of him, tugging her hands from his.

Her body was slumped like a beaten dog and a tear landed on his neck. He gripped her harder. "No you don't! Why shouldn't you have to do this? I do it. Your father does it! I have given up *everything* for you and your father. We were supposed to be a team but we're not. It's me and your father while you pretend that nothing is happening. How can you live with yourself? Watch us walk out the door and not know if we'll come back? But you do it! You let us go while you shop, and date, and have fun. We are not normal! You and me. *That* was the deal, Val."

She was crying in earnest now. As he'd talked she'd stilled, letting him hold her closed fists. Now her hands shifted, twining her fingers through his. The weight of her on his body finally penetrated his thoughts. She was straddling him, sitting on top of him and he wanted to push upwards, get closer to her.

She whispered, "I can't do that. I won't stay, and live a life of death, waiting for you to come home in a body bag or worse. I don't *want* to be dead in five years, maybe less. And I can't spend my life afraid for you." The words were deep and impassioned. Her eyes locked on his, as though she were a vampire trying to capture his gaze and bend him to her will. "The *second* I can get out of here, I will." She let his hands go and pushed away from him, standing and going back to the car.

Jack stood and picked up all of their things then went into the house to see if he could find any information about why the vampire was here, desperately trying not to think about what had just happened.

CHAPTER 4

SAN LOARAN, CALIFORNIA
4 YEARS AGO

It was the longest day of Valerie's life. Today was the day that the University of California admission letters arrived. If she went home and had an empty mailbox she'd shoot herself. Well, maybe not, but she would definitely be depressed for an eternity! She'd gone to school and spent every moment watching the clock and waiting for the day to end.

Berkeley. She wanted to go to Cal. If she didn't get in she would be happy at UCLA, or UCSD. Failing that, she wanted to go to UC *Away*. Anywhere that was away.

She sped the whole way home.

With a deep breath, she opened the mailbox, peering into the metal depths. *Junk mail is a curse!*

There they were. Four letters. She was beyond happy, like being kissed for the first time.

She went into the house and threw her bag on the floor. Several undignified moments passed as she jumped up and down and even squealed like a small pig. Thank God she was alone! She started to laugh, embarrassed at herself but gloriously happy as well. She was getting out of this town! Away from her father and away from Jack!

She started crying, overcome with joy and a little bit of grief. She would miss Jack, she loved him too much not to, but God she wanted to be free. And now she'd be someone new, someone normal.

There was movement in the corner of the room and she saw Jack coming towards her. *Why was he here?* He'd been in Latin America for the last three months.

He looked amazing. His hair had grown out and the back of it was brushing the collar of his blue T-shirt. He wore a pair of dark jeans and Adidas shoes. The shirt fit him well, bulging in all the appropriate places, flat where it should be.

He could be an underwear model, she thought. An image came to her of Jack in underwear and she blinked, looking away.

He was smiling at her.

Someone alert the media.

"Good news? Did you get in?"

Her eyes filled with tears and she nodded at him with a stupid grin on her face.

"Cal, right?"

She gave another watery nod, "Yes! Can you believe it?"

Oh screw it! She laughed and hugged him. Val wrapped her arms around his neck, her chest was flush with his. She squeezed him hard and he squeezed back, pulling her body in even closer, until she began to feel dizzy.

He was tall and strong, stronger than he had been when he'd left. His face was more chiseled, his cheeks leaner, his skin tanned from the sun. But he looked tired too, dark circles under his eyes that spoke of sleepless nights and stress. It made him look older, although he'd never really been young.

It was the awareness of him—his smell, shampoo and nice cologne, all the things that were Jack were cloaking her. And it was heaven.

"I don't think we have ever hugged." She said with a laugh. Was that true? How could they have lived together for years and never hugged?

"You're right." He said evenly.

She looked at his features up close and realized the changes continued. His lips were extraordinary. He was smiling slightly and that was different too. She imagined his lips twisted bitterly, cruelly or angrily, but not happily. Things had been so bad by the time he'd gone away that she'd forgotten he could be like this. Be sweet.

Her gaze returned to his eyes. They were slate gray and reminded her of stormy oceans, with his own dark ghosts trapped within their deep depths. *Save the poetry, Val.*

She pulled away from him and he released her quickly. Val didn't want to think about him like this. He wasn't *her* Jack. She was leaving for college. She would leave him behind and stop thinking of him, dammit.

Even though he'd let her go, she could still feel his hard chest and the strength of his arms. "So, welcome home. How was Latin America. Go to any country in particular?"

He sighed and she thought he was sifting through information trying to decide what to tell her. He wouldn't tell her everything and why should he? She'd made it clear she didn't want to be sucked into his orbit for the rest of her life, waiting for him to die.

"It was good. I got you a souvenir."

Okay, he wasn't going to tell her anything at all. Things became awkward, the levity of the moment gone, all the unresolved issues they had crowding in close between them. "If it's vampire dust I don't want it."

He smiled slightly but it didn't reach his eyes.

"Geez, did you actually bring me vampire dust?" She laughed nervously.

"No. I'm just trying to keep you in suspense. You can have it at dinner."

There was an awkward pause large enough to drive a Suburban through.

"Well, see you at dinner." She smiled again and ran up the stairs. This was too much. She needed to get away before she begged him to never leave, ravished him on the floor, or something equally stupid.

Val forced herself to stop thinking about Jack. It was a skill. Besides, she had to call everyone. Everyone! She was going to college and she would *never* look back.

The day passed quickly and finally she couldn't hide from Jack and her father any longer. She went downstairs and saw her father in the kitchen. He was tearing lettuce for the salad and lasagna was in the oven.

Jack was a great cook, especially Italian food. He could cook Italian and swear Italian—and both were worth watching. It was the only time he was incredibly expressive. He used hand gestures and everything. He'd learned to cook from his mother, and in Val's more tender moments she thought he cooked so that he could remember her and what his life had been before the blood, death and vampires.

She took the salad bowl and set it on the table. The parmesan was still in the fridge, and she found the expensive block of cheese, as well as the expensive cheese grater that was all Jack's Italian roots would accept.

Jack took the lasagna out of the oven, a puff of hot air brushing by her.

They sat down at the old wooden table in the kitchen.

"So Val, you got in. Congratulations." Her father said, his smile an afterthought.

Oh no. Was he going to keep her from going? A vision of her father telling her she could either help them or be on her own rocketed through her mind. What would she do if he made her choose?

She'd say goodbye.

When Jack had left four months ago, her father had stayed with her. She knew that Jack had hoped they'd bond but boy had he been wrong. They'd been strangers in the same house, using the same rooms and space, eating together, but never saying anything worth saying.

There was a reason she always called him 'father' or 'Nate'. He didn't deserve a 'dad'. He didn't do 'dad' things with her, he tried to kill her. So he could be Nate for all she cared.

She was going to have to be on the offensive. "Yes. It's exciting. It will also give you more time with Jack. You guys will have each other, be able to protect each other and not have to worry about me." *Yeah, that sounded natural.*

Her father cocked his head to the side. "Why wouldn't we worry? Do you know how many vampires live in the Bay area? Lucas was there last month."

Self- preservation told her to be cautious. "I've done *everything* to learn to protect myself. I'm going to college. The only question is whether or not I have your blessing." That was the speech she'd worked on all day. She was pleased with herself for getting it all out, but it seemed a shame it had only been three sentences long.

His fingers drummed on the table. He stopped the nervous habit and took a bite of lasagna, chewing thoughtfully, undoubtedly trying to figure out his next attack to keep her here.

"No. I will hate you if you keep me here. I won't stay."

He nodded. "Okay. Jack will go with you."

Val looked at them both venomously. "No! He won't! I won't have a jailer anymore. You need him more than I do. Who will keep *you* safe? Things are worse; there are more attacks than ever. You need help. And I'm sorry, but you are not getting any younger. If something happens to you because he's with me...." Her voice trailed off and she felt her throat closing up with tears.

She looked at the picture of her mother on the wall. How she watched over all their meals with a benign smile. Her father got up and she hoped he was coming to hug her.

He walked past her and went upstairs, closing the door behind him. She wanted to cry. Throw something. Leave tonight and never look back.

Her gaze flew to Jack and she knew that he would hug her if she wanted. Of course he would. He was perfect and a mean part of her hated him for that. As though he could read her mind, he got up, leaving his food half-eaten at the table. She heard him going up the stairs, his long stride eating the distance quickly. He knocked and entered the study, closing the door quietly behind him.

Her father and Jack didn't need her. They kept her but it was a duty. No more. She couldn't be that anymore. Be a disappointment, a burden, an afterthought.

****

Valerie finished packing for college. Her room was stuck in a time warp, perfect for a little girl who loved pink. Light pink painted walls and white wainscoting. It even had a huge wooden doll house in the corner where Barbie and Ken had gone all the way...repeatedly.

She'd packed everything, not wanting to leave anything behind. The pale pink bedspread from when she was a little girl and some of her stuffed animals, like the elephant her dad had won for her when they went to the state fair the year before her mom died.

That was a time before vampires existed for them. They were a normal family: dad had a normal job at a consultancy firm and ran the occasional 10k. Her mom was a second grade teacher and they'd had a dog named Pickles. He was white and fierce. One of those dogs that had a short man's complex. He wanted to attack everything. Kill first, sniff later.

She'd loved that stupid dog.

Jack knocked on her door and interrupted her thoughts. Good, she knew what came next on her trip down memory lane. Seeing mom butchered in cold blood, her dead dog, then her father destroyed. She could skip that memory.

When she opened the door she smiled at him, happy for the interruption. He seemed a little surprised but smiled back.

"Hey, I was thinking we could order some pizza for your last night. Maybe watch a movie or play scrabble."

Valerie raised her eyebrows at him, surprised at the offer. They hadn't spent an evening together in...yeah, it had been awhile.

"Last time we played Scrabble I won," she teased him.

"Yeah, because I was 14. I could *speak* English really well but you were a real stickler for the spelling." His tone was fond and she detected a hint of a challenge.

She thought about refusing. Wouldn't it be harder tomorrow if they buried the hatchet tonight? Could they even try to pretend that they weren't total opposites in absolutely everything now?

He crossed his arms in a defensive gesture and she realized that he knew she was thinking of saying no. He wanted her to say yes but he was waiting for her to shut him down. Val was always going to be weak willed around Jack, would probably always give in to spending a little bit more time with him if she could. What harm could it do to pretend to be friends, one last time, before their lives were forever altered?

After all, his life was changing too. He wouldn't have to watch over her anymore, or stay in San Loaran but could devote the rest of his life to revenge. Why wouldn't he be nervous too? Had either of them had a big life changing event that had turned out positive? His parents murdered, her mother.

Life as they knew it was at an end and looking at Jack with his soft smile made her feel an overwhelming sadness that their relationship had gone to hell, especially compared to when they were younger. Once she was gone she might not see him again for a while, maybe never if he was killed. He reached out to her and squeezed her arm.

She nodded, "Yeah. Okay. But no Scrabble. How about Monopoly?"

"What? That thing's like eight hours!" he said with mock indignation.

She started to laugh. "No, don't worry I'm a *much* better cheater now! I'll have you cleaned out in two hours tops." Val snapped her fingers to demonstrate how quickly time would pass.

Jack turned and went down the stairs. "I'll order the pizza."

She heard the television click on as she followed him down.

"It's the VH1 pop up show! And a marathon no less. We're kicking it old school tonight!" Her voice was gleefully. Jack paused mid-dial but didn't look up, while Val waited to see what he'd say about her lame comment. But he said nothing. Instead, he closed his eyes and shook his head a little, then called for pizza.

Their relationship had always been complicated. They were like two shipwreck survivors clinging to a raft and waiting to be rescued. But no one came to rescue them, and they'd grown up in a house with almost no affection or guidance, beyond how to kill a vampire. It was weird. Like Leave It to Beaver but Beaver was buried in a shallow grave out back.

So, yeah. Complicated.

But not tonight. Tonight would be one last night to have fun, and pretend that their relationship was simple.

They got the game set up and promptly had a fight over who got to be the car. She only wanted it because the car was his favorite and he made a ridiculous screeching tire sound as he moved away from her properties. Then he'd comment about the bad service and how he should get his money back.

She had no idea if it was *actually* funny, but it had been part of their bickering for so long that she thought it was hilarious.

The pizza came and they ate the whole thing. After the last bite, Val said, "Okay Jack. I want a favor."

His hand froze above Park Place. "What is it?"

"It's a *really* big favor."

Jack waited.

"I want to play the drinking game version of Monopoly. It's a weird night anyway. Can't we get drunk together once? You know, be young and stupid." She tried to waggle her eyebrows, but feared she'd accomplished a sick-worm-dancing expression instead.

"I'm not that young, Val." His superior tone got on her nerves and she made her hands into a mouthpiece shape and put them to her lips. "It's three years, Jack! You are only three years older than me!" He rubbed his hand across his eyes like he had a headache but she thought she saw a smile. She watched his hand, those long fingers and neat nails. He had a five o' clock shadow and he looked a little...rumpled? Perfect Jack being not so perfect was really sexy.

Don't. Think. That.

As he combed his fingers through his hair, Val waited, watching him think. "How about we do it on one condition?"

She was excited but then worried. Jack always got his pound of flesh. "What is it?"

Jack stood and went to the kitchen. Opening the cupboard, he pulled out a bottle of tequila and then grabbed something she couldn't see from a drawer, before coming back to the coffee table. In a smooth motion he was down on his knees, the bottle on the table and a... *pager* beside it.

"Go on." Val chuckled uncomfortably.

Jack looked her in the eyes and her heart squeezed. "This is a pager. But it only does one thing. It goes to me. You have to promise me that you will carry it at all times and be prepared to use it if anything peculiar happens or you need help. I mean it, Val. I want us to test it every three months. A prearranged time where you push the button and we make sure it works. New batteries every three months as well."

Okay, he was really serious, "Does it, by any chance, have a tracking device in it?"

A few moments passed where he wouldn't look her in the face. Finally, he nodded. "Yeah, it does."

She squeezed his hand and then pulled away. "You are a shitty negotiator. I totally accept. I would have taken it anyway, if you asked me. I'm not *that* heartless. I know you need to keep track of me. I get it and I love you for it."

"Who are you?" He peered at her face. "You look like Val and speak like Val, what with all the swearing, but you are so reasonable."

"Get the damned glasses."

In no time they were back, settled down on the floor, backs against the couch, facing the T.V., a coffee table loaded with booze and Parker Brother's paraphernalia in front of them.

Jack settled down on the floor next to her, his body turned towards hers, their knees touching. His face was close enough that she could see the amber colored flecks in his gray eyes. The room was suddenly tense, the commercials intrusive to their little world before the couch. *Now or never*, Val thought and picked up the salt shaker.

"Give me your hand," she said and felt a flutter in her stomach. Val stared at his dark jeans, his knee suddenly fascinating as she waited for him to do something. Either he'd agree and give her his hand, or he'd refuse. But she felt stupidly exposed now, like she'd stepped over a line or given her true feelings away. He had no expression. Perfect control.

Who knew what the hell he was thinking? And why did she think that was so hot?

This was a lot like bungee jumping, she decided. She could dick around at the top of the bridge, looking at the view and crapping herself with fear, or she could just jump and feel the rush. That was how she was going to live her life, she decided. Jump first and damn the consequences.

Jack extended his hand towards her, palm up. His body had shifted, both knees flush against hers so that all she had to do was lean forward—five, maybe six inches and she could touch her lips to his. Err, not that that was the plan....

Val wrapped her hand around his wrist, tugging it towards her mouth lightly. He was relaxed, his fingers loose but lightly curled as he waited for her to do something.

Her gaze flashed to his and she smiled.

There was nowhere else in the world she'd rather be right now, and she knew, staring into his eyes, that she'd remember this moment for the rest of her life: the warmth of his hand, the expression on his face.

Leaning forward, she touched her tongue to the back of his wrist. Jack jerked a little but tried to keep his hand still while she licked him.

His knuckles whitened on the shot glass in his other hand.

She pulled back, her tongue tingling from the touch of his skin. Val felt herself blushing and quickly poured salt on his damp hand. She went to lick her own hand, moving quickly, trying to get beyond her own embarrassment, but he made a noise and she stilled.

"Turnabout's fair play," Jack said, his voice slightly husky.

Val thought his comment should have been corny but it wasn't. He was so sexy he could get away with almost anything.

Jack took her hand in his and she noticed how warm and large his hand was compared to hers. He pulled her hand towards his mouth and caught her gaze, refusing to look away.

Gulp.

She watched her hand go towards his mouth, felt his tongue on her skin.

His touch was gentle. Jack was coiled and lethal, focused and practical. This wasn't practical, it was very, very sexual and Val felt like she'd been waiting her whole life for Jack to look at her like she was edible. He tapped the salt shaker, coating the damp mark on her skin.

"Bottom's up," he said, almost in a heavy sigh.

Val couldn't help it, "These double entendres are coming hard and fast, you know."

The shot was to his mouth, the liquid on his tongue and she knew he just about spit it out because he was laughing so hard. He got it down but not without a struggle. His eyes were red and he shook himself exaggeratedly, as though the tequila was vile.

Which it was.

He put the glass down with a cough. "There is no one like you Val."

"Do you want to drink to that?" Her eyes were still watering from the fiery taste, but she waved her little glass at him in challenge.

He shook his head in an emphatic no and turned a bit somber. They went back to playing the game and enough time passed that they each had seven or eight hotels. Every time someone landed on a hotel they had to drink, and it wasn't long before they were both tipsy.

The game had gone on for over two hours when Cyndi Lauper's, "Girls Just Wanna Have Fun" came on Pop up Video.

Jack was almost out of money and heavily mortgaged. She was happy and relaxed; alcohol, Jack and victory all contributing to her good mood.

"Did you see my talent show video from sixth grade where we 'performed'" She used air quotes so that he knew she was using the term loosely, "this song?"

"I haven't had enough alcohol for that. I'm gonna need another shot."

Without hesitation, she poured him another one and he drank it. It was a strict no contact shot, understood without words. After the third one she thought she moaned a little when he licked her, and they hadn't done it since.

Cyndi was belting it out now and Val decided to go for stupid. If in doubt, choose excess. It was a motto *somewhere*, right? She kicked off her shoes and stood on top of the coffee table, the little monopoly dog biting into her heel. She squawked and kicked it away. Val started doing her dance routine from years ago. It consisted of lots of high kicking, shaking and generally lame 80's moves.

I really need some leg warmers.

Jack sat on the floor looking up at her and she wished she had her camera, his mouth was hanging open. He snapped it shut, came to some mental decision, then sat back to watch her.

Val wanted to laugh really loudly but couldn't have said exactly why. Taking the controller, Jack turned up the volume in encouragement. She danced and moved and when the song came to an end he held up his hand to help her down from the makeshift stage.

Handing her another drink, he said, "If college doesn't work out can I suggest stripping? Only if it's tasteful, of course."

"Of course!"

She grabbed his hand and licked his wrist, almost spilling his drink. *Maybe* she'd pulled a little harder than was necessary.

I am totally drunk. Then it was her turn again and he held her hand, looking at it intensely, making the moment drag.

Turning her hand over so that her wrist was up, he bent over her pulse and kissed it lightly. Then he licked her and poured salt on her skin. Her wrist burned from his touch, little tendrils of heat skating up her body and she could feel her body responding. She squeezed her thighs together and they drank their shots.

"What will it take for you to dance, Jack?" she asked him teasingly, trying to get past the desire to rip his clothes off. What *would* he do if she threw herself at him? Maybe she could get in one good kiss and grope before he pushed her away.

That was too depressing.

"Nothing." His tone was strident. "No power on this earth could make me dance.... Well—" He gave a shrug that reminded her he was actually Italian. She knew he wasn't going to tell her what the song would be. Who did he think he was kidding?

"Oh no, Jackie! I know you. You're a good American now, but I know your weakness..." She let the moment draw out and he actually cringed. ""A-Ha". Take on me, right?" She belted out the main lyric, "Taaake *on* me, take on me! Dude, you are so 80's."

Jack raised his hands and again she was reminded that he was European, as he made a flapping or shooing motion with his hands, perhaps to dispel the truth of her words—or some pigeons. "I know! I know! I can't help it! I love those damned Norwegians! It was a crucial stage in my development. Go to any karaoke bar in Italy and I swear you'll hear it at least twice! It's not just me, it's the entire country!"

"Oh sure. When I think of Italy I think of fascism and 'A-Ha'."

And then it happened.

Pop up video came through.

Take on me by 'A-Ha'.

They both looked at the television in mild disbelief while the bubbles bleeped across the screen giving information about the band. They watched as the silly cartoon drawing band went running down corridors. "Hop to it! You are on! This is fate. If you don't do it you could be smote down! You don't go against fate!"

He shook his head.

"Jack, you have had several shots of tequila and will be hung-over in the morning. We may not even remember that this happened! You should do it. You can blame it on the alcohol! Now go get *jiggy* with it!"

He gave a long-suffering sigh. She opened her mouth to offer more words of encouragement, but he held up a finger to forestall her, grabbed the bottle of tequila, took a big fortifying swig and hopped up onto the table. He used the half empty bottle for a microphone and gave a fairly earnest performance of the song, at one point stopping to complain, "Do you know how hard it is to sing this song? I'm not doing the high-pitched parts. That's not part of the deal."

But when the high part came, he gave it a try and she was charmed. She'd also never laughed so hard in her entire life. He reached the third stanza, knowing all the words by heart and she felt like he was singing to her, wishing the words were for them.

Would he always come for her?

Val realized she was biting her lip. He was *actually* graceful. Jack could dance? He tapped his foot and did the occasional hip swivel and point. Then he clapped his hands, careful of the bottle, and she became suspicious.

"Did all these moves come from Dave Gahan?"

Jack winked at her and she knew the dancing was on purpose. She'd been obsessed with Depeche Mode and had seen the concert videos over and over again, much to everyone's irritation. By virtue of living with her he'd been forced to see it at least ten times.

"You are so fucking hot right now."

Jack stopped and looked at her, an inscrutable expression on his face. She clapped her hand over her mouth in horror as he stepped down and put the bottle on the table with careful precision.

"That's it, Val," His voice was dark and she knew he was going to leave. She'd gone too far. But he didn't. He came towards her and extended his hand. Her heart pounding, she took it and he pulled her up off the floor and into him so that she was flush against his body.

She could feel his heat and heartbeat through her sweater. Or maybe it was hers. She couldn't think. She looked up into his face, and held her breath in mingled fear and excitement. He was looking at her hungrily. Passionately. Unconsciously, she licked her lips. With a mumbled Italian curse he leaned down and kissed her.

His lips were dry, soft and warm as he kissed her lightly, almost chastely. Then, he hesitated as though waiting for her to answer a question. Val tilted her head a little, inviting him to kiss her back, but so afraid of breaking the moment and exposing her desire for him, that she couldn't kiss him back.

His tongue touched the seam of her lips, then withdrew. His hands came up to frame her face and he pressed kisses on her quickly. Slow kisses, then harder kisses, at the corner of her mouth and one that sucked lightly on her lower lip which she felt all down her body and made her gasp in pleasure.

The kisses became wetter as she opened her mouth under his, giving in to him with abandon. The feel of his tongue sliding into her mouth with a soft thrust made her knees weak. It was a totally new sensation and she wrapped her arms around his neck, needing support to stand.

Jack reached down and picked her up, so that she was forced to wrap her legs around his waist. He walked with her to the couch, settling his body on top of hers, never breaking their kiss. His hips were wedged between her thighs, moving against her. If they'd been undressed he would have slid inside of her, he was so perfectly placed. The feel of his erection burning against her made her wiggle closer, try to settle her damp heat against him, get that fraction of an inch closer.

They stopped kissing, staring into each other's eyes for a moment, and Valerie wanted to shout at him, tell him she loved him, that she'd loved him for years and that she always would.

Her fingers clenched on his shoulders as she forced herself to stay quiet but she wondered if he knew because he made a whisper soft shushing noise before slowly lowering his head back to hers.

She met him halfway and wondered if they were both being careful for fear of breaking the moment.

Jack's lips touched hers again and she felt her whole body soften, her lips part, welcoming him into her. The kiss was sweet and then it changed.

She couldn't have enough of him fast enough to put out the flames. Val crushed her lips against his, years of build up for this moment wiping out any trace of gentleness, as desperate urgency replaced her hesitancy. He groaned and pushed back with his mouth and hips. His head tilted to the side, trying to kiss more of her, deeper. Her hands fisted in his hair, the dark silken strands sliding between her fingers, like silk.

There was no hesitancy or softness in him as he moved his lips to her neck. Needing the friction, she tried to move against him, grinding her hips into him, wanting every part of their bodies to be flush. Jack's hands settled on her rear, pulling her closer to him. His mouth came back to hers for a wet and open kiss that made her whole body clench in need. She nipped him.

He jerked against her in pleasure, grinding his pelvis against her over and over, mimicking the movement of thrusting within her and she realized how easy it would be—a few pesky scraps of fabric removed and he could be inside of her.

This could be real.

His breath came harsher and she desperately wanted him to palm her breasts. She could hear them both panting heavily in time to the thrust and press of their bodies.

I could come just from this, she thought dazedly. It was just right, a deep pulsing press against her and she wondered if he knew how much this turned her on. How each stroke made her climb higher, want to squeeze him closer and closer.

His tongue swept into her mouth again and she knew this was what it would be like if they had sex; hard and fast, desperately urgent. She'd be making up for years of repression and a future that could be finite.

She moved her hands down his back, under his shirt. His skin was warm and smooth, the muscles bunching against her fingers. He shivered and exhaled harshly next to her ear, raising goosebumps across her skin. She felt powerful.

This was *her* Jack and he wanted her back.

She felt the muscles of his sides, traced his shoulders, feeling the hard muscles tense and relax as she touched him.

Val moaned loudly when his hand cupped her breast. Then he kissed her neck and she put her head back, urging him on. Jack bit her lightly on the neck then licked her soothingly. He sucked her earlobe into his mouth, his breath exhaling in her ear, sending shivers down her body.

"Oh God, Val," The words were dragged from him, his voice deep and agonized. It was the most erotic thing she had ever heard and it was enough to push her over the edge. She felt her whole body tighten, pulse endlessly and then relax as she came with a cry against his mouth.

She breathed heavily and pulled back a little, saw the want on his face. He'd watched her orgasm and in response he was grinding himself against her heavily, kissing her deeply while he restlessly shifted his weight against her as though he could will the fabric away.

And then something changed. The kiss became slow again. An exploration of her mouth as he savored her, tasted her and traced the shape of her lips. His hand fisted in her long, heavy hair and she wanted him to tug harder.

Val closed her eyes and said something encouraging. But Jack released her, striding to the other side of the room like the hounds of hell had a hard-on for Italian flesh.

Jack took some deep breaths and put his hands on his hips, pulling himself together.

That's it?!?

Without a doubt, he was letting her go, she knew it. He looked at her, his eyes raking her from head to toe like he was imagining her naked. His gaze was predatory and she wondered if this could continue if she pushed him.

Taking a deep, fortifying breath, Val walked towards him. "Jack, come on Jack." Her voice was sultry without trying. Val was ready for bed, ready for him, had waited years for them to get to this point and she wouldn't let him leave without a fight.

If she let him go now, she'd always wonder what could have happened, if she'd let her future slip away because of her own cowardice. She couldn't take that risk.

A look of pain flashed across his face and he closed his eyes. She tried to twine her arms around his neck but he held her lightly away from him, maintaining several inches of distance.

"Val, this was a mistake. We are both wasted and out of our minds. In the morning we will regret this."

I won't. But he would. Val tried to disagree but couldn't think of anything to say.

"This has always been here Val. We know it and we avoid it because it doesn't change anything. All it will do is tear us apart."

"We are already apart. How can this make it worse? What if something happens Jack, and one of us dies? I want to know what it's like. I want you and I always have." She tried to step in close to him again but he gripped her wrists, a light squeeze that stopped her cold.

"Do you know what I have in my life? You. You and your father. Everything I do is for you and my parents. You are so conflicted and desperate to run from me and this life.... I don't blame you. But I can't do this every day and have you as my weakness. You hate this life and eventually you would hate me too." There was a pause before he spoke on a sigh. "You'd destroy me."

She shook her head in denial, tears sliding down her face.

Leaning down, he kissed her on the lips. Quickly. He wiped away her tears with his thumb, his hands on either side of her face. "I know the life you want and I can't give you that. And maybe it makes me an asshole, but I don't want to taste what I can't have." He took in a breath but didn't release her. "I had a *perfect* childhood Val and they—it was ripped away." His voice trembled with grief, making her cry harder.

She clung to his hands, trying to keep some link with him for as long as she could.

"I see the life you have, what you have made for yourself and I want that for you. I am trying to be a good enough man to want that for you...so don't torture me with this. I'm not the white picket fence guy. I like you happy, carefree. You're my bright spot, the light in my life." he paused, "And yeah, I read it in a Hallmark card but it's still true."

Val choked on a desperate laugh. With all her heart, she wanted to deny his words. "This isn't funny." There was nothing else to say, she couldn't believe it. *I always have something to say!*

He let her go and she felt numb, like she'd survived the apocalypse.

Each step felt uncoordinated, one foot in front of the other but nothing to do with her. The stairs were hard: heavy and slow. A part of her didn't expect to make it to the top, as though her grief would bring her crashing down.

Wouldn't he change his mind? She'd feel his arm stop her, pull her back and things would work somehow. The fairytale come true. It wasn't even a fairytale she wanted, dammit! She wanted normalcy. A hot boyfriend who loved her, was that an exceptional wish?

But he didn't stop her.

****

The next morning she felt like a husk. And she was the proud owner of the hangover from hell. No returns allowed.

Jack drove her to Berkeley. It took two hours from San Loaran. Neither of them spoke and Val looked out the window. The view changed from dry, flat land to rolling hills and then it was gone, covered in concrete and civilization. What would she do amongst all these people? How would she function without Jack and the friends she had known?

He took her to her dorm in brittle silence. Then, dropping her bags off with a heavy thunk he disappeared for a while. Examining everything, she knew. Her father had already been here and done that, but Jack would do it again.

He came back. Jack knelt before her and she turned her head away from him. She didn't want to see his beautiful face. She could feel the sadness like a weight in him but he was the one turning away from her. She would have tried, would have thrown herself into *anything* with him if he'd asked, screw the consequences. They'd deal with it when they had to.

But that was what made them different. She let her life be blinkered while he planned it all out and he knew how this story ended even if she didn't want to.

Jack took her hand and put the pager into it.

"You didn't have to go to all that trouble to get me to take this. I would have taken it without the mind fuck." She gave an ugly little laugh and he stayed where he was, watching her, ready to take whatever she would say.

"Do you know what, Jack?" Her voice quavered and she wasn't sure if it was rage or pain that caused it, probably both.

He gripped her tighter, as though it was hard to force himself to stay still and not take her into his arms. *Good!* She hoped it was hard for him too. She watched her fingers twist amongst themselves, like unsettled snakes.

She wondered if she should just let him leave, have things unsaid between them like they always did. But that wasn't the life she wanted anymore. "I would have made love with you last night. I wanted you.... I've thought about that so much, fantasized about you and me for...ever. And so I waited. Do you understand? There was no one else. I waited for *you*. But I won't anymore." Her voice broke at the end.

With a grim expression he nodded and rose, went to the door and left—without a single look back.

CHAPTER 5

LONDON, ENGLAND
SIX MONTHS AGO

Val pushed the door open with her bottom, holding the suitcases tightly, knowing that if she put them down, she'd be too tired to pick them up again.

Twenty six hours ago she'd been in San Francisco and now she was in London. The awe, enthusiasm and amazement were becoming buried under a fierce desire to shower and nap. London had been around for hundreds of years, and she figured it'd be there after her nap too.

The hallway was dingy and bare except for a piece of paper taped on the wall. It said 'Hampstead pub crawl tonight at 8pm' and was written in red pen.

A pub crawl. That sounded *youthful*. Nothing said London like a pub crawl! She hoped it was as simple as she thought it was: Go to pub, have drink, repeat until intoxicated, crawl home.

Her room was on the second floor. There were bathrooms at both ends of the hall and a communal kitchen. The walls were shamefully thin but the room was large and had huge windows that opened up to a nice courtyard below.

Val unpacked and took a long nap which forced her to hurry or be late. Somehow she managed to show up at the kitchen at eight o' clock on the dot. The natural look was in, right?

There were twenty other kids there already. *Kids*. She was twenty one. Yikes. Maybe she was too old to be living in a dorm after all. She was going to graduate school and the woman in Admissions had sworn that there would be others her age here, working on their degrees as well. Hmmm.

To say the kitchen had seen better days was inaccurate. It might have been newer, but it had never been anything beyond functional in the cheapest sense of the word. This was a kitchen used to students, which meant everything was dented or slightly broken. Some of the cabinets were hanging askew, like they'd been ripped off and screwed back on by a drunken repairman.

The toaster had what was hopefully butter, smeared all over it, and the table looked...sticky.

I'm too old for this. Could she get her money back? Find an apartment somewhere? But it was only a year, right? Did she really want to be on her own, with no one to talk to? She made a tsking noise under her tongue, thinking then looked around her again. *Oops.*

She'd been staring into the distance, thinking her own thoughts but a young man had been in the way. Now he was watching her, a smile on his face. Oh god. He thought she'd been checking him out.

Val blushed. He *was* handsome. Light brown hair and blue eyes. His smile was slow and reached his eyes. He smiled a lot, she could tell just by looking at him. He just looked like a happy guy. What a novel idea, she thought, comparing him to Jack's doom-and-gloom-persona. Ooh, he had nice teeth too. That was when it clicked, a feeling of rightness and potential belonging. She was in London. She was young and free, Jack and her father were thousands of miles away and she could be someone different.

They left the dorm and began the walk to Hampstead Village. Purple brick mansions lined the streets, narrow steps leading up to ornate doors with heavy brass knockers. Huge Range Rovers and full-sized American cars were parked on the small streets, towering over their European cousins. Not too shabby for a dorm location.

"You know Rod Stewart lives around here."

She turned and there he was. The handsome one. "Really? Do you know which one?"

He laughed. "No. It may not even be true. My roommate told me. But he's Northern and you can't trust them an inch."

"What?" She was perplexed but amused.

"He's from Northern England, near Liverpool. He's nice enough, but they're a very disreputable sort."

"That's a terrible thing to say!" She laughed anyway.

"And snobbish." He contributed helpfully. "Class warfare is alive and well in England. There, now you know. We also have good fish and chips. I'm Ian." He held out his hand to introduce himself.

Val took his hand and noticed he had nice nails too. His palm was smooth and not too warm. They chatted all night. Ian bought her a drink at the Wellington, then bought everyone a round at The Dog and Crook, which resulted in much cheering from her bleary-eyed new friends. By the fifth pub, everything was hilarious. She laughed and danced. Blur came on and they all sang along with abandon. It was so different from America. Liberating somehow.

Ian maneuvered her into a corner and kissed her lightly, waiting to see if his kiss would be rebuffed. He tasted of ale and she knew he'd taste the cider she'd had several pints of. Fermented apple juice was the gateway drink to beer. Who knew?

Ian pulled back. "You taste like apples. I thought girls were supposed to taste like strawberries." He said it in a James Bond accent that came complete with a raised eyebrow and smug expression.

She actually giggled. "At least it's a fruit. Have you ever kissed someone after they ate a loaf of garlic bread?" *That was dumb.* But seriously, she was so drunk he was lucky she could say anything, let alone coordinate a kiss.

Smiling, his lips met hers again. Val closed her eyes and leaned into him, feeling her heart pound and a sweet desire unfurl within her. She twined her arms around his neck and he held her lightly, kissing her until she felt a little light-headed. Val pulled away from him. "I'm sorry. You are so cute, and I am so drunk, but we have got to stop. I need a shred of reputation or this will be a really long year. I can't make out with you in public on the very first night of school."

Ian squeezed her hips lightly. "Maybe you don't need your reputation. Maybe we are perfect for each other and it's a grand passion. Uncontrollable. Forever." Her brain was hazy but that was wrong. Forever was wrong, reminded her of vampires and the life she'd left behind. The Hell she would! She'd kiss him, make herself think about Ian and not worry about—

Why is he watching me? Seated at the bar, back to her, was a man. A mirror ran along the length of the bar and patrons could look into it and see the people behind them. He was watching her, burning her with his gaze.

Her heart fell all the way through her body to land on the beer soaked carpet.

Jack!

The look in his eyes sobered her up. Sort of. He threw back the rest of his drink, something dark in a shot glass. Without taking his eyes from hers, he reached into a pocket in his black, cashmere coat. He pulled out an envelope and held it up between two fingers, summoning her to him from across the crowded pub.

Fucker.

Val made her excuses and went to the bar, Ian letting her go with mild confusion over her sudden departure. All the women were watching Jack either overtly or with sidelong glances.

But oddly, the chairs surrounding him were empty. As though people knew he was dangerous and determined, not someone to trifle with. There was something hard about him. His eyes were cold and flat, reminding her of the famed London fog.

His expression was a mask of boredom with the slightest hint of anger and a dash of disgust. *The recipe of Jack.* He turned towards her, leaning back so his elbows rested on the bar. A cool and relaxed pose.

Val smiled. She was drunk, she couldn't help it. And after the last time she'd seen him, three years ago in Berkeley, he deserved this. She was free. So what if he found her? A sober part of her wondered what he wanted and worried that he'd try to take her away.

Placing her hand on his thigh to steady herself, she felt the hard muscle bunch under her fingers. His jaw locked together rigidly in a sign of frustration. It made her smile.

She was a devil when she was drunk.

Val leaned into him so that if he looked down he'd see straight down her top. Her cheek pressed against his and she whispered into his ear breathily, "What brings you to a merry little pub like this? And where were you six hours ago when I was carrying all that stupid luggage? Look at my hand, it's still red and I chipped a nail." She made sure her voice was a little bit pouty.

She stuck her hand out in front of her so that he could take it and look at her palm. His eyes flicked down but then met her gaze squarely again. He didn't touch her and she had the impression he wouldn't touch her with a ten foot pole. Jesus. After three years he could still rip her open with a look.

"Don't worry I'll get someone else to touch me instead," she snapped, wanting to hide the hurt he'd made her feel.

"You. I'm here because of you. As always. Your father wanted you to have this. Read it. It's a list of areas to avoid, any intel we have about the scene in England. Safe houses that you can go to if something happens. We are going to Africa. We won't be around for a few months. If you need anything, call Gilbert Arthur. We'll check in with him when we can. Got it?"

"How is Gil?" She asked, partially to irritate Jack and also because she wanted to know. He was a sort of unofficial coordinator for the Hunters.

Jack looked around the bar in boredom, "He's good. Says 'Hi'."

She leaned away from him, feeling very sober now. "That's *great*," she said just as insincerely. "And how is dad?"

"Also fine," Jack waited.

"Also great," *Really? This is our conversation?*

Her hands clenched at her side. She should just let him go. But she wanted to see him, even if he was angry and disgusted with her, she wanted to look at him, see the changes of him. His hair was shorter, his skin tanned and dark. She could see a bruise on his jaw and wanted to ask him how he got it. Wanted to touch it.

"Why are you going to Africa?"

He gave her a look and she knew he wasn't going to tell her.

"So if you guys go missing, I'll start in South Africa and ask who's the big bad vampire until someone tells me, or hears about the dumb American girl who believes in vampires and is looking for them." She finished in a sing song voice, "I guess we know what will happen..." Val dragged her finger across her throat, imitating her throat being slit.

He leaned towards her, his face inches from hers. She could feel his breath as he spoke, smell the alcohol and she wanted to kiss him so much that if he'd told her she could have just one taste of him but then she'd have to give up London—she might have done it.

In that moment, she would have left it all behind.

"That is deeply unamusing. Does it really matter, Val? Why threaten to come after us? You haven't before. You don't want to know what we—screw it. I'm outta here."

He's going to leave!

"Jack," she said, voice stricken. What the hell had happened to make him so antagonistic? His eyes dropped to her lips and his gaze fixed on her mouth. It made her stomach tighten.

"You want fun, not family. You have *never* chosen us."

She'd done it; pushed him too far, made him lose control a little and that was even more tempting than anything else. Val had imagined him taking her in a darkened fury more times than she liked to count.

He never touched her but part of her kept hoping he would. That the emotional outburst would turn physical. As though he could read her mind, his lips curved into a half smile that was more sneer than happy.

"You have a good night, Val. We'll let you know when we get back." He stood and she stepped back. He was a full head taller than her and so imposing it was instinctual to move out of his way.

With quiet despair, she kept her mouth closed. She wouldn't do anything, dammit. Wouldn't wish him well, wouldn't say goodbye and sure as hell wouldn't apologize. All she was doing was living her life. He'd rejected *her*. What did he have to be pissy about?

But there was another reason she didn't want to say goodbye to him. She didn't want to jinx it. If things were an emotional mess she knew he'd survive. It was a stupid and irrational way to behave. Crap, it was probably just an excuse to not fix things. But she did believe it, at least a little bit. Happy people died. If he had unfinished business and anger, he'd come back to her.

Anger socked her in the throat and she reached out her hand to his chest, pushing him back down to the bar stool so that they were the same height. He let her, she knew that. Jack could have stopped her, or even resisted a little, but he wasn't.

"We are not done. So what? You had a few days off and thought you'd come to see how I was doing? You don't have a Google account?"

"I see how you are doing. Moving a bit fast, aren't we? Helpful tip, hard to get is *actually* a turn on."

Val threw her head back and laughed, her heart breaking with each forced sound. "Please! *Please*, tell me that you are chastising me for flirting with that guy?

"His tongue was down your throat. Maybe I'm a prig, but that's not flirting."

"You are such a jackass. You are not my father. You just want to keep me in a cocoon. I'm twenty one now. Stop checking on me like this." Even as she said the words she wanted to take them back. *Do check up on me,* she wanted to tell him. *Or else I know I'll never see you again and I like knowing that you will at some point show up.* But she kept her mouth shut.

"Your father worries about you," Jack's deep voice became husky with sincerity.

"Then where is he? Life is fleeting and where is he?"

Jack shook his head and she could feel his disgust. "He saves people. We save people. You go have a drink and screw your English boy-toy. Christ, Val." He didn't look back at her, staring resolutely towards the door, and she knew he was dying to get away from her.

Val wanted to slap him. He always made her feel guilty and small. Grabbing the envelope from him, she stalked away.

Ian was waiting for her, clearly with questions about the man she'd talked to at the bar. *No more questions.* She went back to Ian and grabbed him by his shirt, pulling him in for another kiss. He looked surprised as she wrapped her arms around him and kissed him hard. He pulled back a little and gentled the kiss. A brush of lips over hers, instead of the bruising grind she'd greeted him with. Relaxing, she forced each contracted muscle to not tense over Jack. The kiss was slow and had the excitement of newness. When she came up for air, Jack was gone.

****

Jack left the pub, his blood boiling as usual. What a spoiled brat! He walked silently through Hampstead to the Northern Line tube stop. The flight left at six am, back to America. *Not soon enough.* He'd done what he was supposed to do and given her the information. He'd checked on her and seen her. Val was fine. Shit, she was better than fine: she was going to slut her way through London for the next year. Maybe he'd leave that part out when he saw Nate.

He got to Heathrow at one in the morning. He checked in and sat down in a chair, his back to the wall, so that he could see everyone as they came towards the gate. Closing his eyes, he tried to sleep.

Someone in his line of work could sleep anywhere, under any circumstances. He rested his head back against the chair, crossed his arms, and sprawled his legs. He tried to think of nothing. Clear his mind and sleep but he kept seeing her in his mind. She was gorgeous. So fucking gorgeous. Not in an obvious way. She was probably considered pretty by others, but to him she was like an inferno.

Tonight, she'd worn jeans that looked like they had been painted on they were so tight. Jack remembered the flash of generous cleavage as she'd leaned over him, daring him to look at her. He scrubbed his hand over his jaw, wanting distance from the memory of her body.

Who was he kidding? He was too tired and too lonely to fight his memories tonight anyway. Thoughts of her hand on his thigh. Her breath in his ear, made him hard. More memories came to him unbidden, her straddling him, her-

Christ.

He thought of the night before she left for college. Just once, he'd wanted to give in to her. After all those years of her looking at him with adoration and lust, while he feigned ignorance.

Why was it so hard to keep her away and not want her? Just last week a vampire had attacked him outside of his home. That was not the life for Valerie. She'd been through enough and worked hard to be on her own.

In a way, maybe he was her weakness too. So he kept himself away from her. Now he saw her as little as possible. It was too painful. Especially after he'd held her, kissed her, felt her shudder in climax against him. God, he wanted her so much. But, he wanted revenge... and they both knew that he wanted revenge just a little bit more than he wanted her.

And yet, in his weaker moments and in his dreams, he'd thought of her thighs over him. Val on top of him, clasping his hands, but gripping him, pulling him up and towards her—*this is not restful*. He loved that hair of hers, so thick and rich. A hundred browns. Dark hair that glinted in the sun.

Her eyes drew him too. He could look into those dark eyes forever. See himself reflected in them, chocolate brown with gold flecks. When he looked into her eyes, he knew she loved him back. Or at least she had. She appeared to have no trouble moving on now. What a cluster fuck they were in.

He tried to push these thoughts away, focus on the mission in Africa but instead he dwelled on Val and Nate. The man wouldn't even try with her. He claimed that he didn't want to draw attention to her. Whenever Jack had to go see Val, Nate made sure he was somewhere on the other side of the world drawing attention to himself. Usually, pissing on Lucas's doorstep. Since half the world was his doorstep they had gotten away with it. They planned each attack thoroughly, planned with contingencies and they had succeeded and lived this long because of their caution.

The mere thought of Val trying to do what they did made his blood run cold. She wasn't calm enough or methodical enough to keep herself safe. She acted first and thought later. So why did he always taunt her, want to convince her to stay with them?

With him?

Because he was a selfish bastard and he wanted to know that he meant something to her. He needed to know that if they died someone would think of him and remember him as family or as *hers*.

He needed another drink. Jack didn't drink very often but he was in the airport and it was almost daylight. He was safe for today. So he'd drink and torture himself with memories of all the times he'd let her go.

CHAPTER 6

LONDON, ENGLAND
TWO MONTHS AGO

Valerie sat alone at a small square table that had a nice view of the High Street. Her three hour long Monday class was over and she'd decided that staying conscious during an incredibly boring lecture on Ptolemaic History deserved, maybe even *required*, a nice lunch as a reward.

Cafe Rouge was near her dorm. It was a chain restaurant that Val feared she liked more than it deserved. Everything was black, white, or red and pictures of burlesque dancers, cats and bicycles decorated the walls. The decorations were meant to be French, but Valerie suspected that the decorator thought this was how people expected a French cafe to look, rather than how one actually did.

The waiter, a stinky and authentic French import, was busy talking at the bar and had been ignoring Valerie's bring-me-my-check-or-die stare for at least five minutes. Reaching into her bag, she pulled out her wallet, deciding the flash of cash might help speed things up.

As she righted herself, she saw a man sitting at her table across from her as though he'd been there the whole time.

Oh shit! Her bag dropped to the floor in shock.

"Lucas," Val said in a hush, like saying his name too loudly would give him power—or wake her up from a dream. What could he want? She lifted her hand, nervously tucking a strand of long brown hair behind her ear.

His eyes—a blue so Arctic and cold that it could give freezer burn—followed the movement, shifting ever so slightly to watch her hand before dipping down infinitesimally, and she just *knew* he was looking at the pulse of her wrist. Was that the equivalent of a guy checking her out? Scoping out her pulse? She was *fucked*.

"It's daytime!" she said, like it wouldn't have occurred to him that he could burst into flame at any moment.

"A benefit of my longevity," He said quietly.

"Can other vampires come out during the day?" She looked around the restaurant as though she might see a huge group of vampires dining on blood pudding and eyeing the patrons hungrily.

"No."

How old is this guy?

Hastily, she looked away from his face, not wanting to be caught by his gaze—again. Everything she knew about him rushed through her mind like a tidal wave. Ever since he'd saved her she'd tried to learn about him. She didn't know much; just that he was rumored to be well over a thousand years old. And back in his mortal days he'd been a warrior. He was intensely private and no one knew anything about him.

No one ever found his bodies. Whatever he did with them, there was never anything to associate a death with him. She realized she was kicking the table with her leg in agitation and stopped.

He *looked* like a warrior. *Repress all thoughts about being conquered!*

His looks were cold and Nordic. Patrician features, a blue gaze, square jaw and grim mouth. And yet, when Valerie thought of warriors, she thought of action, passion and speed. Lucas was contained, almost reptilian in his quietness. He was still, patient and detached, as though he had utter mastery over himself, his emotions and everything around him. Everything orbited around him without effort because he was so magnetic.

If there was action and passion to him, it was buried deeply under a mantle of icy boredom.

Lucas waited for her, almost politely, his legs crossed, power and confidence reined in, as though not wanting to startle her. He gave her a small smile. He was beautiful. Inhumanly so.

He scared the crap out of her.

His hair was long and thick, the color of ripe wheat ready to be harvested. It fell beyond his shoulders, heavy and straight. His lips were a pale pink, lighter than a human's would be, but fitting with how pale the rest of him was.

His hand was suddenly extended across the table to shake hers. Val blinked hard, she hadn't even seen him move.

"Valerie Dearborn. We meet again." She hadn't remembered that he had an accent. It was like he'd blendered up twelve languages and drunk them down in a gulp, so that when he spoke the words had odd pauses and cadences.

I will not harm you, he'd told her that night in the forest. Did he remember that now? Any chance it still applied?

Valerie looked around her. The waiters and waitresses were oblivious. Why wouldn't they look over here and see the beautiful and incredibly scary man sitting at her table? She sure as hell wouldn't be able to look away! Her gaze went back to his, then dropped to the hand that was still outstretched. Would he kill her? Could she run? She had to *know*! Fear blossomed within her—not like a flower, but like blood welling from a gunshot wound, spreading throughout her entire body.

"I will not kill you, but I do wish we could get past the formality." He nodded towards his outstretched hand.

Her voice was shocked and thready, "Can you read my mind?"

"No, but I understand your expression."

Hesitantly, Valerie slid her hand across the table until it was clasped in his. A current of sensation ran up her arm and swirled over her body like water sizzling on a stove.

She shook her head, denying the feeling. She tried to pull away but he didn't let go, gently keeping her hand in his. The almost painful sensation retreated like he'd turned the volume down.

Lucas still held her hand and there was something odd about the handshake but she couldn't figure out what it was. His hand looked normal...but it was perfectly conformed to hers, as if bones didn't matter or stop him from moving in any way he might choose.

It meant that his palm was slightly closer to hers, her hand encompassed by his. She pulled her hand away and he let her, leaning back, then idly picking up her iced chocolate milk.

He stared at it curiously for a moment, as though it were a small animal that had crawled into the palm of his hand. Almost hesitantly, he lifted it to his lips. He took a sip, his brows raising slightly.

What the hell did that mean? "Would you like some? I'd happily order you one. Even twenty if you let me out of here, you know, *alive*."

Lucas stared at her in a disinterested way, not acknowledging her words, and the moment became painful, her heart thundering in her chest, as she wondered and dreaded what his silence meant, why he was here and what he wanted from her.

An eternity ticked by. "No."

"No, what?" Her throat was parched.

"I will not kill you."

Gulp. She was waiting for him to say 'yet'.

"I am sixteen hundred years old, Valerie Dearborn. Your emotions shine from you, your expressions convey every thought in your head. I can chase you down in a moment. But I will not. Would you like me to promise you again? I promise I will not hurt you. I swear it on my very being."

"Lucas, is that like Cher?"

He continued to watch her in his reptilian way, so she kept talking, nerves prompting her to speak, "Only one name, no last name or family name?" *Shut up, Valerie!*

"Would you like to know my full name? I do believe it's hard knowledge to come by. Lucas Tiberius Junius." Each word was like a stone, a rock thrown into a pool that rippled outwards and all around the world.

"Tiberius Junius? Isn't that Roman?" she asked, fascinated despite herself.

"Are you familiar with the Visigoths or the Goths?"

"Probably not as much as you are. I thought they were separate."

"They are. But I was uncertain of your historical education."

What, he wanted to know if she got a good grade or something? The chocolate drink was in front of her and Val knew she was going to finish it. If she was going to die she wanted to go out with chocolate in one hand and a shopping bag in the other. She hadn't realized that she'd been quiet for a few moments until he spoke, breaking the silence and interrupting her deadly contemplations.

"My Hunter is dead."

His words yanked her back to the present. "Excuse me?"

He didn't repeat himself and so she had to think about what he'd said. "You had a Hunter? Like what my dad and Jack do or the Hunters who hunt animals?"

Another small smile was bestowed upon her, as though there were no difference. Perhaps there wasn't. Was he actually telling her that one of the Hunters helped him? That would be a huge betrayal.

"How else would you humans find us?"

She was surprised by his easy arrogance and snapped back, "Because people are intelligent and can follow clues and decipher patterns. Hello, CSI. Or Sherlock Holmes, if that helps you. I know you vamps get a little stuck in the past."

He actually laughed. It was rich and dark, relaxed and happy, not a laugh appropriate for a vampire. *Uh oh.* It slid through her, twined around her thighs and slipped inside of her body, making her twist in her seat, an unwelcome, no, a terrifying, glimmer of desire covering her like glitter.

She flashed a look at him. The laugh had stopped abruptly and he was looking at her oddly. Did he know? If so, how?

"A vampire is a master at deception and can travel faster and farther than a human. A vampire is stronger and more experienced than a human can be, centuries of practice honing our abilities to kill and survive. A human's skill will always be paltry in comparison. It's never been a fair fight and it never shall be. Every time a Hunter kills a vampire, it takes preparation and help. I provide it. The man I used to give information to is gone."

She had a horrible suspicion she knew who it was. "Gilbert Arthur."

"Good." He didn't sound particularly pleased with her, despite the praise.

"Why would you sell out the vampires?"

"Every creature needs to be policed."

"Yeah, right."

"What is a vampire's instinct but to kill and take? The division between gluttony and survival is slight.

Val spluttered in outrage. "Then you are doing a really shitty job, because lots of people—children and parents get slaughtered by vampires every day and there doesn't seem to be any policing going on." She flushed and looked away. Taking a deep breath, she wondered if she should apologize. *I'm sorry I don't stop and think first. Don't kill me, pretty please?*

"Do not let your emotions be your undoing." His words were deadly quiet.

"Are you threatening me?"

A lengthy pause, sky blue eyes boring into hers. Fucking hell, she needed to look away. She looked down but he leaned towards her, crowding in close to her so she could smell his cologne, see the strands of his hair inches from her fingers that rested on the table. She had to look back up and keep track of him.

"I am not threatening you. I am speaking to you, the very heart of you, asking you to be more careful with your emotions."

"I have a temper. I know it's stupid. I'm sorry."

He waved away her apology, "I presume you don't have a temper. In fact, you are undoubtedly quite tolerant. Loyal. And have a strong sense of right and wrong."

The words sounded like a compliment but his tone had been almost sad or cautionary.

Lucas leaned towards her, his hand on the table. His hand was large, long fingers, buffed and short nails but there were faint scars on top of his hand. A lot of them.

"Why do you have scars? Shouldn't you be...blemish free?" She'd wanted to say 'perfect' but thought poor word choice might lead to her doom.

"Injuries received when one is mortal are permanent." His hand was on the polished wood and Valerie found herself staring at it intently, forgetting where she was or the danger she was in, conscious only of the long, tapered fingers and the back of his pale hand before her.

She acted thoughtlessly, would later wonder what the hell had possessed her as she reached out and traced one of those fine white scars across his hand from his wrist until it disappeared between his middle and ring finger. His hand stayed still, allowing her to touch him without interruption.

"They are from swords and knives when I was a boy."

Val could imagine him with a sword, an avenging angel who could kill with an effortless swing. His scars were intriguing, humanizing, the flaw adding to his perfection since it was a reminder of his former humanity. His vampiric good looks were almost harsh in their otherworldliness, intimidating, while the scars made him seemed fragile, approachable.

Fallible.

Val realized what she was doing and yanked her hand away from his, hiding it beneath the table. He was watching her almost warily.

Sure, big bad wolf afraid of Little Red Riding Hood.

"I take great care to keep the killings down. Vampires have feeding partners, which ensures some stability and keeps loss of life to a minimum. We become attached to mortals, just like mortals do to each other. To take blood elsewhere can even be an affront to the relationship if a bond is strong enough."

WTF? "Where'd this come from? You make it sound like there is some kind of, what, love involved? Equality? I've seen what vampires do to their victims. I know how they...eat. If this is how you think vampires are, then no wonder you do such a crappy job policing them." Her heart started pounding. What the hell was wrong with her? Did she want to die? There was no way it was a good idea to push him.

"You are a Hunter's daughter and therefore you only seeing a vampire at their very worst; when they have behaved so poorly that the world notices. Why would you think there was anything kinder?"

Closing her eyes, Val tried to calm herself, wanting distance from her emotions so she wouldn't keep provoking him. "Can I just apologize, very sincerely, for saying things that are...bad for my life expectancy. I have *no idea* why I can't seem to shut up."

He was silent and finally she opened her eyes to see him watching her with an almost curious fascination. "Do not concern yourself; it is in your nature to provoke."

Huh. Maybe he does know me. "Is that on my face too?" she said sarcastically.

Lucas blinked slowly, then drummed his fingers on the tabletop.

That night, long ago when he'd saved her and forced her to kill the attacking vampire, he'd said he wouldn't kill her, maybe he'd even said he'd *never* harm her. She couldn't remember. Not if he'd actually said the words, implied them, or if she'd made that up in her mind.

But her idea of him, the golden vampire who'd saved her, would never hurt her. She trusted that like she trusted the news from the National Enquirer, and yet....Shit.

His hand smoothed across the checkered tablecloth in a gentle and distracted gesture, as though he were brushing bread crumbs away from him. It was an oddly human gesture but she suspected he was angry, that the gentler he became the more worrisome it was for whoever pissed him off.

Lucas sighed, and again it was a surprisingly human gesture.

"There was a time when things were different. There was a balance in the world. There were Others. Not only vampires, but werewolves, Fey, witches, empaths—they were all real. All powerful. If one group became too bloodthirsty or powerful, the others could unite long enough to restore a balance." A long moment passed.

"What happened?"

"Only vampires remain and I rule them all." His tone held no inflection, he was simply reciting facts, and the depth of his detachment raised goose bumps on her arm. It was really weird.

"Vampires have changed. Grown darker. The humanity leached out of them, stewards to nothing. There is no longer a balance."

"Hindsight's a real bitch."

He gave a Gallic shrug.

Lucas turned his head away to look outside. People passed by on the street, talking on cellphones, carrying groceries, and shopping.

A sliver of sunlight fell across his chiseled cheekbones; his skin was flawless, poreless and pale as marble. Val breathed in, expecting him to burn in the sun but he didn't. Nothing happened. He closed his eyes and tilted his face upwards, letting the sun touch him fully for a few moments before he turned back to her.

He could stand the sun?

"Even the sun cannot kill me now." he said, no doubt reading her face again, or her mind, or whatever it was he did so that he knew the answer to questions she didn't ask.

"My expectation from you is this. You are to research for me and do as I bid. I shall give you information about the groups that I once knew of and you will see if you can find traces of them. If they exist, I want to know of it. I want treaties with them and their integration back into the human world. From time to time I shall give you information about vampires that can be exterminated which you will pass along to the appropriate Hunter.

He hadn't mentioned her father or Jack. "Why would I do this for you? If they're so powerful and you're the Grand Poo-bah, why don't you take them out?"

"I kill vampires for specific infractions that are known to all. When a vampire dies his maker sees the death through the eyes of the departed. They know who has executed their progeny. If the last thing a vampire sees is a Hunter, then not only does it take attention away from me but it makes Hunters seem stronger than they actually are. I use Hunters to maintain distance as well as give the vampires something to fear. The older vampires are my responsibility. You and your men could not hope to kill an older vampire. Like Marion."

He paused, no doubt to watch her reaction and keep her in suspense. "She will kill Jack if he does not desist."

Her heart squeezed. Thinking of what he said made her stomach roil. "So, basically you have humans do your dirty work?" He didn't respond, didn't get offended. And why on earth was she still trying to provoke him anyway?

"I do find you interesting Valerie. Val. Like Valkyrie. You speak when you shouldn't. You do not cower. You have abandoned those who love you—even though it creates a hole inside of you. You are perfect for my purposes. An insider on the outside. Also, there is leverage for me which insures your loyalty."

My father and Jack.

Lucas leaned forward again, crossing his arms on the table, his heavy biceps flexing under his white, collared shirt. "Do you not find it interesting that your men have lived so long? Most Hunters do not survive more than a few years. They can only run for so long. Like a mosquito buzzing around, finally they draw enough attention to themselves that someone gives them a swat. And yet, your father has been hunting for more than a score of years and Jack for near a decade."

Trembling, Val dug her fingers into her thighs to try to contain herself.

"They are protected by me and shall continue to be so." His cold blue eyes burned into hers and she couldn't look away from him. Unless she created a problem, they'd live. He didn't bother to finish the threat. Yeah, she got it. She was really trapped, wasn't she?

His hand extended towards her and a file appeared in it, seemingly from out of thin air. "This information is for you. Search through it. I shall come to you again and tell you what to convey and to whom."

"Where should we meet?" Could he be ambushed? Could she get Jack, Nate, every Hunter in the known world to come and try to take him out? Would that even be enough? Forty odd Hunters to one bad-ass monster? Probably not.

"I will come to your little room."

He wanted to come to her dorm? *Hell, no*! Like she'd invite him in. "Here!" she said quickly, "I'll meet you here."

"No. Too public."

"But all these people have already seen us. Who are you worried will see you?"

"I have no concern for myself, only you. I do not want other vampires to know of my association with you. As for this cafe, no one has looked in here. And they won't. But expending that much power, to make all passersby disinterested, is foolish and might draw attention as well. It would not be wise of me to do so again." He had shielded them somehow, done something to make people not want to look into the cafe.

"But what about these people? They have seen you too."

The cold, almost haughty look continued, as though he didn't exert energy for facial expressions. A few tense seconds passed and Valerie felt compelled to fill the silence. "Have you ever played poker? You'd clean up, let me tell you." Her voice trailed off and she cleared her throat, crossed her arms as though she was cold and leaned back, pressing her spine into the hard wooden chair.

"You do not understand me and what I am. I am king to my kind. You must know me and my capabilities."

Lucas raised an elegant hand, prepared to snap his fingers and Val felt an overwhelming dread of what he might do. "No!" She lunged forward across the table, spilling the water and chocolate, felt the cold liquid seeping into her shirt as she gripped her hands around his to stop him from doing-*something*. Whatever he'd been about to do.

He allowed her to grasp his hand, pausing in midair while he looked at her with a painful intensity and animation. Her eyes went up to his, imploring him. "Don't do it! I understand. I'm sorry. I can't help it. I know what you are. I do!"

"What would I have done?" The words were spoken quickly, at odds with his previous unnatural calmness, almost as though he expected something of her.

"I don't know." She felt his hand beneath hers, icy cold and dry, light callouses on his palm. She feared letting go, tightening her grip to keep him still, even though her instincts were screaming at her to pull away and run as far from here as she could.

Lucas shifted in his chair, lowering his arm slightly so that his elbow rested across his crossed thigh, opening his palm in an almost peaceful gesture. Shifting her hands, she continued to hold on, only readjusting her grip.

The fear of letting go and what he would do if she did was greater than her desire to flee. His big hand engulfed both of hers so that when his fingers closed gently over hers, they were almost covered by his one.

His voice was soft, still interested, almost a bedroom voice used between lovers. Like he didn't want to be overheard but her answer was important to him, "You knew something. Tell me what it was, be it foolish or not, what did you think I would do?"

"Nothing. I just felt...dread. Fear I guess."

He nodded at her in a brisk motion and opened his hand, releasing her then gesturing to the room around them, the other diners and waiting staff. "I will only erase their memories of us."

"Does that mean I don't have to pay the bill? Crap- *I mean-* why would you feel like you needed to wipe us out of their memories?"

He didn't explain.

She sighed in irritation and he continued, "Events are happening that I am not in control of. There is no need to draw attention to you from my kind."

"Humph. Then maybe you should leave me alone altogether."

She thought he was thinking about it. He looked at her lips and her hair then away from her, brow knit in concentration. "I cannot imagine letting you go. Many would kill you just because of your relationship to the Hunters. You are not safe. You cannot get out of this destiny. You can only go forward."

"I don't want a destiny." Just thinking about it made her feel a little broken. Val wanted to scream at him to go away. Force him to understand that she'd just gotten her life the way she wanted it and that he was ripping it from her. Her dreams and future had just been thieved from her. Helping him would probably kill her.

"What about Jack? Your father? Even you? Do you think you are all safer with my help and protection or without it?"

What could she say? Certainly Jack and her father would be better off with his protection. Her? Probably not. But she couldn't turn her back on them to save herself. Her father and Jack would say that she'd already abandoned them, that by coming to England and going to school she'd run away. She couldn't believe that was true. They chose their lives and she was choosing hers. But if she told Lucas she didn't want him to protect Jack and Nate... there was a real chance they might die. And that would be her fault.

"If I don't help you, what will happen to them?" *Might as well get this situation crystal clear.* How crappy of a situation was he going to put her in?

"Your father is too old for this job. Jack is bloodthirsty and angry, but passion is not always a useful attribute."

Here was the question she was scared of asking, although the answer probably should have been obvious to her. "Do you want to kill them?"

Lucas ran his hand through his hair and the action startled her. He'd been so still that she had taken it for granted. "I don't enjoy killing or dislike killing. It makes no impact upon me either way. But, I remember a very long time ago that I did care, and that I used to believe human life had value. I curb my vampires' excesses because of those memories." There was a small pause where he watched her so closely she wanted to cover her face with her hands to break the penetrating contact, "Don't forget what I am, Valerie."

Tears filled her eyes. She didn't really see how she could forget that. But it conflicted with her memory of him. When he'd helped her and saved her. Val hadn't realized how important that memory was to her until he'd shattered it just now. "Why did you save me that time if humans mean nothing to you? Was it even me? Why were you there?" Each word seemed to become a little more desperate and high pitched so that by the end she could have won an Emmy.

Lucas negated her words with a gesture. Apparently, the time for conversation was at an end.

"I will come to you. And you will invite me in." The file was on the table as he stood and walked out the door. The sunshine touched him, glinting off of his long, heavy hair, making a halo around him.

There was something about his presence that gave a feeling of peace, of death so quietly offered that it was drawing. Alluring and relaxing.

The sun kissed him and a slight breeze ruffled his hair.

He disappeared.

Val left the restaurant as quick as she could, throwing money on the table and bolting out the door. Crossing the street, she walked by a small church and glanced at the old gravestones before hastily turning away. In that little churchyard there were mausoleums that were so old and weathered, the lids were broken in and cracked on the sides. More than once, she'd tried to peer inside, half afraid she'd see a skeleton or the glint of a coffin through the broken rock. But it was pitch black and she'd never seen a damned thing.

She'd never look at that cemetery the same way again. She'd be like that. Dead and time marching onwards so that she'd be forgotten, dust to dust and Lucas would still be perfect, immortal, making every place he visited glow with his splendor.

How many people had he watched die? Had he ever loved a one of them? No one could be that cold and have cared for anyone or anything.

And yet, he'd been so compelling and fascinating, looked like some sort of medieval champion in Gucci, that if he was the face of evil, what the hell did good look like?

Not only had Lucas saved her life, he'd helped her—been patient with her, taken away her fear, gone on to star in some of her better fantasies. And now, to see him again?

What did he want from her? *Really want*? Help, maybe. Did that guy need help from anyone? Nah. So he was here for something else. Is he here for me? Desire—heavy and smooth as gold weighed on her.

He'd been reserved and icy but every so often, when she crossed her arms, licked her lips or moved her hands he watched her avidly.

How do you say 'no' to *him*? She huffed, it was probably just as difficult to say 'yes'! Sure she liked the idea of being with someone so hot but man that was a lot of pressure. No amount of waxing, buffing or painting could make her feel secure enough to sleep with him. *Don't forget the fact that he might fucking eat you!,* a tiny and sane part of her brain said.

Eat and kill. That's what vampires did. She'd be just like her mother.

CHAPTER 7

LONDON, ENGLAND
PRESENT DAY

Sex. The horizontal mambo. Humptoberfest. The beast with two backs. Stuffing the turkey. Although that one probably didn't make it out of the United States and was only said in November. She was going to have sex with Ian tonight. It was like a compulsion, an urge. Like a lemming going over a cliff. Christ, she was the lemming. She was going to have sex tonight if it killed her!

Get it out there—loud and proud, she was not interested in Lucas because she was banging someone else. *Ta-da! If I'm sleeping with Ian, I can't sleep with Lucas. It's like a magic trick. Probably sleight of hand.*

Surely that wasn't *totally* evil. They'd been dating for three months, she'd met his parents and all of his friends from home. In fact, they were all refreshingly normal. His parents had even given her tea and fruitcake. Not that fruitcake qualified as cake. It didn't even belong in the desert category. It belonged firmly in the category of things-one-ate-to-live-longer-but-really-hated.

Ian was fun to be around. He was smart, charming, rich and a good listener. He was also handsome and genuinely cared for her. The real question should be why *hadn't* she slept with him before now?

Because he wasn't permanent.

He wasn't serious.

They dated and he was sweet but she had kept herself back from him physically as well as emotionally. But now that the big bad wolf was at the door, she was going to rush into the sack with him. *Oh yeah, this is a really good decision.*

For the umpteenth time she wondered if she was being melodramatic. Lucas had said nothing that implied he wanted her. Sure she'd touched him a little and he'd let her but it wasn't like she'd ripped her clothes off or propositioned him. Maybe she could resist him. Maybe she didn't even need to resist him because he wasn't interested.

No, he wants me and if I don't send a signal that I am unavailable, I'll be coffin bait for the rest of my life.

Alright then.

Val showered and dressed carefully. Ian came to pick her up and took her to Pizza Express. She loved their thin pizzas and salads. Why didn't California have pizza like this? Probably the same reason England had terrible hamburgers. Some things just didn't cross the pond.

Ian took her to the theater and they saw The Phantom of the Opera. Val had seen it before and loved it. They had considered going to see Cats but the Time Out review called it 'moth eaten' so Phantom it was.

Valerie had always loved the Phantom. Who liked the boring old knight in shining armor anyway? Oh no, she always liked the bad boy. As if the happy ending would last past the first orgasm. The irony was not lost on her.

When the opera was over and they left she was near to tears. Val had spent the whole time thinking about her life, the future and her current options until she was a wreck. Ian took her home and she started crying. He held her sweetly and even sang her a song to cheer her up.

He had a nice singing voice and like most English guys it seemed he'd been in a band for all of his formative teenage years. Pulling her wet act together, she splashed water on her face and convinced him that she was crying because of the play. He actually bought it.

When she turned her face to his and kissed him deeply he eagerly joined in. Almost aggressively, she pushed him back on the bed. He tried to protest a little, slightly disturbed by her change in emotion but she didn't stop and the protest was half-hearted at best. She reached between them, felt him through his dark jeans, then unbuttoned and unzipped his pants, maneuvering her fingers through his clothes until she felt his hard, silky skin in her palm. *This was right.*

Right now, with him, she wanted this. Let him possess her, she thought frantically, someone human claim her. Because she knew, in a terrified little part of her, that things were changing. Ian's hands were shaking when he put the condom on, rummaging around in his drawer and then his closet, trying to remember where he'd stashed them. Val laughed, surprised that he wasn't carrying one on him, just in case. With a mock frown, he told her it was her fault. He'd given up on thinking he was going to get laid and had told his roommate to have at them. Apparently, he had.

He kissed her over and over until they were both panting and then she spread her legs, felt him pressing against her.

Finally, when he was in her, moving gently, telling her how much he loved her, she believed it, clasping him closer, feeling only him as he blocked out the rest of the world and kept her safe in his arms.

Val slept in his room, trying to ignore Ian's roommate who came stumbling in, blind drunk at three am. Sleep came to her fitfully as her mind went over the events of yesterday, attempting to process just how much her life had changed in such a short amount of time. Lucas, sex, the secrets she now had. Also, the bed was made for one and Ian had disgracefully sharp elbows.

At 6:30 am, she was awoken by the cleaning ladies coming in and banging around in the kitchen. It was still dark outside and Val was exhausted when she snuck back to her room. The old ladies started in the communal kitchen, then did the bathrooms and finally opened every door so they could take the trash out and have a good gander at the irresponsible inhabitants. The last thing Val needed was to be gossip for the cleaning ladies.

When Val opened her door, she was struck by the cold and breeze. She froze, her gaze drawn to the open window.

Jack was sitting on her bed, his feet on the ground, back against the wall. His hands were laced across his stomach and he was the picture of relaxation. Sitting up, he put his elbows on his knees, turning his head towards her.

He looked her over, scrutinizing every inch of her. Her mussed hair, clothes that were rumpled because they'd been on Ian's floor all night, and she just *knew* she had mascara on her face from all the crying she'd done. She also knew her lips were a little swollen and that he could tell that too.

His lips thinned into a fine and angry line, his jaw clenched. He squeezed his hands together once, like he was restraining them from violence.

"We're back."

"Are you fucking kidding me?" He was here, now? Twelve hours ago she would have jumped him! He would have had to fight her off.

"Hard night?" Jack asked, his voice taut.

She put her hand out in front of her like she could capture his words and keep them from hurting her. Where had he been twelve hours ago? She drew in an unsteady breath. He stood and came towards her, wrapping his arms around her and holding her tight. Clumsily, her arms went around his waist and she tucked her head against his chest, listening to his heavy heartbeat.

"Are you alright, Val?" His voice was tender. Of course it was, this was perfect Jack. She could tear his fucking heart out and he'd want to know if she broke a nail. But the next time he'd wear armor.

She nodded against him, having no idea what to say. Then he was all business.

"Why do you have this information?"

She pulled away from him, following his gaze.

He'd opened the folder from Lucas and spread all the papers on the bed. She saw photos of Marion, the vampire who'd killed Jack's parents. She'd been off the grid for a decade. Not a whisper and yet here was a photo of her holding the hand of a young man in what, Switzerland? The bottom of the picture said Geneva and a date. Two months ago.

She felt his confusion.

"Why are you here?" she asked instead.

"Your dad and I went to clear out Gilbert's house and there was a note with your name on it. I just needed to make sure you were safe." He searched her face.

"Yes, because Gilbert's dead." She said absently.

"Yeah, he is. But how do you know?"

As far as he was concerned she didn't know anything about this stuff, had cut herself out of the loop on purpose when she'd chosen a normal life instead.

"These files look like his. That's even his handwriting. Why is it here with you?"

She thought quickly. "I've been doing some thinking for a while now and I wanted to help...a little." It was a good idea to stick to the truth as much as possible. "You guys were gone. I called Gilbert. I didn't want you and dad to know."

Something wasn't right and Jack knew it. "Why wouldn't you want us to know?"

Man, she hoped she could lie her way through this, "Because I didn't know if I could do it. I wanted to try to help on a trial basis. Why get your hopes up or involve you if I just decided to cut and run instead?"

Jack crossed his arms, surveying her like a teacher with a cheating student. His legs were spread a little, making him a bit closer to her eye level—but it was also a don't fuck with me posture.

"So, Gilbert sent you this?"

She nodded.

"What were you going to do with it?" Anger and disbelief threaded his voice.

"I was going to look up records in Switzerland, see if I could pin her down a little. Check obituaries, rentals, look for aliases or weird disappearances, stuff like that."

There was a lengthy pause as Jack organized his thoughts. She was surprised he didn't explode, cartoon style, he was getting so worked up. "You were going to try to get information on Marion? The monstrous *bitch* who stole my family? You were going to sniff around her and see what you could find, is that right?" He was moving towards her and she didn't realize she was backing up until her back hit the wall. "This I will take." He looked her body up and down, and she knew he meant her sleeping around, "But I won't let you get near her. You don't give her *any* reason to notice you. You shouldn't even *think* about her, do you understand me?"

She thought of Lucas killing Jack or her father if she tried to say no.

"You don't have the right to tell me what to do!" She was overcome with rage. Rage that he'd shown up too late. Rage at being forced to lie to him. Rage at being cornered by Lucas. She pushed him hard and he barely moved, allowing no more than a few extra inches between them.

"You passed me up, remember? It's my life and I'll do whatever I want to. If you want to be involved—great. But if you think you can dictate to me, then I will throw out that fucking pager and leave here in the middle of the night and you'll be lucky if you *ever* see me again." Val wondered if maybe she was laying it on a bit thick, but he was so infuriating!

Jack invaded her space again, voice lethally quiet. "First of all, you would never escape me. I would hunt you down, wherever you go. And secondly, you will do what I tell you when it comes to her. She is mine!"

Val nodded. He was at a breaking point and this was getting ridiculous. If Lucas hadn't forced this information upon her, she wouldn't have gone digging for information on Marion. She had a damn good reason to leave Marion alone: if Jack found out where she was, he'd try to kill her. And there was a big chance he'd wind up dead.

"You're right. Anything I find goes to you first. I won't do *anything* to get noticed. But I've made a decision that I can't keep sitting by and waiting for a phone call to hear that you are dead. I'm going to help. Wasn't that one of the problems, Jack? That I turned my back on my family and wouldn't help? Well, here I am. This is what you wanted, so don't try to shut me out." Val sighed, looking out the window at the lightening sky, "Let's face it, any vampire who wanted me could have killed me a long time ago. I just wasn't worth the time and attention."

Until now.

"Jack, I'm good at this. Did you know that Lucas is almost 1600 years old? Well, give or take a few centuries, the math is a bit fuzzy. I even know what he looks like."

He looked at her like she was a Sports Illustrated Swimsuit model. Lucas was elusive. Vampires had been tortured and talked of him but neither Jack nor her father had ever seen him.

"And as for Marion, I've found out more about her in my limited time of searching then you have in ten years. You're more likely to get her with my help. That's what you want, right?"

Jack paced away from her. "I don't know. I'm exhausted. I've been up for 36 hours, then I come here and your room is empty, yet you have pictures of Marion everywhere and now...."

Yeah, he'd just seen her come in from shagging her boyfriend and was turning his life upside down. *Great night.*

So, Lucas was giving them Marion. Guess she should have read the file sooner. He walked over to her desk and started writing. "Whatever you get, you can reach me here."

He put down the pen, and walked away from her desk towards the door. "Good night." He opened her door and stood in the doorway, not looking at her. He seemed momentarily frozen, then he rolled his shoulders a little and exhaled. "Val, it's really nice to see you. I'm sorry I've been such a dick." Then he closed the door and left.

His comment made her smile in a wobbly sort of way. Maybe that was the only conversation they would have about her dating other people. Maybe now they would move on and there wouldn't be this weirdness between them. She thought about how she might act if she saw Jack the morning after being with someone. Sad. Even after all this time a part of her would think that it should have been her.

Would she always feel that way? That if things had been a little bit different, Jack a little less haunted, that they would have made it work? He was her childhood love. Even though she was grown up, he was still around and in her life. He'd show up, be all alpha male, say something about how important she was to him and she just...couldn't quite get over him.

He was the fantasy. And a small part of her still hoped that if he killed Marion he'd be free. She could then convince him to give this all up and settle down with her.

She went to the piece of paper and looked at his tightly scrawled writing. The cell phone she had, mailbox she didn't. A secondary email address she'd never seen and a fax number were also listed. All with a strange country code. 420. What was 420? She turned on her computer and looked it up. The Czech Republic. Why was Jack based in the Czech Republic?

She put the papers and Jack's information back into the file and wondered about where to hide it. She didn't need Jack looking at that information again and she didn't want Lucas to find out about Jack. Folding it in half, she put it in the bottom of her box of tampons. That'll scare everyone off, she thought and then went to take a shower.

She walked down the hallway in her robe. It came to mid-thigh and had a definite 'lived in' look. It used to be a dark blue but had been washed so many times that the color had lightened to pale blue. Like Lucas' eyes, she thought. *I'm so stupid.*

The dorm had a communal bathroom. It sucked. Happily, no one else was taking a shower.

She thought about Jack. What if it had been him last night? Torturing herself, she imagined him taking off her panties, that it was Jack moving into her and over her.

Val imagined him stopping, gentling her and kissing her while she got used to the sensations. It made her heart break and she wondered when loving him would end. Would she spend her life wanting him, loving him, despite herself? *Pathetic.*

Jack had a death wish. And she knew that on some fundamental level he ranked his life lower than hers or her father's. That part of him had died when his parents died and he'd just never recovered.

Jack would live as long as she and her father did. So long as he could make the world safer for them. He was like a prisoner marking time and there was a depth of hurt and darkness in him that he hid and probably didn't want her to be stuck with. Sometimes she thought he'd snap. Like the last straw would settle on his shoulders and he'd go nuts.

A man who wouldn't have children with her, get a normal job, and laze about on the weekends reading the paper. Surely that was part of the reason that he kept himself away from her?

Pretty to think so.

He'd leave her and destroy her life by dying if it got him a crack at Marion. Was it selfish to want him to not be a hero? Sigh. Probably.

Val also knew why it upset him that she would get involved in the vampire biz now. He'd given up on her. Released her to have a happy life and now she was turning back. God, if he knew about Lucas he'd kill himself trying to get to him.

Val finished rinsing and then stood under the water for a good ten minutes. Watched the water swirl down the drain and tried to not think about anything important.

In England, she didn't have to think about wasting water, it rained all the damned time anyway. But bizarrely, England had a lot of droughts, even with all the rain. The pipes had all been set up during the Victorian era and were now falling apart. Huge quantities of water were lost because of leaks. That's the sort of crap a one hundred thousand dollar education got her.

It was time to get out. How long could one person hide in the shower anyway? She wrapped herself up in her Hawaii towel that she'd brought from home. It had lots of dolphins, and a couple of crabs with Hawaii written in big red letters.

Val walked back to her room, her little bucket with soap and razor clanking against her leg. She unlocked her door and walked in, thinking that her room was basically a cell: little sink in the corner, a chair to read in, a wardrobe, her desk and desk chair plus a twin size bed.

She put down her toiletries and closed the curtains so she could get dressed. She was about to drop the towel—

"Mortals seem preoccupied by nudity."

She whirled around. Lucas was sitting in her chair in the corner of the room. He'd been hidden when she came in the door. She needed to get a fucking security guard.

"What?" Her voice was thready with surprise and a healthy dollop of fear.

"You may not want to discard the towel yet."

Her anger from before was still near the surface, almost like a layer of warmth enveloping her skin. Lucas being in her room was too much. Instead of being meek and pleasant—which could keep her alive—she was angry and surly. "Well if you left, it wouldn't be a problem. How the hell did you get in here anyway? You're a vampire and I didn't invite you in. As I remember, that was the ultimatum, 'You will invite me in, Valerie,'" she said, imitating his deep voice and weird accent. Unfortunately, she sounded a bit like The Count from Sesame Street.

His eyes wandered down her body and lingered on her toes for a moment. They were painted purple.

"You have a helpful, yet surprisingly contrary, cleaning lady."

She scowled. *They do hate me!*

"Don't you think I'm at enough of a disadvantage without having to be naked in front of you? Go away!"

Three fingers rested against the side of his head, elbow propped on the arm of the chair, as he scrutinized her intently. "You are surprisingly insolent,"

Valerie looked at him quickly. He'd sounded amused. *Maybe. Who could tell?*

His eyes dipped down her body lingering on her legs and the hem of the robe at her thigh, like he was wondering what was under there. Why, it hadn't changed in the last thousand years, had it?

"I can assure you that no one else would dare speak to me in such a way. Usually, they say please, thank you and my favorite.... Yes, master." His voice was more of a drawl, with a definite hint of seduction at the end.

Oh, what a voice! She suppressed a shiver. It was so rich she thought of chocolate. Not a little bit of chocolate, but an overdose, like when Val wolfed down a whole bar and realized that if she didn't get water immediately she might dehydrate into nothing.

She blinked. What had he said? He wanted her to call him master? *Screw that.* "Yeah? Slavery is out dude. Catch up," she muttered, as she rifled around her drawer looking for underpants.

Lucas threw back his head and laughed. "You are terribly amusing,"

She'd better stop that! "Not really."

Suddenly, he was in front of her. Mere inches between them and she was trapped against the wall. His height was incredibly imposing, and she felt a little lightheaded being so close to him. He had his forearm resting against the wall, the other hand brushing lazily across the top of her towel. His touch was electric, little prickles of pleasure dancing across her skin wherever he touched. She could feel the echo of his fingers, even as his hand dropped back to his side.

Lucas captured her eyes with his and she didn't look away. She could hear her blood pumping slowly through her body and felt like she was in a trance. The whole world was slowing down, this moment with him an eternity as he encompassed her world.

Val looked from his eyes to his lips, their perfection drawing her in until she felt an overwhelming need to touch him back. Her hand reached up and slid through his long hair until she reached the ends, twisting her fingers so that it twined around her hand. *No man should have hair this great.*

She could smell him, expensive cologne and something under it...she didn't know what it was and while it wasn't unpleasant, she wasn't sure it was human either. Imagining smelling him, her nose pressed to the hollow of his throat, she had a sudden urge to lick him.

Her hand lifted away from his hair and went to his cheek. It was hard and cold like a statue and she pulled away, disturbed by the sensation.

Not human.

Taking a deep breath, she realized where she was, who she was with, and most worrying of all, what she was doing. Her thoughts were sluggish, her breathing deep and unnaturally slow.

Lucas shook his head, his hair swaying gently. Her gaze slid back to his mouth, watching his lips move.

"No, again," he said in an intimate whisper. Any hesitancy fled, and she reached back up to touch him. The cold, hard skin was now as soft and warm as a human's.

"How do you do that?" Val kept touching him, the backs of her fingers going from his cheek to his full lips. They had more color, looked soft instead of cold and cruel.

Val licked her lips unconsciously, wondering what it would be like to kiss him, but it was almost unfathomable as he was so... alright, she'd call a spade a spade, he was hot. Too hot for normal her. And he might eat her in a non-sexy way.

Lucas was emotionless and that radiated from him, an almost negative energy that had weight to it.

As her finger passed by his mouth, he opened his lips and licked her knuckle, a quick flick of his tongue, almost teasing. It was deeply erotic and her heart sped up, as though that tiny lick had been between her legs instead of on one ignominious knuckle.

Val was hyper-aware of her next breath, and felt her nipples tighten in desire. His breath was warm against the pad of her thumb. Lucas took her palm in his warm hand and turned it over, so he could kiss her palm, the sensation making another beeline to her sex.

His every touch was hardwired to her core, startling her into a breathy moan of pleasure. Lucas smiled, brought her hand to his mouth and breathed in her clean skin, his eyes closing as though he was just as fascinated by her as she was of him.

He placed another kiss gently in her palm before opening his eyes and licking her again. The touch stabbed through her, warmed her everywhere. He was only kissing her hand but moisture pooled between her legs and she moved a little restlessly towards him. *This isn't normal.*

Val felt like she was on the edge of an orgasm and all he'd done was kiss her palm. He let her hand go and she was so weak limbed that her hand plunked back down to her side, jerking her out of the strange trance.

His voice was like black leather, "I can play at being human too. Do you know what I can sense? Sex and Jack. Does he know about last night?"

It was like he slapped her. She shoved against him but he was solid as the wall. Angry, she ducked under his other arm and stepped away from him. "Don't touch me! I want ground rules for this relationship. *Working* relationship!" Her voice became shrill. "And one of them is you don't barge into my room and try to seduce me." He raised a brow and she knew he took exception to the word 'try'. As though he hadn't been trying and was offended that she thought that was the best he had.

"But most importantly, don't screw with my mind! You've got to *swear* to me you won't compel me."

"I confess, I had no intentions of... touching you when I came here. Your emotions affect me, even the remnants of them, like a fire that's died out but still gives heat. I did not expect it and was unprepared. I shall be more guarded next time. This does neither of us any good." He sounded almost sheepish, which was so incongruous to his ruler-of-the-world persona that she didn't know whether to believe him or not.

"*And?*"

"And...what?"

Furious, the words were loud, "You won't mess with my mind?"

Lucas looked very smug, a slight smile on his lips. "Ah, Valerie. I did nothing to you, I swear."

Her mouth fell open, gaping fish-style. *He's serious*! "Well, it's because you're a vampire then, right?"

His eyes narrowed. "What are we discussing?"

How mortifying! He wanted her to say it. *Didn't you make me act like a nympho using your vampire wiles?!*

Well, she wouldn't start keeping her mouth shut now! "Look, buddy. That ain't natural. You don't just touch someone and have them... *combust* unless there is some kind of supernatural mojo going on."

"In what way does the answer matter? If it's because I am a vampire, you are still affected. If not, then perhaps that's even more worrying for you? Do you want to know?"

Okay, maybe she didn't. This was all too confusing. "Just let me get dressed! Why don't you go find a Starbucks or something."

Twenty minutes later, Val was dressed and in the kitchen, eating her bowl of cereal while reading about Prince Harry in Hello Magazine.

A pale hand dropped a white bag in front of her.

Val froze, the spoon halfway to her mouth. She forced herself to keep eating, chewing her granola, even though it tasted like sawdust. Or Weetabix—both were bad.

"If I open this bag will I find a human heart?" Val couldn't believe she'd said that. Was it a joke?

"I paid for a croissant. If it is a human heart I shall be quite put out. And you would need to share."

Val leaned back in her chair, disbelief in her voice. "Really? You paid for this?"

He shrugged.

Maybe, maybe not, the gesture said. She could not imagine this... *manpire* standing in line for anything.

Whatever.

"Why did your Hunter get killed? Gilbert Arthur."

"I am not entirely sure."

That was rich. "Really? My guess is that you either murdered him, someone else murdered him to send you a message- not comforting by the way- or he got himself killed chasing down a vampire. So what was it?"

"I didn't kill him. His remains were found in a burned out warehouse in Melbourne. Everything was gone. I don't know why he was there or if another killed him. I couldn't sense anything. There was too much..." he seemed to be looking for the right word, "char."

"That's pretty unfortunate. Sounds like a message to me."

He waited.

Exasperated, she explained. "It doesn't make sense for a vampire to burn the place down if Gilbert was already dead, unless they didn't want you to know who did it. It's like, overkill." His gaze flicked to the door and one of the boys from down the hall, who was coming towards the kitchen, turned around and went back to his room.

Now that's a handy trick.

"Gilbert Arthur was under my protection. Whoever killed him would not want me to know they had done it. I would have avenged him."

Val gave him a sarcastic smile. "That's sweet. I'm sure he'd give you a big high five of thanks if he weren't dead. So whoever did it knows you can't trace a smell if it's been burned badly enough. What other weaknesses do you have?"

A long pause. "Empaths."

"What's an empath?" Val looked at her cereal then pushed it away. She couldn't eat with this guy sitting across from her.

"One of the Other kind that has been long gone. Vampires can feel things to a certain extent, but it fades over time, especially positive emotions. The older a vampire gets the more they are drawn to slaughter because they are emotions that can still be felt. But an empath can convey emotions to a vampire. Evoke, even restore... everything." His tone was carefully neutral.

"But you killed them all? And I thought people were trigger happy. You think that if vampires could feel positive emotions, they wouldn't kill?" Val admitted to herself that the idea was intriguing, but she couldn't believe that vampires were anything other than murderers. They survived by eating people, for God's sakes.

"It is in our nature to hunt humans. But we do not need so much blood as would kill a person to survive. That's simply gluttony. Look at Marion, for example. When she was human, she was a mother. Now she takes children for companions, but it is a habit. She no longer loves them, they do not make her feel love or affection and so she discards them. Always looking for something long gone. Once upon a time, she was kind to her companions."

"So now that she's crossed a line, she can be killed? Marion was still, is still, feeding on children. That's not love, that's sick."

"I do not know. I have lived a very long time. Most children, if they survived birth and were not instantly killed by their parents, died young. They died from disease and famine, simple cruelty. If they had a family they would be fortunate if they were raised by their own mothers. Mortality rate for a woman dying in childbirth was very high. Domestic violence did not exist, it was life. Often I am surprised people have thrived at all. But now we live in a time where all life is thought to be valuable."

"So you let her eat and kill children because it was better than death?" This was too weird, too ruthless. "What do you want?" Val looked down the hallway and saw Ian heading towards the shower, a towel around his waist. Her heart started thundering and Lucas turned his head towards Ian, like a wolf who'd scented a hare.

She reached out and grabbed his hand to keep him at the table. Lucas was ice cold, his hand marble again. He closed his eyes and then his hand became warm and soft.

"Why don't you just keep yourself warm all the time?" She was trying to distract him.

"It takes an inordinate amount of energy to maintain. Also, it is daylight and I have already dematerialized twice today." He turned his head back towards her. "I am not limitless." The words were just above a whisper, his face close to hers. The comment made her stomach clench, like fingers were sliding along the walls of her stomach. An image came to her of him being totally sated, so used and exhausted he could barely move.

His head tilted to the side like he could hear her thoughts, eyebrows raised slightly as though he was surprised by her. Valerie blushed and looked away while Lucas smiled at her slowly.

"He loves you."

She pulled her hand back.

"Who?" It was defensive.

"The young man you gave yourself too. He cares for your happiness."

She nodded.

"You believe Jack would have been gentle too?"

Her voice was a whisper, she was petrified now. "What?"

"You believe Jack could contain his rage and lust, so that he could have lain with you purely?"

Did he really expect her to answer?

"Perhaps you have more faith in him than you should."

She reached her hand out again but he was ready, her fingers met his warm palm as he turned his hand to lie face up on the table. The warmth of his hand was like a caress. "Please don't kill them. Please," Val couldn't keep the quaver from her voice.

"I will not harm someone who only means you well."

Lucas was watching her intently. "Your thoughts radiate across your face."

She remembered what he'd told her. "That's right! And it makes me really boring, doesn't it? Mr. Seen-it-all. Now, what do you want?" She took the bag off the table and opened it. The croissant was really flaky and butter had made grease stains on the inside of the bag. This was going to be a really good croissant. She took a bite. "This beats the ones at the train station."

He looked affronted. "Well, yes."

The pastry melted in her mouth, and she tasted orange marmalade in the middle.

"Honestly, this is so good it's like it came from France."

He squinted a little. "It did."

She almost choked.

Lucas waved a hand to dismiss the conversation. It was nothing, the gesture said, 'I go to Paris to get croissants for all the girls'. Crap, maybe he did, but it was worrying. Because it was a *very* romantic gesture.

And I'm a sucker for shit like that. See, romantic?

"I want you to do some research." Another file appeared on the table and she flipped it open. There was a report about wolves in England and how they had been hunted to extinction centuries ago. A list of reference books was included and stapled to that were excerpts of local werewolf legends. Part man and part wolf, they roamed the woods, their change dictated by the lunar cycle. *Yeah, yeah, yeah. Werewolves were always the same—dogs.* Woodcut pictures of wolves stealing children from their beds or destroying livestock were at the end. The pictures were creepy and odd. Almost out of place as well, but Val couldn't have said why.

"So you think there are werewolves, huh?"

"Possibly."

"Hmm. And you think I could find them?" She said skeptically.

"If they exist, you have the best chance of finding them. They will not come near a vampire, especially not me. Also, my people do not need to know my plans. I suspect they would be irritated."

"Why do I feel like that's an understatement?"

"Because you have both beauty and intelligence."

Nice. "You said they were violent. Why start with them and not the Fey or some friendly wiccans?"

"There are no friendly wiccans. It's impossible. Do not concern yourself with the choice I have made, simply carry it out."

Like a please would kill him.

He continued to stare out the window and she thought that Lucas was not normal. It was like he played at human, but then when it all fell away he was not quite a corpse, but not alive either. It was hard to determine what made him seem so inhuman.

"It's because I don't breathe." He didn't turn towards her but continued to stare out the window so she could only see his profile.

How the fuck does he know these things?

"You look at me and I can sense your…conflict," he said the word very precisely.

She wanted to contradict him but anything that kept his interest in her at bay was probably for the best. Besides he was a vampire, it didn't really matter if he was beautiful.

"Let's pretend I find a werewolf. Then what? Take some doggy treats and hope for the best? What do you think I am going to do? Why would they even talk to me? You say they are in hiding, population decimated and you want me to saunter in and talk to them?"

"I endorse you."

"What does that mean?"

"You would be a neutral party, given safe passage through their lands."

"But, I'm basically your puppet."

"Your father is a Hunter. Known for killing my kind. That will help."

"Won't they just think you brainwashed me?" She thought about her response to him in her room and wondered if she was under his thrall even now.

"If they have the methods of their ancestors they will know how to discern your mental freedom."

"What are they going to find? Am I 'mentally free'?"

"Do you feel compelled?" He watched her like a cat looks at catnip.

How would she know? He held out his hand towards her, "Come to me," he said commandingly.

She stayed where she was. Did she feel like going to him? Only cause he was sexy and she liked him saying 'come to me'. But she didn't feel controlled.

"No mind control?"

"That is correct."

"Maybe not right now, but what about earlier today or even tomorrow? If you wanted to, could you make me do what you wanted?"

"Go to the wolves. Norfolk first," he said, avoiding the question. He placed a card down on the table. It had two phone numbers on it with two different country codes, 44 which was England and 420.

Oh, Christ, Jack! "The Czech Republic, huh? Is that where Marion is too?" Please let Jack be looking for someone besides Lucas.

His penetrating gaze rested on her and she wondered if he knew that Jack had a base near him. Surely, he was trying to make a bid for Lucas if he was there. "No. She is not allowed in that part of Europe."

Her stomach suddenly hurt like she'd eaten a dozen jalapenos.

"What are you expecting me to do about Marion? With that file?"

"You have given it to Jack?"

Val decided to leave her tampons out of the picture. "Not yet."

She didn't want him to know Jack was in town. How could she trust that Lucas would really protect him? She needed time to think and work through all the information that had been thrown at her.

"Then give it to him."

"Do you honestly believe that the only reason vampires have been killed by Hunters is because of your information and help, whatever that is?" She didn't mean it in a snarky way, she just wanted to know.

"There is a lot of preparation involved in killing a vampire. If he or she is over a few hundred years it would be near impossible, without my intervention."

"With wooden bullets and silver and holy water? They all seem very effective."

Several seconds went by before Lucas spoke. As though deciding how much information he would tell her. "He'd be better off with a sawed off shotgun. It's more draining for the vampire to eject multiple pieces of wood than a single wooden bullet. Small slivers consume near as much energy to heal as a large one."

"That doesn't make any sense. It seems like it would be harder to regenerate a wider hole than a smaller one."

"It's mental focus and direction of power. That's never a pure process. Energy is lost in the transfer. The pieces are smaller and require more power to be precise." He nodded his head slightly, "I will see you tonight."

Tonight?!?

And then he was gone.

Val spent the day in her room and drove herself crazy trying to put everything together. She wrote down everything Lucas had told her about vampires and even wrote down most of her encounters with him. She left out the towel situation. If she turned up dead, she wanted Jack and her father to know the truth. But that didn't mean she needed them to know that Lucas made her hot and bothered.

She recoiled from the thought. Wasn't it enough that he was a vampire? That alone should make him unattractive. The fact that he was dead *and* a killer should push him over the limit to barf-worthy. Sure, he dressed well and was good looking, had all that hair and rocked the Viking chic look better than anyone had in several hundred years, but honestly, if she thought her and Jack were a bad match, her and Lucas was suicide.

Hers.

She went to her jewelry box and found a silver cross that her father had given her years ago. She put it on and hoped that would help. Her feelings were not natural. *And that's all there is to it.*

CHAPTER 8

LONDON, ENGLAND

That evening, Val was fed up with her dark thoughts and being stuck indoors so she headed outside. Lucas could find her if it was so important. She didn't go towards the Heath at this time of night, since it was supposed to be a gay meeting point and the last thing she needed was to stumble upon two men shagging in the bushes.

The small streets leading to Hampstead Village seemed like the safest choice. Inside the purple bricked mansions were people with families having dinner. Smoke came out of the chimneys tingeing the cold air with the smell of fire. *Normal life.*

Sure she was looking in on normal life from the outside, but so what. *So what! Don't think about how quickly everything is going down the crapper and what you may not have.* Val didn't know if she wanted kids. In theory they were fine, sweet and little but the reality contained more snot and naughtiness then she felt she could handle.

She tried to imagine having children and a husband. An image of Jack laughing and happy came to her. No! No more would she think of Jack when she thought of the future. Jack didn't want happiness. She thought about Ian instead. He had asked her to stay over for Christmas and be with his family. How sweet was that?

Oh God, Ian. She had to cut him out of her life. Being around her wasn't safe and she'd have to change everything.

Get rid of everyone.

Be alone again.

In danger again.

Her mind rebelled, looking for alternatives.

Could she confine Lucas in any way? Find some way to make him let her live a normal life? No, because she had nothing to bargain with. She was the pawn. Val kicked a pebble down the street dispiritedly.

Part of her wondered, like a whisper in her mind, if maybe she was that interesting. That whisper of a voice was like a devil in her, telling her that she could have Lucas in the palm of her hand if she chose.

And that he knew things he wasn't telling her. *Nice deduction Captain Obvious.*

Perhaps he was not nearly as self-contained as he pretended to be. It was the same voice that told her she wouldn't be having a normal life no matter how hard she tried or how far she ran. It was probably the same little voice that addicts heard right before inhaling a monstrous line of coke.

She needed to ignore that voice.

Steps echoed hers, Lucas falling into step beside her. She kept walking, refusing to acknowledge him.

"Such turmoil." His words were silky, quiet and deep as shadows.

"You can't be the biggest of the big bad without being seriously evil." She waited, but he said nothing. "But now you are trying to convince me that you are...helping. *Good*."

"No. Not good. But neither am I inherently evil. There is a field of gray between light and dark. I tell you most vampires are like sun down with hints of light in a sky of black. They were people once, just a very long time ago. There is a moral code to vampires, albeit nothing you may appreciate. We do not make murderers into vampires, for example. There are rules."

Val stopped walking and turned into him, forcing herself close. He backed up a step, giving ground, but she followed. He seemed to stand a little straighter, and then her hand was resting on his chest. "Will you take them from me? Do I need to give this all up? If I do what you want, will you leave everyone alone?" The questions burst from her.

The agony of not knowing was too much, and while part of her was afraid her rash words could imperil everyone more, her instincts and fear won, forcing the words out.

She felt his breath whisper over her hair. "Who do you ask sanctuary for? What promise would you have from me? Am I to protect people from myself or others? Supernatural and natural harm? Perhaps even protection from their own actions?" He looked down at her, and she noticed his hands resting on her shoulders.

Val didn't pull away, wasn't sure she even could. She felt like a planet orbiting around the sun, unable to change course.

Was he threatening her? He could hurt them and make it look like an accident. Was that what he was saying? This moment was important, she knew that, but he watched her like she was a clairvoyant about to predict the winning lottery numbers and she wondered what she was missing.

"You should leave school because your responsibilities to me will take all of your time and because you don't want to draw unnecessary attention to the people you care about. I have told you I will protect Jack and your father. You must believe that. But also, you must recognize that I am not solely an evil man, or else you will betray me and be manipulated by the Others if we find them. The Others are neither good nor evil either. Werewolves, witches, the Fey—all are creatures who interact with mortals and do so for their own benefit. Humans become pawns and shields. Loss of life is expected and irrelevant to most supernatural beings."

"So your goal here is to terrify me *and* get my help in bringing more evil to humanity, is that it?" Val spun away from him, walking quickly, the street sloping downwards towards Hampstead Village.

"I do not interact with humans often. The last two hundred years especially, I have been away from life."

What the hell did that mean?

Lucas stopped speaking and she thought that this time he was trying to find the right words rather than being evasive. "I have spent hundreds of years unchallenged and in isolation, both emotionally and physically. But now I am drawn back to this world and it is astonishing to want things again. It is better for humans if the Others returned. All of the Other races need humans and like them in a way that most vampires have forgotten."

She could feel his sincerity swimming over her. He did want balance for the world but he also wanted things from her specifically. This moment convinced her of that. The insidious voice was back, telling her to pay attention, that he was being honest. Or as close to honest as he was gonna get.

"What level of protection should I be asking for? What would it take to get you to promise not to harm anyone that I come into contact with?"

Lucas looked at her for a long moment and she thought he would tell her. Her eyes implored him and she realized she was touching him again: her hand on his arm. She jerked back her hand, his gaze tracking the movement as she pulled them away from him and fisted them at her sides.

"Nothing. There is nothing you can offer or give that I would accept." He changed the subject, "What do you require for your task?"

"You don't think it's a little ridiculous that you ask me to trust you and do your bidding, yet you won't give me the one thing I want? Promising to leave these people alone doesn't cost you anything."

"I take promises very seriously. All of my kind do. Breaking of oaths leads to death and war. I won't make a promise that vague. Not even for you."

She tried to stay focused, waiting until later to analyze his words. "I need money so that I can move and I guess.... I guess I have to drop out of school. Also, I'll need a way to stay in the country." *Am I really doing this?*

The grief of giving up her life hadn't totally hit her yet. It would when she was packing. Or when Monday morning came and she wasn't in class. Then the aloneness of it all would crush her.

He frowned. "This upsets you."

"Um, yeah! This is my life that's changing. It's getting swapped out for a crappy one with a bloody death at the end of it. Tell me I'm wrong."

"I will protect you. It is my understanding you have been studying for many years now. At what point would you have stopped?"

"Are you trying to be a jerk?" She said angrily.

"You do not need to do this. I will leave your life and never return. Ignore Nate, Jack and you."

"Yes, how magnanimous. Then they'll die, right? That's not a real choice."

He rubbed a hand over his face and looked around at the houses while he decided what to say. His tone was mildly curious, as though he found this only slightly more interesting than a conversation about the weather. If he'd been human, he would have been gesturing, his voice would have been raised. Maybe he would have touched her or moved. But he was a vampire, so he stood still and didn't fidget. His hands rested in the pockets of his wool slacks. His matching suit jacket was open, his gaze fixed on the distance.

"I was made a vampire against my will a very long time ago. This luxury of choice is a new phenomenon and I fail to see how you can be so upset by it. You are saving your family. What wouldn't people give to have that opportunity?" Lucas seemed genuinely bewildered by her attitude.

"Did you get to save your family?"

His eyes bore into hers, "No. All I did was for them. And it wasn't enough. I would have bargained my soul to the very devil for their survival."

Valerie flushed. He made her feel like a selfish child.

"Do you honestly believe that doing your grunt work is the best thing for my family?"

Would he tell her the truth? She stepped forward again, close to him as though the closer she was the easier it would be to sense his honesty.

He looked down at her, a very severe and remote expression on his face, lips compressed hard before lifting his hand slowly and running a warm finger down her cheek. Valerie fought to keep her eyes open: his touch making her feel weak with a languid desire. Then sensation was unlike anything she'd felt before, like he drew the weight of her sadness, anger and sudden desire up through her body—a waterfall of feelings flowing uphill and into his waiting hand.

"Don't do that," she murmured.

Lucas pulled his hand away, rubbing his fingers together and frowning at them slightly. His lips thinned into a hard line and he took a step backwards, putting a slight distance between them.

"What else do you need?" he said tonelessly.

Val wanted to slap her cheeks, wake up and talk some sense into herself at the same time.

The fog cleared and Val remembered the conversation they had been having. "I also need to get access to the British Library. I want to research all of this and there are so many sources that I can't get to because I don't have clearance. It's like the Pentagon in that place."

"The library." He reached for her. His hand went to the hollow between her shoulder and neck, lightly holding her still. The contact was minimal, the distance odd, like she had the plague. Then he was disappearing and taking her with him.

Disoriented and cold, a whirl of wind blinded her and bit into her flesh. Then it was over, the wind died down and she felt the sharp contrast of being outside then coming indoors.

They were standing in a huge basement filled with books. Monstrous stacks of books that extended in all directions. There was even a conveyor belt so that books could be taken from the shelves and whisked to the public quickly, a practical addition since the distance across the cavernous basement was too far to reasonably have someone make frequent trips.

She took a deep breath, inhaling the musty smell of books. Truth be told, she thought the smell was kind of sexy. She'd had fantasies of having sex in a library. That was probably what happened when one spent those crucial hormone-filled years surrounded by books instead of boys.

This, however, was not the fantasy. She liked close stacks and dim lighting, carpet and quiet, being surrounded by books that no one ever checked out. Knowledge waiting for anyone who cared. But this library wasn't about the experience. This library was cold and clinical. Like the difference between going to a gynecologist and having sex in Hawaii—she might get penetrated but it wasn't gonna be the sexy fantasy.

Then she looked over to Lucas... it wouldn't matter where he had sex, he was the fantasy. She quelled the thought and looked around again, taking several seconds to get the lay of the land before looking back at him with a smile on her face.

He was giving her his inscrutable look and she almost laughed. The scariest man she'd ever met was looking at her as though she was the one to worry about. Actually, that wasn't true; the man who killed her mother was the scariest being she'd ever met. Trapped in a room with the two of them, she'd cower behind Lucas every time. And didn't that say something, she thought darkly.

"Why am I not more scared of you? I start off frightened and then it goes away."

"I have told you I will not harm you." He said, as though surprised she still worried for her safety.

"Yes. And to some extent I must believe you. But why? I've been raised to kill vampires, to fear them, hate them. But with you it's like..."

She searched for words, an example came to her mind but it was so inappropriate, she kept trying to think of something else to say. Lucas shifted, looking around and she knew her silence was becoming awkward. Nothing else came to her so she plunged ahead, "You know what it's like? It's like being on a diet. I remember that I am on a diet until a cookie appears or some chocolate, then I eat it and the moment it's gone I suddenly remember, 'oh yeah, I was on a diet!' but during those few moments when I'm shoving cake in my face, I honestly can't remember. You are like that-"

"Shall I be flattered then?" His voice was hard and he turned his back, walking away from her.

Val blushed, embarrassed by her example, but it was out now and she wanted an answer, "I don't know about that, but why? Why don't I stay afraid like a sane person would? You can't tell me you don't inspire terror into the hearts of one and all. Is it something you've done to me?"

"I have given you my word. That must suffice. I can only assume that a fundamental part of you knows I am sincere."

Was that it? Val felt like there was something missing or left out but couldn't think what it might be.

"What books are you looking for?"

She understood that he wanted to change the subject. Val decided to go with it, she'd go home and think about it a little, try to decide if she really did believe him or not.

He said he wasn't manipulating her but there wasn't much she could do about it either way, was there? If he wanted to kill her, she was dead. If he wanted to compel her, then she would be. It kind of sucked to be human.

Val walked towards a computer and turned it on. They waited in awkward silence for it to boot up. Well, she thought it was awkward. He was older than dirt, he probably didn't even notice the two minutes it took for something to happen. Why was it that everyone complained about government agencies and their spendthrift ways and yet their technology always sucked?

"Maybe you want to come back later? Give me a couple of hours?" She thought about how much easier it would be to work if he wasn't there, looking over her shoulder and watching her like she was a cake on legs or an unusual insect.

"No."

She was irritated. "*Really?* You are supposed to be king of the vampires and you're going to hang around a library with me in the middle of the night? You have *nothing* else to do?"

"An effective leader delegates. Right now your communicating with the Others is the most important thing in the world." Was he joking?

He wandered away from her and disappeared into the stacks.

Sitting down at the computer, she made a concerted effort to lose herself in the research. She wanted first-hand accounts of people from those areas from as far back as they would go. This was why she'd needed to get into the British Library. Some writings stayed in the family, or if the person was famous enough or interesting enough it might stay in a local town museum, but a lot of it was kept at the British Library where it could be preserved and used by scholars. Since she wasn't a scholar she didn't get access, but now she had her vampire teleporter to get her in. This might actually count as a perk of being blackmailed by an evil fiend.

When Lucas returned she had piles of books and documents settled around her. He held an old book that had worn leather binding with faded gold lettering. It almost looked like an old copy of the Bible.

He placed it on the table and she glanced at the title. Not English. *Old Norse, anyone?*

Val sighed and looked at him. "I have found two villages that speak of wolf attacks. One from 1550 and one from 1575. By 1680 wolves were extinct and James I said that werewolf victims were delusional. That's a very long time ago. Do you really think that the wolves are still there?"

"If you can find none in England then we will check the colonies."

"Yeah, we call that America now."

"They could have gone anywhere. Australia, North America, Mexico, even India. I meant you should look to places that were colonies at the time."

Oh.

"But why? What do you think they can do if they are that decimated? How will they restore the balance? A couple of wolves and a handful of pixies, presuming you can even get that, doesn't seem like much of a threat."

"Then you know nothing of wolves. They are very dangerous to vampires. They can track them. Follow them through the streets and into buildings. Their speed is equal, the desire for blood matched and usually the wolf wins."

"Then why would they be hiding instead of picking you guys off one by one?" She asked.

"Either they are no more, or they have been regrouping."

"For four hundred years? That's some serious regrouping."

"Yes. And yet legends of them still exist, humans claim to encounter them. There may be a reason for that."

"But to hide for this long?"

"It's the nature of wolves. Their priority is to protect their pack at all costs. And yet, wolves are easy to provoke and it has proved a fatal weakness. The clans were stronger when there were still Fey and empaths in the world, because both have always had a strong influence on wolves. A guiding hand. When the Fey were gone the destruction of the wolves was simple. Steal a young or kill a juvenile and their hierarchy could fall apart without a strong leader. They would erupt into violence, attempt revenge. Disorganization and passion have always been their downfall. All we needed was to wait. A vampire is a calculated creature and it's been an unfair advantage. If they still exist and have been this quiet, it is only because the Fey shield them."

"So when did Faeries disappear?"

Lucas sat down across from her. So quick she could hardly see it. She wondered if it took him conscious effort to move like a human. "A very long time ago."

"Did you have your hand in that too?" For a moment he looked pleased. A master tactician appreciating the beauty of a perfectly executed strategy. Then he sighed as if in regret.

"What else did Faeries do besides ...wolf tame?"

"Another time."

And there endeth the lesson.

"Take what you will. We will depart now."

She looked at her watch surprised that it was almost three am. No wonder she was so tired. She made a pile of what she wanted and it disappeared. It was a neat trick and she was unwillingly impressed. Lucas extended his hand and she gave him hers.

"You need to be closer." He didn't pull her closer but waited for her to move. Val moved slowly, waiting for some sign that she was close enough. Finally she was bare inches from him, wholly in his personal space. His other arm swept behind her waist and pulled her flush to him. It felt like he was about to sweep her into a dance and her heart fluttered. Very sternly, she told herself that it was fear she felt.

The cold whirlwind assaulted her as they dematerialized across town and she felt herself sagging forward as the frigid white darkness rushed up to meet her and she felt Lucas' arms tighten around her, cradled her close. And then she knew no more.

When she awoke she was in a strange apartment and light was coming in through a large bank of windows. If the sun was up it was either a freakishly nice day for March or she had slept for an incredibly long time. There was a clock on the bedside table. Two pm. She'd slept for 11 hours! When she stood up, she stepped on her flats and stumbled forward. Confusingly, she had no memory of taking them off or coming here.

The scuffed black shoes slipped on easily and she walked across the deep beige carpet to the main living area. It seemed like a new apartment, the paint was fresh, the carpet brand new, the kitchen modern.

Looking around, she saw no personal affects. Curious, she looked in the bathroom and the bedroom closet but both were empty. She found a letter on the small kitchen table. The script was small, with sprawling letters that twisted unusually.

"Yours. Your belongings will be transferred two days hence. An account is established for you at Barclay's. Cards to follow. Tell me if you need further assistance."

Feeling dazed, she read the note twice more, not wanting to absorb the words. Just like that her school life was over. She would go back to school and pack, tell Ian thanks for the memories, hate to shag and run, but there were no other options. She was on her own.

CHAPTER 9

LONDON, ENGLAND

Two weeks had passed since Val left school. She hadn't seen Lucas again, but true to his word, she had a bank account with a ridiculous amount of money in it and she had come to love her apartment. It was near Holborn and centrally located. She could walk almost anywhere and was close to the British Library as well as several London colleges that had extensive book collections.

Being a loner who spent most of her time in the stacks wasn't awful. She still saw some college friends for lunch or a drink every now and again. And while she was boyfriend less that was alright too. She'd liked Ian—but it was never going to be anything permanent.

Her daily routine was to get up around eight, shower, have breakfast and then walk to the library. Sometimes she'd come home for lunch, but usually she went to Pret a Manger and had a sandwich. She'd have a latte and a lemon bar, then go back to the library until three when she'd come home and try to put everything in order.

Several nights a week she exercised. She ran a lot, perhaps with a hint of desperation but it helped her feel like she was in control of her life, even if she wasn't.

She had been waiting for Lucas to give her the go ahead before going to Norfolk, wanting to see if he had any more information to give her or advice but after the third week of no contact from him she assumed he wanted her to set off on her own.

She packed a small bag and taken the train from Liverpool station to Norwich and everyone she spoke to warned her about the rail works at Colchester. If she came back on a Sunday there would be no service as they fixed the railroad track and she'd be punted onto a bus which would take hours! The locals were beside themselves.

Norwich seemed like a nice enough town, a picturesque little river ran near the rail station and a few cathedrals with towering spires had been visible from the window. She rented a car and drove to a forested area near the coast, bemoaning the dismal state of Norfolk Radio. What were there, like three stations? And one of them was taken up with talk of hunting and local animal husbandry, something so dull that the radio disc jockey would have been fired if she'd been in America.

The journey to North Walsingham took a little over an hour and she was never more than a mile or two from a house or tiny village. How had werewolves ever lived here when it was so densely populated? A werewolf would surely have been noticed, let alone a pack of them.

Her bed and breakfast was in the middle of the town, population three thousand, with a few intersecting main streets and thatched cottages that radiated out from the center like a small star.

The owner was a friendly widow named Mrs. Jenkins, whose husband had passed on a few years ago. Val's room was on the second floor, up a set of creaking stairs. A black and white cat seemed to own the little house, refusing to leave her room while she unpacked.

She'd just finished putting her toiletries into the bathroom when Mrs. Jenkins knocked on the door and announced that it was tea time if Valerie was interested. Interested? Tea was one of England's biggest selling points! Mrs. Jenkins put on a good spread which included clotted cream and freshly baked scones. Clotted cream was one of the purest joys of Val's life. Pure because it was all cream and fat. It was like a mix between whip cream, frosting, and ice cream.

A heart attack waiting to happen.

The owner puttered around the dining room and tried to talk to Val, her movements birdlike and a little brittle. But she was a fountain of information and willing to talk. If Val was being polite she'd say the woman had a gift for gab. Really, Val was sure the woman wouldn't be able to shut up if her life depended upon it.

Before Valerie could decide where to start her questions, Mrs. Jenkins took the helm. "And what brings you to North Walsingham, my dear?"

"Oh, I'm a history student and I'm writing a dissertation on the occult. There are quite a few supernatural tales associated with this area of England." Val said, hoping her story didn't sound too rehearsed. It was almost true.

Mrs. Jenkins was middle aged and clearly believed that a scone a day was part of a healthy diet. Her gray eyebrows rose heavenward when Valerie explained her purpose. She had a very soft voice and a melodious accent that made Valerie feel like she could be in the middle of a murder mystery on PBS.

"Yes. Indeed we do. One could spend several days in North Walsingham alone. It's a very superstitious town."

"Really? Is it still superstitious?"

The woman tilted her head, perplexed. "Well it depends upon what you mean by superstitious." She paused dramatically while she stirred her tea and added more sugar, nodding sagely when it was just right, "Right there on the fireplace, do you see the flowers? It's an offering to the little ones. You mustn't ask for specifics about *which* little ones, as it's very bad luck to speak of them and gain their attention. But, every week I put up new flowers."

This was better than Valerie had hoped. "Are the... little ones friendly?"

"Heavens no! One can only try to placate them and hope they make mischief elsewhere."

"Did they live around here?"

"You wouldn't go looking for them, would you?" There was real concern in Mrs. Jenkins voice. The woman leaned forward, looking at Val's face as though to see the truth more clearly.

"No. Oh, no. I was just wondering if I should avoid any places in town."

The woman seemed mildly appeased, slumping back in her chair.

"They are gone now, though?" Val asked.

Mrs. Jenkins shot her a canny glance and Val decided a bit of sympathy might go a long way to getting more information from the woman.

"Actually, Mrs. Jenkins, I have to confess that I also put flowers up every week. I just buy them from Tesco down the road- nothing fancy- but I have studied so much and heard so many strange and true stories that I would almost be afraid not to!" Valerie laughed nervously.

There was a lengthy pause and Val heard a clock ticking somewhere nearby.

"My husband, bless his soul, he wasn't a believer. Thought it was all hogwash. So I went away, for eight days, to see my sister and when I came back, the flowers were gone and poor Harold was dead on the floor. A heart attack." Mrs. Jenkins patted her sweater absently as though looking for a tissue. "I should have come back a day earlier. Seven days, you see."

"Yes. I see." Valerie felt cold and uncomfortably clammy. She hadn't disbelieved Lucas when he'd told her about the Fey, but she supposed she hadn't really expected to find anything either.

It was possible Mrs. Jenkins was wrong, or a kook, but Val feared there was at least some truth to her story. Mrs. Jenkins found the tissue and blew her nose noisily.

"Would they have been so cruel? After only a day's lapse?"

"Oh yes. Our little one is very vengeful. I suppose they all are though. But most of them are long gone."

"Why do you think they are gone? Why would this one still be here then?"

"Every village and town has its history and gossip and so does ours. We all know what used to be here and we know when they left."

"But why do you think there is one little creature left behind?"

Local legend says that there is a little goblin who roams the woods crying, sad that he had been forgotten. I'm not saying it's true...but most legends have some basis in history."

Val smiled weakly. "So why do you think he's still here if the others are gone?

"If I had to guess I would say he got lost when the others left. Or he could have been abandoned. It's even possible that he was too tied to the land to leave. I don't know."

"When would it have been abandoned?"

"Well, people will say different things, but I suspect it was 1587."

"That's very precise," Val said, surprised.

"1587 is a pivotal year in our town's history. The town was divided, half of them leaving for America and half of them staying."

"You think the Fey went to the New World?"

Mrs. Jenkins got a sour expression on her face. "I didn't say Fey," She said defensively.

Valerie took a bite of her scone and chewed slowly. "I thought the little ones were the Fey?"

Mrs. Jenkins shrugged and looked like she was getting ready to excuse herself, smoothing her tweed skirt and dusting crumbs off her lap.

"Why leave any behind?" Val asked quickly.

"I couldn't say. I don't know if they did it on purpose or not. Just like them leaving: It could have been they went to America, or they could have gone somewhere else entirely. But after they left, our town became more in step with the rest of the country, less *backwards*."

Mrs. Jenkins said 'backwards' oddly and Valerie couldn't decide if Mrs. Jenkins was angry that the old ways had been abandoned, relieved or maybe even frightened. Her tone had been weary, her faded brown eyes roaming the room restlessly.

"I don't think we should talk about it any longer, just to be cautious, but if you are still interested, you should go to the town museum at the end of the road."

Valerie finished her tea and a second scone (with an even larger helping of clotted cream and strawberry jam) then took her leave to find the museum. Stepping out the door, Val was doused in a drizzle, which she despised. A drizzle had all the wetness of rain but was more insidious, like a rain sneak attack.

The museum was open but no one was there. Valerie made the requested two pound donation and looked around, captivated by the history of the area.

In 1587, almost half the village left for the New World, going to Roanoke, South Carolina. The name was familiar, but she wasn't sure why. She found an explanation on the other side of the room.

Roanoke was 'The Lost Colony'.

115 men, woman and children had vanished, never to be seen again.

The first English child born on American soil had been Virginia Dare, born just a few months after the colonists arrived.

When a ship had come from England bringing supplies, they found the colony abandoned. No sign of attack or illness—just vanished.

The fate of Virginia Dare captured people's imaginations, leading to stories that she'd survived and been adopted into an Indian tribe.

There was something so sad about all those people missing. Thinking they'd made a choice for a new life only to vanish.

On her way back to the bed and breakfast she saw Dare Lane and decided to take a detour. The little lane ended in front of a Tudor style home that had a wolf carved into the lintel above the front door. Had the Dare's been werewolves?

Was that why it was carved there? The house was empty and owned by the town, used only for meetings which made it impossible for her to go in and look around.

The rain picked up and Valerie hurried back to her room searching the internet for more information about the Lost Colony. She also wanted to reread the information Lucas had given her.

The colonists had vanished, leaving behind three letters carved into a tree: CRO.

She found the file Lucas had given her and read through it again. There was nothing in the wolf reports for CRO but in the index she found a single mention *bunadh na cro* which was Celtic and translated to Host of the Hills, another name for The Fey.

Assuming everything Lucas had told her was true, then the villagers who had left had been werewolves, fleeing England to escape persecution. They had landed in Roanoke only to disappear three years later.

Was that why CRO had been carved into the tree? To tell people they'd been abducted by the Fey?

Back in her room she checked the time table for trains and discovered that if she hurried, she could make the last one out and sleep in her own bed. She packed quickly and left, calling Lucas on her cellphone as she drove back to Norwich. What would his voice sound like on the phone, she wondered and felt a little breathless at the thought.

The call went straight to voicemail with no message or greeting. Considering how terse Lucas usually was, it shouldn't have been a surprise. She left a message saying she had found something and would be home late tonight.

It was 10:30 p.m. by the time she got home. She went into the kitchen and was startled to see a huge bouquet of flowers sitting on the counter. There were hydrangeas and roses, tulips and some others she couldn't name. There was also a bottle of wine sitting next to it with two glasses. She found a note. It didn't say anything, just an incredibly luxurious L written boldly on the page.

Val dropped the note like it had thorns, and wiped her suddenly sweaty palms on her jeans. Geez, she was in trouble. The Vampire King was sending her flowers and setting her up in an apartment. As a bonus, if she didn't do what he wanted, he might kill everyone she loved or at least let it happen.

And yet her heart was pounding and she was wondering if she should put on some lipstick. She was drawn to him. No, it was worse than that. When Lucas was near her, she almost *craved* him. It was sick and weird.

The moment Lucas was gone, sanity returned and she could see the danger she was in, how close her death might actually be, and *then* she was afraid. But when he was with her, the fear was almost gone. She had to remind herself to be afraid of him since all she wanted was to touch him.

She heard a knock on the door, surprised at how quickly he was responding to her call. If she was this closely monitored she should be worried. Opening the door, expecting to see Lucas, she was surprised to find Jack instead.

Her heart gave an extra beat as she looked at him. He leaned against the door frame in a pose of total confidence and boredom. Jack straightened, giving her a huge smile before grabbing her in a hug.

She had the urge to tell him everything. Confide in him and have him fix her problems like he used to. But he couldn't fix this. She took a deep breath, enjoying the smell of him, the feeling of being squeezed tight and then he let her go.

His gray eyes were dark, his skin pale as though he was tired from days of too little sleep. His dark brown hair was too long, the ends curling against the back of his olive colored cashmere turtleneck. She stood back and swept her arm wide, inviting him in. Giving her a small nod, he walked into her apartment, looking around him with curiosity.

"This is nice. Makes much more sense, who wants to live in a dorm?"

"Thanks." She wondered if he'd ask anything else. Like he'd suddenly turn around and shout twenty questions at her until she started blabbing about Lucas.

She'd left college and sent him an email telling him she didn't like the dorm and had decided to use some of the money her mom left her to move out. As far as he knew, she was still in school.

Shit the flowers!

Jack was already in the kitchen, the paper in his hand. "Who is L and why has he left you a very expensive bottle of wine?"

"Hello," she said sarcastically, "and how nice it is to see you too! What business is it of yours?" Carefully, he set the piece of paper down on the counter then walked out of the kitchen.

"Why do you even know how expensive the wine is?" Was he a big wine connoisseur?

He went to her sofa and sat down on the crème leather, slouched down and put his arms on the back of it possessively. Stick a beer in his hand, turn on the game, and he might never leave, she thought.

Jack looked at her again and straightened. Why was he so fidgety? "It's Italian. The vineyard was near my home. The owner threw a party once a year when the grapes were in. It ain't cheap."

The coincidence was scary. How likely was it that the one winery Lucas had chosen was coincidentally next to where Jack grew up? She felt sick to her stomach knowing that it wasn't chance. Did Lucas also know that Jack would see the bottle of wine? Was that why he'd left it and brought the flowers? To piss off Jack and tell her that he knew Jack's movements and what he was up to? She wouldn't be surprised if this was all some elaborate game of Lucas'. He'd told her he'd spent the last 1600 years scheming. She hoped she was being paranoid.

"What's going on Jack?" Val asked, needing to focus on one thing at a time.

"I'm worried about you. I came to bring you some weapons. Make sure you were okay here."

"Why?" Her anxiety cranked up another notch and she felt like she'd had six cups of coffee; wired and nauseous.

"There are too many vampires in town. It's weird. I've never heard of so many being in one place at one time since Italy." His eyes met hers quickly and studied her.

"Why do you think they are here?" she asked.

"That's what I wanted to ask you."

Her heart pounded. Did he know about Lucas? What would he do if he did? Oh right, he'd get his death wish fulfilled.

"You've been sniffing around for a couple of months and now a whole cadre of vampires turns up in your city. Maybe you were not careful enough."

The jerk! Why did he assume it was her fault? He was the one who went around killing vampires and he thought *she* was responsible? Val wanted to tell him that there was no way it was her fault. All the information she'd given them over the last few months had come straight from Lucas. Her sole job was to fact check it and then send it on to Jack.

Lucas was still holding back information on Marion and had given her nothing more since that meeting in the cafe. Jack had nothing to go on. He'd gone straight to Geneva after leaving Val in Hampstead, determined to find Marion and no doubt kill her.

After tracking down where the photo was taken, staking out the major hotels and even hacking into some local computer systems, including the police department, he'd run out of leads.

Now he was getting impatient and Val feared it would make him reckless.

Val slumped down onto the couch next to him.

"I brought you a sawed off shot gun with wood and silver shot, along with 30 bullets."

She was surprised. "That sounds like a lot."

"I wanted to get you more but it's taking a while. We've been distributing it to Hunters all over and it's made a big difference. The kill rate has increased while injuries have decreased. So, good work on that front."

"Yeah, but it's not easy to walk around with a sawed off shotgun and be unobtrusive."

"It's also illegal to have guns in the UK. Which is why you are taking this too." He sounded pleased with himself, holding something small and black out to her.

"This is just a taser." Val said, sounding a little disappointed.

"Oh, ye of little faith. It's more than a taser. It's been specially modified, and interestingly, it will incapacitate a vampire for about thirty seconds."

This was fantastic. "How did you get this?"

Jack shrugged, "I'm not sure you really want me to answer that question."

She gave him an irritated expression.

He sighed and answered her, "Now that we've been using the shotguns we have wiggle room. The vampires are weaker, manageable so we don't have to kill them immediately. We've been trying out a couple of things. This is the most successful."

Torture, that's what he was telling her. Val imagined bleeding vampires being chained to a wall and experimented on. Her mother had been killed by a vampire, and maybe if they'd had these weapons her mother would still be alive. Her conscience could live with evil vampires being tortured before they were killed. Resolutely, she kept her eyes fixed on the taser instead of looking at Jack.

"What are you going to do now that London is infested with vampires?"

"I've got back up for you. Smith and Duncan flew in today and are going to be shadowing you just in case."

That was not a good plan. "I'm sure they could be put to better uses."

"It's not worth the risk." Jack patted her leg in forced casualness. She knew he'd be devastated at her death. How he'd endanger himself worrying about her, when he should be fighting vampires. But, what if having the two extra Hunters as back up saved his life? If he died when backup had been stuck babysitting her ass, she'd be the one who couldn't live with the outcome.

"What will you be doing?"

"Lucas is here."

"What?" Terror iced through her.

"Don't worry. He won't come near you, I promise."

Of course, he'd misunderstood her reaction. She knew Lucas was here. Her concern was that he'd go after Lucas and get himself killed, not that Lucas was coming after her.

"How do you know he's here?"

"We have our sources. Actually, we have more than a source. One of his own vampires is feeding us information. She told us he was here and even gave us a picture of him." He pulled out a picture of Lucas. It was black and white, taken with a telephoto lens.

"Who is she and why is she giving you information?" This was odd.

"Her name is Rachel and she says there is dissension in the ranks. She wants Lucas gone and has offered her support if we try to take him out. She says there are others who will follow her lead. But I think that last part is bullshit. She's working for someone else. She's just the representative."

"How do you know?"

"She's not powerful enough to control the vampires. Don't worry about how I know, I just do. Research her too. She's given us some other stuff that's checked out but there is no reason to take her at her word.

"What are you going to do?" Her voice was surprisingly steady.

"Taking out Lucas would solve a lot of problems and disorganize them which could only be good for us."

"When?"

"I'll let you know. It's going to take people. I have six Hunters here but two are dedicated to you. I've got three more coming in tomorrow and then we'll see. We know his movements."

"Really?"

"Yes, don't go to the Dorchester Hotel and Val if you see him, you run." Tension radiated from him.

"Jack, it's stupid to keep two guys watching me when they could be helping you. I swear I won't leave here until you tell me to. Keep them with you. Please?"

He looked at his watch, indecision on his face. "No, I want them here with you."

Hysterical laughter bubbled within her, "I'm just as worried about you as you are about me. You know how much I care about you. Don't waste them on me when they could back you up. I'll stay here and read a book. Please." Reaching for him, she took his hand and he squeezed her hand back, nodding his head jerkily.

"Shit. Okay, I have to go. You *swear* to me you won't leave here until I tell you?" Val nodded. Jack wasn't convinced he was making the right decision, she could see the doubt on his face. On his way to the door he threw a final glance at the kitchen, examining the flowers and wine. He gave her a tight smile but kept himself carefully neutral.

"Have a good night. Don't leave this place, got it? I'll call you tomorrow and we can discuss this again."

They hugged, her arms wrapping around his waist and filling her with a sense of calm and peace. Jack was made for her, she thought, curving herself against his muscled frame. A soft kiss landed on her head and he was gone.

As soon as Jack left she went to her purse and found Lucas's card. Even in her state of near panic, she admired the thickly textured card. Very classy. She called both numbers but he didn't pick up, forcing her to leave another message.

There was nothing she could do and Val desperately needed to do *something*. She went to the computer and checked the society pages, wondering if any of the vampires had turned up in there. She checked all the names, adding Rachel to her list of vampires that she was always looking for, including Marion and Dmitri.

Because she was always looking for them. They were glory hounds and she'd found pictures of both Marion and Dmitri holding a glass of champagne, and smiling brightly for the camera more than once.

Nervousness ate at her and she felt like she needed to get out and go for a walk, or a drink, but she couldn't. She'd told Jack she'd stay here and she would.

In resignation, she closed all her curtains, then opened the wine. It really was very nice. If she couldn't help, she'd drink. Food would be good too. No need to be worried on an empty stomach. She hoped there was more than yogurt in the fridge. She needed to go to the grocery store.

Opening the fridge, she found one of the most amazing fruit and cheese plates she'd ever seen. There were little squares of toast and water biscuits, brie and chevre as well as some roasted nuts. Even some fig compote, which was to die for.

For someone who didn't eat, Lucas sure knew his food. She was totally distracted and absorbed with the cheese when she realized she wasn't alone. Lucas walked out of her bedroom and into the kitchen. Val finished chewing and washed her hands, then poured him a glass of wine and handed it to him.

How domestic, she thought sickly.

"What is going on?" She asked him immediately.

"To what do you refer?"

"Why are all these vampires in town? The last time there were this many vampires around, or at least obvious, Jack's parents were killed and there was a huge bloodbath. This can't be good."

Lucas was very still for a moment, then brought the wine to his lips and took a drink. Was he buying time to think?

"Where is your information from?"

Val might need to be careful here. "The Hunters know. There are several on their way now." He didn't need to know that there were several Hunters here already.

He gave her a predatory smile and she didn't know why. If it was just meant to unsettle her, it worked.

"Do you still promise that you will protect Jack and Nate?"

"Yes."

"What does that promise mean? We talked about that before, how binding something was. What my expectations were and there was no agreement. How much protection do they get?"

Lucas went to her couch and took a seat, motioning for her to join him. He was dressed in black wool slacks and another white collared shirt that had two buttons open at the top so she could see the hollow of his throat. His long hair was loose and she was again struck by the beauty of him: square jaw, blue eyes, full lips and large, heavy limbs. He ate up her couch. A sunlit knight with power and lethal grace.

The fancy clothes couldn't disguise him.

"What do you think they need protection from?" His eyes studied her and she tried not to flinch away from his gaze. "They have my protection from myself and other vampires that I command and you want to know if there is a caveat?"

She gave a jerky nod.

Lucas set down his wine glass and spread his arms along the back of the couch, making her wait. Each second that ticked by stressed her out just a little bit more so that she wanted to pull her hair out by the time he spoke again. "You ask me what I will do when he attacks *me*?" That final word was deeper and darker than the rest. "Will I protect them at cost to myself?" His voice was preternaturally soft, his gaze locked on her face, making her feel like he was reading her again, knew all that she was thinking just from her expressions and his centuries of existence.

"Are other vampires giving information to the Hunters?" Val asked.

"No." He rubbed a hand across his eyes as though he had a tension headache. Was that possible?

"You're wrong. Maybe that challenge to your authority is coming sooner than you think." Val wanted to sigh in relief; perhaps she did have a bargaining chip. She blinked and he was standing before her, yanking her off the couch like a ragdoll, pushing her against the wall, his forearm across her windpipe in a slick move that was too fast to see.

His body was almost flush with hers and she felt the threat of his weight and strength, even though his arm was barely touching her neck. None of it had hurt, he'd been gentle with her, but it was still a threat. Still shocking.

His eyes changed color to a blue so dark it was almost black.

"Who?" he asked and his voice sent shivers down her spine. That was the voice of a king. A voice that held conviction, authority and death.

Val closed her eyes, afraid of him compelling her. "I want them safe. I want all the Hunters safe." Her pulse thundered through her veins and her voice came out a whisper.

"No. I cannot save them all and I will not save them all. We are discussing Nate and Jack alone. The name for their safety should they attack me. That is what you want, yes?"

His body was ice cold, frost seeping through her clothing, touching her skin until her bones ached. Her eyes opened and fixed on the pulse point of his neck where his shirt was open so she didn't meet his gaze. A pulse beat there as though he were human.

She cried out at the painful cold.

Lucas said something unintelligible and quiet then dropped his head down, his lips close to her throat.

The need to fight and scream urged her onwards. Raising her arms, she tried to push away from him before he bit her. But he was too strong, too wide and tall. His whole body covered hers easily, kept her locked in place and unable to move like he was a large cage.

Lucas lifted his head from her neck, a look of purpose on his face as he maintained the effort to warm her.

"It's not enough." His voice was gravelly and she didn't know what he was talking about. Val breathed in slowly, her breasts touching his chest with each inhalation and tried to remember the conversation.

Oh, the name wasn't enough for their protection if they came for him.

"It is enough. You are making up all the rules. You can accept that if you choose to!"

"Then I choose not to. It's not enough. I can find out who the traitor is."

"But not with subtlety, not without giving away that you know someone has turned against you."

"If you don't give me the name, I will be forced to allow the attack upon my person. Then they will all die. All your Hunters....As a display of what I can do." The last was a whisper.

"Mass murder is not going to get you into my panties." She wondered why these stupid things came out of her mouth. She tried to change the subject, talking of her panties could only cause her trouble. "What if one of them gets lucky? Six Hunters attack you at once? At least one of them has to get a good shot at you, right? Is that enough to tip the scales? Vampires and Hunters come at you at once, are you sure you can you survive that?"

Inexplicably, she felt a tear roll down her cheek. It was for Jack and her father only, she told herself. It was fear for good men and the danger they were all in, herself included, none of it was for Lucas.

He saw the tear slide down her cheek and frowned. He tensed and for a second she thought he might lick the tear from her cheek. Instead he pushed away from her, leaving her cold again, her back to the wall and her breathing ragged.

Lucas walked to the window, looking down at the street, then turned back to her "Are you so skillful at deceit? I can see your sorrow on your face and feel it in my body." She wondered if that was true. Could he sense it, feel her emotions? He said it like it made him feel dirty.

She took a deep breath, then another, refusing to look at him.

"They will be safe. Tell me the name." His rich voice cut through her, caressed her, the weight of his promise almost tangible on her skin.

"You won't hurt Jack and Nate even if they attack you?"

A terse nod of agreement.

Gulping, Val said the name before she lost her nerve, "Rachel."

Smiling, he put down the glass again. His hands went to his pockets and he casually walked back to her. *Playing human again.*

"Tomorrow night there is a party. I will come for you at six. I am sending a modiste at ten. Choose what you like."

She went to the couch and sat down, looking at him from across the room. He stayed standing, walking to the window to stare at the traffic below and the lights of the city.

"Is Rachel likely to kill you?"

Lucas shook his head slowly. "Rachel is nothing. She is barely old enough to kill a human bare handed. She would not dream of attacking me outright. She works for another. But I am surprised that either of them is willing to try."

"Why? You can't be that indestructible, can you?"

"My ability to recover from injuries is unparalleled. It is my strength, speed and age that have kept me unchallenged for centuries. I can go into the sunlight, dematerialize repeatedly and feed infrequently. For one as old as I am, the dangers are different."

Val waited for him to continue and watched his broad back, her gaze dipping down to his ass, imagined sinking her nails into it as he—

What the fuck is wrong with me? Stupid, nonsensical reactions.

She looked at her nails instead. They were painted shiny red, the nails short. She wore a silver ring she'd bought in Covent Garden that had two semi-precious stones set in the middle.

He sighed. "Boredom and ennui are the true dangers for a vampire over 500 years old. What is left to live for when everyone we have loved is long dead? Relationships become repetitive and trite. We become exhausted. At my age, suicide is the most common form of demise."

Oh. "Do you want to kill yourself?"

"Not just at the moment," He said dryly. "I have goals, things to accomplish before I consider anything so permanent. I want change for my people. That is a goal worth living for."

"Why wouldn't they just wait for you to kill yourself instead of challenging your directly?" Val asked, trying not to think of the ramifications of his dying, but keep the questions matter of fact.

"Either impatience or because those who would rule do not have the power to do so unless they steal it from me."

"Vampires can steal power?"

He turned from the window, came back towards her and sat down in the chair opposite her. His hand covered his eyes for a moment as though he was tired. "Blood is power. My strength is contained in my being. I can will power into my blood and transfer it to those below me, if I choose. It means I can both feed and reward my people. It can also be a punishment. I can drain power from those below me if I feed from them."

"Do you get extra powers, like turning into a bat, by being older?"

"Speed, strength all increase. Dematerializing is something that only comes with age. But most things are myth. Even capturing someone with a gaze is atypical. It is a neat trick, but very rare.

"But you can do it." She'd experienced it. The memory came to her of when she'd met him in the woods, looking almost the same as he did now, and how he'd offered to take her fear from her so she could kill the vampire who was attacking her. She'd gone willingly, let down every shield she had, giving herself to him.

"Yes, I can do it."

He stood and walked away from her, going towards her bedroom and disappearing as he reached the short hallway.

She hadn't told him anything about the wolves. Although a revolution probably trumped that anyway.

A modiste, huh? She didn't know anyone said the word modiste outside of a regency romance novel. Maybe they didn't and he was two centuries behind.

That fit.

CHAPTER 10

LONDON, ENGLAND

At ten a.m. sharp she heard a sharp knock on the front door. A French woman bustled in with two harried looking assistants pushing a rack behind them. The assistants wouldn't make eye contact which made Val think that the woman either ran a very tight ship or had a lot of vampire customers.

Closing the door, she walked back into her living room watching as the assistants unzipped garment bags and shook dresses free from their plastic covers. Dresses were draped haphazardly around her living room and a large mirror with three panels was set up, so she could *really* know which dress made her ass look fat.

The woman knew fashion but as to why Val needed the gown, she either wouldn't say or didn't know. The modiste called the event a ball and all the gowns seemed to support that statement. Huge princess dresses that required corsets were brought out.

Honestly, if Spanx wasn't enough, she wasn't sure she should go. She wouldn't eat anything else for the rest of the day. The dresses were suited for the Academy Awards or the Golden Globes, not for someone like her.

There it was again—the unreality of her situation. She was a normal girl and he was...well, dead.

The modiste studied Val critically and decided against several dresses instantly. The woman said the color clashed with her hair and skin tone but Val wondered if the dresses clashed with her personality instead. They were soft dresses that required a dainty woman to wear them. Val didn't do dainty. She did hysterical, angry, lusty, afraid and irritated to perfection.

Eventually, all the clothes and accessories were decided upon. The gowns were rezipped and packed away, the modiste bustled back out again, taking her assistants with her and Valerie was alone. Waiting for Lucas and wearing a deep blue gown the color of the ocean.

Her breasts were high and mounded, her waist nipped in thanks to the corset. She really didn't need to look this desirable.

An extra accessory had been given to Valerie which made her realize this was not going to be a normal party. It was a little purse that dangled from her wrist. It was black velvet and had a gold 'L' embossed on the front with a fleur-de-lis pattern woven through the material. The modiste said it was so everyone would know who she belonged to.

With almost no time to spare Val put on her lipstick and was ready to go. Her hair was pinned up into a mass on top of her head that exposed her neck. Something she thought might be fantastically stupid, but that the modiste's assistant insisted was a requirement.

Val thought taking her hair down, but she wasn't sure if she needed to be that petty. She suspected there would be bigger compromises asked for before the night was through, so she left her hair alone and waited.

When the clock struck six she was looking out the window and watching people walk by, hurrying through the eternal rain to go home, probably to a family and hot dinner. A small rush of power wafted over her like pinpricks against her skin. She turned and saw Lucas come out of her bedroom, one big hand fixing the cuff of his crisp white shirt. Good Lord, he could be in a magazine modeling anything from $50,000 watches to expensive cologne.

He wore a black tuxedo minus the bow tie. Again the collar was open and she could see the hollow of his throat, her eyes drawn there despite herself. His deep blue eyes lifted and took in her appearance, starting from her voluminous skirts, to her corseted waist, passing quickly to her face. The gown matched his eyes, she realized, wondering if it was on purpose. He looked at her lips and she had the urge to lick them but frantically tried to hold still.

A velvet cloak rested over one arm, which he opened and held for her to put on. Smiling slightly, he watched her come towards him and Valerie blushed, looking away. He fastened the collar around her neck, red rubies glinting on the clasp.

He flipped it around her shoulders, like a matador baiting a bull. *I don't want to be the animal.*

The cloak was lined with fur and her hands stroked the softness rhythmically, in an attempt to calm her nerves. She could smell his cologne and felt like it was just as heavy and enveloping as the cloak upon her. It was him, this masculine smell that made her relax and feel almost drugged.

Val watched him placidly as he adjusted the drape of her hood. She took in his long lashes and harsh cheekbones, admired the full plumpness of his lips and his near human heat. Lucas reached behind her and pulled the hood of the cape over her face, shifting it so she would be shadowed to anyone that looked.

He'd just fed, she wasn't quite sure how she knew but she did and the sudden image of another woman in his arms, her neck bared for him to penetrate her skin as she gave herself to him had her clenching her hands in dark agitation.

Had he slept with her too?

As though he sensed her change in mood, he finished adjusting her cape to his liking and stepped away from her.

Who was it? Who had he fed from? She knew whoever it was had been willing. How could they not be? Who would, even could, tell him no, he was so beautiful? In her mind she could see it, his hand on some woman's neck as he tilted her just how he wanted her. The power of his body as he stepped in close to her, and even worse, the utter focus he'd have for her. This faceless bitch gave him something he *needed*.

Something she didn't.

Her lips pressed together in a hard line to stop her accusations. She took a deep breath, aware that she was being irrational.

Lucas waited, saying nothing while she composed herself but watching her with a look of mild curiosity. She was so contradictory in her feelings towards him. She hated him and lusted after him, feared him and wished to never see him again. Yet the idea that another held his interest made her jealous and angry. It all added up to a death wish, she just knew it.

His hair was straight and thick, hanging heavily down his back, waiting for her to sink her hands into it, pull him towards her and kiss him. She'd show him how angry she was, make him take only her.

In a red haze, she imagined what it would be like to bite him and claim him, make him hers. Her knees weakened, the idea of marking him so powerful and heady that she feared she might collapse. She looked down and saw his hands, one open but tense, like he might have to push her away, while the other one was fisted and she wondered if he somehow knew the insanity whirling through her mind.

She took a deep breath to clear her mind but the jealousy grew. *He is mine*, her mind seethed. The dark rightness of them finding a home deep in her body.

Fixated on his neck, she thought about breaking his skin, the blood of another woman pouring out of his neck so she could replace it with her own. She made a noise in her throat. A feral sound of anguish and anger.

"Do not Valerie." His voice was quiet and commanding.

She closed her eyes against him, against the overpowering desire to hurt and mark him. Her breath hissed out from her and she dragged in another equally ragged breath of air.

Air that was filled with the scent of *him*. She was overwhelmed by him, her senses heightened, making her hands tingle with the desire to touch him. Her body opened, ached and she felt herself becoming wet and urgent. She needed to be with him.

He'll let me. He wants me just as much as I want him.

Val leaned in towards him, taking a step closer, but he backed up from her, maintaining distance.

He did it humanly slow and she wondered if he was trying to play hard to get or trying not to startle her with a sudden move. Smart man, she decided, feeling like a wild animal, provoked by him.

She was hungry for him, all of him, blood, flesh, anything she could steal from him, she would. Part of her mind was screaming at her, telling her the desire wasn't right, but reason meant nothing to her.

Quickly, she darted forward, trying to hurtle herself into his arms, no intent beyond getting to him when he stopped her easily. "Valerie, Valerie, this is my fault. My mistake. Sit for a moment and let me fix this."

Lucas began to set her away from him gently, trying to extricate himself from her hold without hurting her, but that was the last thing she wanted and it made her aggressive, harder to get a hold of while staying gentle. With one hand she tried to grab onto him. His shoulder, his hair, his flesh—she didn't know what she was reaching for. But she came into contact with his neck and felt her nails rake down his skin.

He froze, his lips becoming a taut line and she was arrested by the beauty of him, a beauty that had been momentarily humanized and therefore magnified. Blood welled in fine lines where she had scraped him. Her gaze fastened there and she wanted to lick those wounds, taste him and then bite him. She imagined her whole mouth filling with his blood and feared she would have an orgasm right there.

Val tore her gaze away, examined her beige carpet, the feeling of wrongness increasing and she tried to shake herself free from what was surely some sort of madness.

Lucas was speaking but she was concentrating so hard on trying to control herself that she didn't hear his words. She felt his cool fingers lifting her chin and then she was looking into his eyes. She heard his voice commanding her, low and urgent. *Open to me*, he said and she wanted to tell him that she didn't understand and she didn't know how when his eyes became a swirl of blue and silver.

She fell forward into the depths of his eyes until the apartment was gone, she was gone and all that was left was blue.

When she came back to herself she was on the couch. Lucas sat in a chair across from her, watching her with a closed expression. She felt fine, rested actually, but then the memory of how she'd acted and what she had wanted to do came back to her.

"What was it?" She knew that wasn't her, the sick desire to have his blood, to tear him apart, aching with hunger and jealousy for this man who was a monster.

"A miscalculation on my part. My apologies."

"What the fuck does that mean?" She sat up and her hand went to her neck, checking to make sure he hadn't bitten her while she was unconscious.

He sighed as though it irritated him to have to explain. "When the Fey were part of this world they had great magic which was often traded or given as part of a good faith bargain or a gift. I wore a ring that I was given a very long time ago which I had hoped would reveal those who were plotting against me."

"You wore a ring that would make people want to sleep with you and tear your throat out?"

He looked to her, away, and then down, finally hiding his expression altogether and he could have been laughing or maybe, even slightly bashful? Seemed unlikely. When he looked at her again his expression was inscrutable.

"The ring erases caution and prompts one to act. It's almost a compulsion to follow their...impulses. Their dark desires. In this case I had expected that it would make those vampires who were not in support of me speak out."

She had lots of questions but most of them she wasn't sure she wanted answers to. "What kind of party is this where you want a big formal-wearing brawl?"

He inclined his head slightly which she took as a 'touché' sort of response. "It's never prompted a *brawl* before. Again you prove to be unique. Tonight is the ball for those that are claimed, human companions that share blood with only one vampire. They are chosen by that vampire and marked as exclusive. To touch a vampire's companion is an insult, answerable with a duel to the death. I don't want my enemies to be prepared and choose their moment well. If I can have them act rashly and individually, there is no question of my victory."

"Don't you have quite the ego?" she said waspishly.

"My dear, I am 1600 years old. It is not ego, but fact."

"How old are the other vampires?"

He shrugged negligently, "No one is over a thousand."

The time periods he discussed so casually were mind-boggling. She returned to the earlier subject, "Doesn't it seem *slightly* unwise to go wandering into a ballroom with a magical ring that's going to make everyone give in to their darkest impulses?"

Lucas gave another fleeting frown. "It is supposed to be more controlled than that. Parameters were put on to limit the effects of the magic. I cannot explain how it went awry."

Val gritted her teeth in frustration, wondering why it was so difficult to get information out of him. "What was the ring supposed to do?"

"The effects should have been limited to those that I have a blood bond with. That would exclude all the humans. Additionally, it only works when someone is within contact distance and the focus of my attention. Not everyone would act out at once."

This scared the crap out of her. "We don't have a blood bond! Do we? I don't remember that!"

"No. We do not have a blood bond." He said in a placating tone of voice.

But she was still unconvinced and the look on her face must have let him know.

He drummed his fingers on the arm of the chair for a moment before saying, "If it puts your mind at ease, I have no desire to take your blood." He sounded snooty, almost English.

For a moment she wondered if she should be offended, what was wrong with her blood? Surely she was snackable, like dessert even, or a fine wine perhaps. Then sanity returned, and she didn't care what his reason was for rejecting her blood, it was a good thing and she'd go with it.

"Why is that exactly?" she asked impatiently.

"That is not something we need to discuss now. Come, we must leave."

He held out one pale hand towards her but Val didn't take it, still stuck on why he wouldn't drink her blood. "Am I sick or something?"

"I am a very old vampire Valerie, certain types of blood are not compatible with my...physiology."

"What, like I'd give you heartburn or something?"

He inclined his head regally, "If it gives you pleasure to put it in those terms you may, but I shall not drink your blood."

Valerie had an image of him drinking from her, cradling her close and piercing her neck with his sharp fangs. There were people who became vampire junkies, their bite could be so pleasurable. But it was only pleasurable if the vampire chose to make it so.

It could also be an experience filled with terror and pain, like living a nightmare or whatever the vampire cared to show you.

Neither held any appeal.

Why would someone be that vulnerable, put themselves in a vampire's possession and hope they wouldn't get carried away and kill them? Wasn't it akin to an attempted suicide or Russian roulette? People could be so stupid. Then she thought of herself here with Lucas, how she was being dragged into his world and was even attracted to him. *I'm stupid too.*

"How did it go so wrong with the ring?"

He dropped his hand back to his side. "I do not know. But I have returned the ring to its case. The silver contains its power; silver has an effect on most mystical things."

He unbuttoned his jacket and pulled out a silver ring box from the inside pocket. He held it lightly in his fingers, showing it to her. The metal was dented and dull.

"How old is that thing?"

"I do not know. It was a gift from the Fey king a very long time ago."

He stood, extending his hand to her, apparently deciding the conversation was at an end and he was ready to go. *Men!*

"Hold up, Fabio." She put out a hand to keep him at bay. "I am not your companion. You cannot have my blood and I will *never* want to give it to you. So why do you want me to go to this...this...bloodfest?"

His fingers clasped hers, soft and warm, his fingers threading through hers tenderly. "Your safety, Valerie, is paramount to me. I need the others to know you are protected by me. By accompanying me tonight, a vampire will not dare touch you."

Val's stomach did a little flip flop. She was such a chump for falling for this.

His arm wrapped around her and he pulled her tight before taking them to the ball. "The ring will stay behind. You now have no excuse to draw my blood. As endearing as it was."

Val felt herself blush and spoke quickly. "I was just trying to kill you, don't be too pleased with yourself. That's not a great effect to have on the ladies, you know."

His head moved down so that his lips were inches from hers, his scent and power enveloping her like a blanket. Both of his hands, warm now, cupped her jaw, tilting her face up to his. She swayed forward a little, her body arching towards him. "You also said you wanted to sleep with me."

Now she wanted to smack him. "Thank you for the painful reminder. I also want to go skydiving, *but I won't*. I have some sense of self-preservation."

His voice was dark as she felt the wind begin to whip around them, "So do I, my Valkyrie, so do I."

They materialized next to a building. The weather was chilly and Val was glad for her cloak. She felt the fur slide against her bare arms and suddenly understood why people had fur coats. Cruel but fabulous. Actually that kind of summed up vampires too.

It was pitch black but she could hear traffic and people nearby. He took her hand is his and she felt small and delicate. They twisted through alleys, the lights in the distance coming closer. The buildings two to three stories high but crowding close in the narrow streets.

Suddenly, they were on a main street and she looked around her. "Where are we?"

Lucas stood next to her, his body behind hers, one arm coming over her shoulder to point to something in the distance. If she turned her head she could kiss him, he was so close. What was he trying to show her?

"Is that the Coliseum? We're in Rome?" *Oh, culture.*

"Yes."

"It's beautiful."

"Rome is a city of change. They all are, I suppose," he said in an odd tone, wistful perhaps.

They entered a very expensive hotel situated on a cobbled stone plaza, huge chandeliers dangling overhead from the high ceilings. Gold gilt and cherubs adorned the walls. *Hello, rococo.*

Liveried staff were unobtrusively stationed around the entryway or scurrying around with luggage, juggling patrons. Cockroaches would be envious of their stealth. Richly dressed guests were crossing the floor—staying and leaving, but Lucas pulled her through them all, noticing that most of them moved away when they caught sight of him.

He had that effect on people, made them run away. She wondered if it was an unconscious act of self-preservation. Maybe on a fundamental level people registered him as a predator.

Two footmen stood before massive carved wooden doors, pale and expressionless. Their outfits were made of velvet, the colors maroon and forest green, different than the hotel employees. When Lucas approached, they bowed, opened the doors, and scurried out of the way.

Her hand rested on his arm as he came to a halt just inside the door. Scanning the room, Val tried to let go but his other hand came atop hers, holding her in place, his hands cold again. Lucas leaned towards her ear and whispered quietly, "Do not relinquish my hold else I cannot keep you safe. There is something here. One circuit of the room and then I shall return you to London."

He stood upright and continued to slowly search the room as he led them towards a wall filled with open verandas, gold curtains rustling in the breeze. The ballroom was large, over two hundred people filling the space. Most everyone had a glass of champagne and Val was happy there were no obvious goblets of blood being drunk as the sight might have been more than she could handle.

Couples danced on the floor, the women in long gowns, the men in tuxedos like Lucas. In every pair, she could identify the vampire easily. Their paleness and speed was slightly off, the humans radiated life and something indefinable in comparison to the vampires beside them. Vitality, perhaps? Valerie didn't see as many puncture wounds as she would have expected and some wore high collars which made it hard to tell.

Fascinated, Val looked around her, the humans were all at ease, the vampires looking at their partners with affection, like a normal date should. Really, the number of people laughing and chatting was surprising. Everything was so *normal.*

As they neared an alcove, Valerie saw a couple in an embrace. The woman was blond and petite, her companion had skin the color of coffee with cream. His hair was short and he towered over her. Despite his muscular build and height, the woman was clearly the one to watch out for. He looked like he should be on Wall Street instead of at the Vampire Debutante Ball, or whatever this was.

She raised herself up on her tiptoes and put her arms around his neck while the man scooped her up, twirling her around playfully before bringing her higher, towards his neck. She laughed as he spun her and then she struck, sinking her fangs into his throat. His eyes closed and he smiled in pleasure. He sat them down on a chair, taking care to arrange her carefully on his lap so she wouldn't have to stop drinking and reposition herself.

His arms wrapped around her protectively, cradling her, and Valerie was both fascinated and repulsed. The woman pulled away from his neck, licked him lingeringly and raised a happy gaze to his. If she'd only seen a photo of that moment, the woman's adoring gaze as she looked into her suitor's smiling eyes, Val might have been envious at the obvious love and happiness they had for each other. But she knew what the woman was. Were any of their feelings real?

The blond put her finger in her mouth, the gesture slightly obscene, then she bit her finger and Val saw blood glinting in the light. The vampire's gaze never left her lover's, his mouth opening promptly, sucking her finger greedily. His cheeks hollowed out as he sucked hard on her finger.

His eyes closed again and he pulled her hand from his mouth, kissed her eagerly, his hands frantically lifting layers and layers of her dress until the woman's legs were exposed, the pink garters she wore on her thighs visible. His hand followed her leg and he gripped her high, his hand disappearing under her dress. He stood, quickly walking further into the alcove where it was dark.

The vampire woman laughed as they disappeared into the shadows.

Val blinked and blushed, realizing that she'd been stopped and staring. Lucas was watching her, his expression unreadable. He quirked a brow at her, waiting to see what she would have to say about the lovers she had seen. She shook her head, at a loss to say anything and they continued around the ballroom.

Lucas transferred her hand from his left to his right and moved so that she was closest to the windows and he faced the crowd.

A tall woman with auburn hair in loose curls came towards them. Her hair was long, halfway down her back and glossy. Her face was narrow, lips thin. She was pretty but there was something hard about her, and almost fevered.

Her eyes were a tawny gold and had a scorching quality. She raked Valerie with her golden gaze, and Val felt like she was being measured and dissected, as though the woman were imagining how she would cut her up, which limb might come off first and how much of it.

Valerie stepped back a pace, tucking herself into Lucas so that her body was close to his. The woman smiled like a villain, as though Valerie had done just what she'd hoped for.

Lightly, she held the arm of an elegantly dressed woman in a narrow cut, black tuxedo. The woman in the tuxedo was tall, a few inches taller than the vampire beside her. She was fresh and pretty, her brown hair had a light wave, hidden beneath a jaunty feminized top hat. Her eyes were brown, with thick fake lashes that made her look like a doll and accentuated an air of innocence. But the eyes themselves were hard. She'd seen a lot, the eyes said. This was a mask. The woman's lips were bright crimson and would have made Robert Smith from The Cure swoon with envy.

Lucas gave her hand a squeeze and she tried to make her expression as bland as possible, feeling the subtle tension go through him. The auburn haired vampire turned her menacing smile to Lucas.

"Lucas, my darling! I did not expect to see you here with a companion. What has it been? At least a hundred and fifty years since...." She stopped talking, letting the sentence trail off and Val thought it was meant to be a little malicious, the implication being that companions were forgettable.

Valerie felt dread come over her. Oh no, she thought. She wanted to back up further and move away. Flee from here with or without Lucas.

Marion.

Lucas confirmed her fears, "Marion, Rachel, allow me to introduce you to Valerie. Valerie, Marion and her consort Rachel."

Oh, shit! Valerie tried to keep her emotions from rushing across her face. She was standing in front of the woman who'd murdered Jack's family, who Lucas now wanted dead. And Rachel was her consort, whatever that meant, who was giving information to Jack about Lucas.

An inferno of anger rolled through Val. Lucas and Marion both wanted the other dead and instead of confronting each other directly they were getting humans to try to do their dirty work for them, making her and her family pawns in their stupid political games.

Rachel's eyes were cold and unusually distant, even as she watched Valerie closely. She held out a white gloved hand towards Valerie, and Valerie looked to Lucas who nodded in consent. She put her hand out to Rachel and was surprised it wasn't shaking. Rachel grasped it in hard cold fingers and brought her hand to her lips. She wanted to yank her hand away and realized she was gripping Lucas hard. She didn't loosen her grip, didn't even breathe, just waited to see what Rachel was going to do.

A moment passed as though Rachel was deciding if she was going to harm Valerie, her gaze flicking to Lucas then back to Val's clasped hand. Then she lowered her lips quickly, the merest brush of her lips against Valerie's hand. Her lips were chilled, but not as cold as Lucas could be.

Desperately, Val wanted to leave, be away from these people and things and their petty politics. She was just a pawn. Everyone she loved was part of their game and they were all going to die at the whim of these monsters. She felt her throat close with tears and tried to calm herself down.

"Valerie." Marion's voice was like ice, brittle and discordant. "I am sure I know you, Valerie. Guess, my dear. Guess how I know you." She gave Valerie a real smile, enjoying Valerie's discomfort, and Valerie knew this woman could bat at her like a mouse, play with her while her chest was ripped open and think nothing of it. Worse, she wouldn't even remember it, just another murder for Marion.

Val shook her head slightly, struck dumb and waited.

"*Jack*. I know you, because of my boy Jack." Each word was said slowly, clearly and lovingly. Marion watched Val hungrily, waiting to see what affect her words would have.

Valerie stared at Marion's well shaped eyebrows, not looking her in the eyes, deciding no response was better than saying something inflammatory like, 'I'll be sure to pass along your regards' or 'Funny, he's never mentioned you'

Marion laughed, as though someone had something amusing, turning to look at Rachel who was giving everyone a small, benign smile.

"And you, Lucas. A Hunter's daughter? What sort of father must she have that she runs straight into your arms?"

She looked back and forth between the two of them, as though waiting for one of them to tell her the punch line from a joke.

"Keep him close, darling. He's a tiger, but once he gets bored... and with the things he'd seen *and done*, he gets bored quickly." It was clear she wanted to sound like she was giving motherly advice, but a bitterness underlay her words, unintentionally or not, Valerie couldn't decide.

Lucas stayed quiet, watching Marion lazily as she spoke and poked at Val with her barbed words. Val wondered why he didn't do something and clearly Rachel wondered it too. Her free hand was atop Marion's, squeezing her fingers as though to urge caution.

His voice was calm, "I would speak with you later. Where will I find you?"

Marion's voice was breathy, her grip on Rachel's arm tightening so that her fingers appeared even whiter. "Paris. I'm at the Paris flat."

Lucas smiled slightly, "I thought you were at the Dorchester."

Marion raised her free hand, bringing her black silk clutch purse to her chest as though for protection while Rachel looked to the ground studiously. "Why do you think that?"

Lucas gave a tired sigh, his voice weary and low, "Do not, Marion. How many times do you think you can be forgiven?"

A look of fury flashed across her features and Lucas moved his arm, draping it around Valerie and tucking her close to him, almost shielding her as they stepped around Marion and Rachel, careful to keep her to the outside of them. He was walking towards the open French doors where Val could see a balcony, the city below.

"Lucas, wait."

He turned back to Marion and then he was pushing Valerie against the wall, shielding at least part of her body with his own. She felt the cold begin at her feet, felt the press of his hips against hers, the way his arms were bracketing as much of her body as possible.

There was the faintest whisper and thud, a hiss in her ear from Lucas—then the cold died.

There was the slightest vibration in his body and she smelled burning flesh. She looked down and saw two arrows embedded in his side, smoke curling upwards and stinging her eyes. He exhaled and it sounded wet.

People were screaming, the floor trembling as everyone ran for an exit at the same time. Of course, the vampires would leave; their humans were too vulnerable to risk.

"Silver and poison. I need a moment. I will get you—" Shots rang out and she felt his body jerk with each shot.

He made a slight noise, almost a growl, near her ear and then his head fell forward, his silky hair sliding in her face and he began to sink, his weight pulling her down to the ground with him.

She felt his blood on her gown, dripping down her hands. He was so heavy. Lucas was dead. Still. No breath, his limbs slack, a corpse pulling her down into the grave.

She tried to scream.

The crowd was panicking, some of them leaping from the windows, others standing to the side to protect their companions while most of them fled to the doors for a quick exit or dematerialized.

Several guards came for them, following Marion's direction as they pulled Lucas off of her and towards the center of the room. He was unconscious, two guards carrying each arm, his head lolling forward. They were moving quickly, Marion trailing them with a gun in her hand. She'd shot Lucas.

But he wasn't dead. Couldn't be dead or he'd be ash, wouldn't he?

Rachel leaned down for Val and grabbed her hard by the elbow, yanking her to her feet.

"I know what you're thinking. If only you'd known, you would have worn black to hide all that blood. I've been there." Then she gave Val a look, like they were high school friends who talked smack about each other and tried to steal each other's boyfriends. "Lucas *and* Jack? I'm impressed and surprised."

Rachel jerked her along, forcing her to follow Marion and Lucas. Marion was almost preening, hips swaying, spine straight in victory. Lucas was still unconscious, his clothes shredded and bloody. The shots were fired at almost point blank range, but through the fabric she could see skin. Whole, unblemished skin that was knitting together as she watched.

Please be alright. Not just because she wanted to get out of here alive and she suspected that would only happen with his help, but because she didn't know how she'd react to his dying.

She stared at him hard as though trying to will him back to health.

And then his head snapped up, feet planted to the ground as he brought his arms together and the guards holding him crashed into each other head first, unable to let go fast enough.

Lucas was free. Turning and eyeing the guards who rushed forward to restrain him again. But Marion was there, back at Val's side, her arm around Val's neck and the gun at her temple.

"Stop!" Marion yelled loudly making Valerie's ears ring.

Lucas paused, drenched in blood like Carrie at the prom, looking Valerie over in a quick sweep to make sure she was uninjured. He waved a hand in acquiescence and walked to the dais that the guards had been leading him to in those brief moments that he'd been unconscious.

Climbing the steps slowly, as though tired, he sat on the throne, his jacket gone, white shirt shredded to pieces and hanging from him in bloody strips, while his long golden hair was matted with blood.

He sat in the throne, the wood so dark and ornately carved that Val knew it was centuries old.

Anger blazed from him, every moment that passed allowing him to heal and regain his strength back. But his skin was paler than usual and he didn't have the same rock-like hardness he usually had.

After a quick glance, Lucas didn't look at her but watched Marion. He made an expansive gesture, his palms facing up and outwards. It was a regal, 'Here I am, now what?' gesture. Marion gripped Val tighter, the gun pressed so hard to her temple that the pain was constant and distracting.

"I'm sure I could guess what you want, but it seems a shame to deprive you the pleasure of making your demands."

"Restoration," she said with a hiss.

He gave an ugly laugh. "What does Rachel get? And your followers- have you any? I fail to see how anyone besides you benefits from your restoration to power." His eyes scanned the room, calling attention to its emptiness.

"I have followers. Step down, tonight, restore me and this will go no further. You can take your little Hunter home and be done."

He laughed. A deep, hearty and human sound, "You would not let us go!"

He slammed a palm down on the wooden chair and leaned forward, his blood stained hair sliding forward over his shoulder, full lips quirked in a bitter smile.

Val blinked dazedly, she'd never seen him so animated, so life-like as he settled back into his chair nonchalantly, confident and brazen.

"Let me tell you what is going to happen. *Nothing*." The words were a snarl, "You will release us if you want to *live*. You have made enemies Marion. Rachel is so weak others will use her at the first opportunity. You are a stalking horse and nothing more. You think to rule in my stead and for what purpose?"

He leaned back in the chair, hands curled over the arms' edges. "Are you bored again, sweetheart?" His tone was seductive, his gaze trailing Marion's body lazily as though he had the antidote to her boredom.

Val shivered at the pleasure radiating from his voice. She saw the fine hairs raise on Marion's arm, his voice affecting her as well.

He shook his head and rubbed the bridge of his nose as though he had a headache, his mood instantly changed. His voice was tired, maybe pain filled, when he said, "They will not follow you. You will bring war upon our race."

She laughed hollowly. "How does that compare to you? You who want to give us to the Fey? Back to the wolves? How can you do that to your *children*?" Her voice held genuine grief.

Noise exploded, two shots fired into Lucas without warning. There was a hole in the chair where one had missed, but blood bloomed from his shoulder where the other bullet struck him.

"I'll keep you so full of silver you won't leave, do you hear me Lucas? God *damn* you! And this girl here too." She pushed the gun against Valerie's temple, pushing so hard Valerie could feel her skin being scraped away. She cried out, tears stinging her eyes.

Lucas was still, almost frozen as though not to startle anyone.

Marion hissed at him, "Tell me she means nothing. Tell me and I'll prove you wrong." She cocked the gun and Valerie felt tears roll down her cheeks.

Lucas watched Marion intently, his gaze never wavering, ignoring Valerie and her tears completely.

"I will not leave so long as you hold her. She is your hold upon me, Marion. Be careful lest you break her," he said calmly.

Lucas shifted his weight and crossed his legs, a king at ease. He flexed his bloody arm and Valerie saw his large biceps bunch and tighten, straining the shirt. Blood flowed freely, a small black river of it gushing out before a silver bullet writhed out of his arm and fell to the ground with a ping.

He settled his hand on his knee. "If you shoot me again I cannot restore you, I will not have the strength."

Marion nodded, acknowledging his statement as true. She passed Val to Rachel, who held her the same as Marion had, Val's back to Rachel's front, gun at her temple. Marion began to walk towards Lucas.

Lucas held up a forestalling hand and Marion stopped automatically. "What of Rachel?"

Marion's voice was angry, "What of her?"

"Will she take power from me as well? Or will you share power with her later?"

Marion gave a wicked smile and turned to Rachel. "My love?"

Rachel's voice was soft when she said, "This is for her. I do not need more than she has already been forced to give me."

Lucas frowned briefly. "You would be her second? I cannot see how that is good for the dynamic of your relationship."

Valerie wanted to laugh hysterically. Was Lucas a marriage counselor now? Heaven help them. He couldn't emote his way out of a paper bag.

"I want her happy. And she is correct, the path you would lead us down is lunacy."

He gave a sad smile and shake of his head. "Rachel, you are too new. You cannot make her happy and you certainly won't make her happy by giving her what she wants. Marion will always want more and nothing will ever be enough." He paused as though deciding whether or not to say more. "And you don't know what things were like when the Others were here. There was balance and beauty. This gray existence we have now is the aberration."

"No." Marion said vehemently, "*you* have nothing and live in a gray world, but the rest of us are happy. We feel things. Numbness is your curse! You put yourself before us, would chain us for your attempt to feel something."

Lucas turned his gaze back to Marion. "What happens after you are restored? Will you let us go?" His voice was ugly, the question insincere, knowing she couldn't leave him alive.

Marion stepped forward, her hand going to his face and touching him lightly. "You have been misguided but generous. I know you have acted towards me with love. It will take time to restore me. I want eight hundred years Lucas. That will take at least a week or two. And you can feed from her, then you can change her. Make her your consort. And you will be her second, just like you did to me. Then you can go free. It won't be worth killing you anymore. I don't want you dead, Lucas. I only want you to be miserable."

"You would leave us defenseless as children, cast out in a sea of enemies."

Marion shrugged. Lucas' weakness was not her problem the gesture said. Things were moving too quickly, Val thought. She didn't want to die, didn't understand the political maneuvering around her but she sure as shit didn't want to become a vampire. Was she a strong enough person to choose death instead of becoming a vampire?

She thought about her mother, opening the door to those memories that she kept tightly locked and saw the pain and fear on her mother's face as she had died. The way her mother had sought her out, watching Valerie's face as though seeing her in those final moments was the most important thing in the world.

Her throat closed up with tears. Yes, she would die. She couldn't do that to someone else's mother, didn't want to be a monster. She could die. She'd do it and once it was done, it wasn't like she'd feel regret, she thought morbidly.

Valerie blinked and looked up, her decision made, that she'd rather die than become a vampire and realized her vision was hazy, tears spilling down her cheeks. It wasn't like death was a great option.

She wiped her cheeks and looked at Marion, blinking until her vision cleared. Lucas held his hand out, his wrist exposed to Marion's hungry gaze.

"Go ahead, my love." Marion said, absently, her whole body focused on Lucas' outstretched wrist and the power that waited behind that thin layer of skin.

And then Rachel's grip tightened around Val's neck and she felt the displacement of air near her body, then a stinging sensation raking down her chest.

Blood welled out of her body. Her chest had been slashed open with a knife, a long jagged wound she could see through her torn dress.

Rachel stood beside her, the bloody knife lightly grasped in her hand. Valerie screamed in shock, watching her blood flow out of her like a dam releasing water. At first there was just a small stain and then it grew into a patch, then it was coursing down her dress and pooling on the floor at her feet. *That's too much blood.*

At first, there was no sensation, but then the pain began to build and get worse, her nerves screaming at the injury, dots floating before her eyes and she feared she might faint. *A killing wound.*

"Think of that as insurance for your good behavior. As long as you don't dawdle and give me the power quickly, she just might live." She took Lucas' wrist in hand and sat beside him. His gaze was locked on Valerie's as she tried not to cry. Each gasp made the pain worse.

Her knees gave out, Rachel letting her slip to the ground. She saw Marion's head descend to Lucas' wrist, striking like a cobra.

Valerie turned away from his intense stare, unsure what, if anything, he was trying to convey to her. Marion was drinking from Lucas, gulping frantically. She raised her head, turning it at an unnatural angle, and looked up at Lucas, his blood smeared around her mouth.

"Faster. The sooner we are done here the sooner you can get your little human fixed."

Lucas turned to Marion, his expression blank. Blood began to drip from his arm faster and faster like honey pouring out of a jar. Marion cackled in a way that would have made the Wicked Witch of the West jealous and continued to drink from him. Obscene little noises of pleasure came from deep in her throat.

Even *sitting* on the floor became hard. Her chest felt like there was a campfire raging on it, burning and sucking all the oxygen from her so that even breathing was too hard.

Just rest. Val tried to lie down, using her arms to brace herself, but they gave out, the sound of her head cracking on the ground like another gunshot wound to Lucas' chest.

Valerie gave up.

CHAPTER 11

ROME, ITALY

Lucas felt Marion drawing from him, stealing the power from his veins as he funneled it to her slurping mouth. He couldn't give her too much, tried to be careful and give her enough so she'd believe him sincere but not enough to keep him from getting Valerie out of here the moment the opportunity presented itself.

Valerie would need his strength if she was going to survive the night.

Marion's head bobbed up and down, sighing in pleasure when all he wanted to do was rip it off her fucking body and shove it down Rachel's throat. How could he have been so lax over the last few centuries? This wasn't a plot that was hatched overnight. It had taken centuries of Marion watching Lucas falter and drift before she would even think to wrest control from him.

She'd always been so obedient, so *simple* and now she thought she could disrupt the world he'd created? It was madness.

Staying still was a struggle. He could easily grab Marion and kill her. He had no doubt in his mind that a little evisceration would show who was really the master here.

But Rachel was ready. She held the bloody knife in one hand while the other held a gun. She'd crouched down, following Valerie when she slumped to the floor and lost conscious, not willing to let the gun be further than an inch away from Val's temple. If he did anything to upset Marion's plan, Rachel would kill Valerie without hesitation. Faster than he could get to her.

This was a revolution. Would he sacrifice his throne for her? All he'd built for centuries upon centuries. Could he give it up for a girl he couldn't even drink from?

He heard steps from outside and leaned forward in the chair, ready to move if the opportunity presented itself. He would hope that at least *some* of his followers would return to investigate what had happened. There had been a hundred vampires here. At least half of them must have stayed loyal, so where were they? Shouts came from outside, the sound of guns being fired and the doors burst inwards, guards and men spilling into the near empty ballroom.

Marion jerked away from him, tearing the skin at his wrist, a piece of his flesh in her mouth. Lucas ignored it, his eyes switching to Rachel. A predator's smile flashed across his face as he waited for her to look towards the door. He only needed a moment. The barest hesitation and he could get to her. Rachel knew it, tried not to shy away from the weight of his gaze, nor look towards the noise coming from the doorway.

He shook his head at her slightly, warning her, 'kill her and there will be no escape for you if you lose this battle.' Her eyes widened, lips frowning, his message received.

Rachel made the barest motion, a nod or a flinch, then looked at the door.

Lucas leaped from the dais, moving in a blur of motion, in front of Rachel before one of the newcomers could fire a shot. His palm slammed into her chest, throwing her across the room and away from Valerie, hearing Rachel's ribs crunch from the impact.

Men were spilling into the room, guns pointed as they formed a tight defensive circle. The shots were loud and echoing as they fired at the vampires in the room.

Lucas pulled Valerie from the ground, wrapping himself around her protectively. She was too hurt. If she was hit in the crossfire, he would never be able to save her.

He focused his will to get them out of there, trying to dematerialize, but bullets pierced him in the back. He dragged her tighter, gathering himself, focusing his energy for one last blast of power before he was spent.

The effort was draining. And it wasn't enough. He blinked hard, blood in his eyes. This was it. They left together or not at all. She'd die in the crossfire if he couldn't get them out.

He tried again forcing his energy outwards to encompass her, feeling a burn and exhaustion in his bones and mind that he hadn't felt for centuries. Lucas roared in agony, demanding his body respond and somehow, find the energy to take her with him.

In a final rush he had her, a cold wind whipping around them, her apartment the destination fixed in his mind as they vanished.

The apartment was quiet and still, the only noise a slight hum from the refrigerator in the kitchen. The anarchy of the moment before was now thousands of miles away. Lucas walked to her bedroom and laid her down on the bed. His legs shaky, movements as graceful as a drunk.

Christ, how weak am I?

Valerie was alive but the chest wound was nasty and long. He pushed at the flesh lightly, attempting to ascertain how deep the wound was but she cried out in agony and he realized it was an absolutely appalling idea for him to coat his fingers in her blood.

His fangs were extended, the desire for her blood painful and getting worse. It felt like a fist was wrapped around his entrails, jerking tighter in a frantic compulsion to lap her dry. Not only was he in desperate need of blood, but here Valerie was, the most exotic forbidden drink. Better than water in a desert, her body splayed out invitingly before him.

Her scent and blood surrounded him, seeped into his clothing and coated his hands and skin. Lucas heard a noise and realized it was him, a gasp and desperate groan of hunger and weakness he couldn't control.

Valerie wasn't just nourishment, but excitement and pure life that could course through him.

All he had to was drink.

Base desire. He tore his gaze away from her jerkily, rocking backwards on his heels, the movements uncoordinated so that he fell backwards, landing hard on the floor.

He had to give her his blood. That would heal her even if the consequences to himself would be severe. The urgent need to feed her almost overwhelmed him, chased his own hunger to the back of his mind. He bit his wrist quickly, the wound from where Marion had taken out a chunk of his flesh, already healed. He moved his wrist towards her mouth but paused.

Slow down.

Think.

He was acting like a rash young man when both of their fates could be changed forever in the next few moments.

Lucas inhaled deeply, pressing the flat of his palms over his eyes as he tried to cut through a haze of blood lust, weakness, and desire for her.

Was this the only option? Giving her his blood would give her power over him. Already, he was drawn to her. How much worse would it be if they had that connection? His fingers went back to the wound on her chest, hovering above it, wanting to see and touch the internal damage. His hand shook to touch her, but he held himself poised and still.

God, he wanted her.

He thought of those who were still loyal to him. Who could he trust, how soon could anyone be here to feed her instead of him doing it himself? It wasn't feasible. Things were so unstable it wouldn't do to have another vampire feed her, have a hold over her and thus over him, especially as Marion already knew about Valerie and his interest in her.

The dilemma was simple. Feed her or let her die. No alternative. He sat on the ground next to her bed and brought his wrist to his mouth again, the second wound closed but pink. Wrist pressed against his fang, he reopened the skin, saw his black blood sluggishly pool to the surface and leaned towards Valerie, a riot of emotion in him like birds batting against a cage. Even though he dreaded this moment and how it might alter the future and give her power over him, it was still a sacred act. An act of devotion to give of himself to her, in order to sustain her life.

Feeding another was intimate, the act sexual, personal and not done lightly, with emotional ramifications and vulnerability.

Her lips were cool, a faint tinge of blue around them and he feared he had already waited too long to save her.

Val didn't open her mouth but turned her head away in resistance, her brow furrowing, her body trying to arch away but too depleted to even roll over.

Lucas spoke to her gently and stroked her cheek with his other hand, speaking words he would not later remember, half threats and half pleadings in his native tongue that he'd not spoken in a long while.

She turned to the sound of his voice, her head tilted towards him again. He saw her features smooth out as she relaxed, her body sinking into the mattress as she responded to his words and the compulsion he put in his voice. Her lips opened and he felt her tongue press against his flesh.

Oh God.

Her mouth was scalding and he dropped his head onto the bed, a harsh breath exhaling from him. A rough groan was jerked from him and he cursed. How many more times could she force utterances from him?

She sucked harder, her throat working as she fed from him.

Each tug and swallow cascaded through his body inflamed him. Lucas felt himself breathing in time with her movements. Quick, jerky, breaths that were unnecessary for a dead man. He forced himself to stop. Stared hard at the wall across from him and tried to get his mind off of the erotic act that was being played upon him.

But his mind wouldn't focus and he kept thinking of this woman, this mortal who was becoming a dangerous obsession. Why lie? She had been his obsession since he'd first discovered her existence. He'd gone to see her after drinking her mother's blood, mixed with Roberto's, all those years ago.

A lovely child who cried herself to sleep because she missed her mother and the happy father she'd known.

He'd been uncertain of what his actions would be: either kill her or take her for his own. The blood of an empath would have been his whenever he wanted. All he had to do was take her and he could feed from her whenever he chose. He'd wanted desperately and feared just as much. Imagined himself as a blood junkie desperate for his next fix of her, a species he'd thought eradicated, but not.

He'd watched her and left her, the temptation for her death or her person warring in him so strongly that he knew he couldn't make any decision then.

But he'd remembered the exquisite pleasure her mother's blood had brought him, how it had lingered in him for weeks afterwards and made him feel things he'd thought long gone.

When he'd seen the little girl in her bed sobbing, he felt sad for her, had felt tears running down his face in sympathy. He'd remembered his own mortal wife and children, how he'd felt when he became a father. The grief from when his brothers had died the night his vampire maker came to his home.

This girl was dangerous.

So he'd let time pass. Let her grow, even protected her family. Even when it expanded to include the human male she loved. He'd seen that happen too and had done nothing. Human emotions were fleeting and distasteful, it made no difference to him where her heart was engaged, it was her blood that called him.

At least that's what he told himself.

But he hadn't expected her to be so strong. So resistant to the darkness. As her father and Jack succumbed to a life of slaughter and protection, she broke away. The empath in her unable to thrive in that dark environment.

He understood her actions and need to break away from the death they craved. While some might consider her actions callous or cowardly, something her Jack always accused her of, he thought they were reasonable, especially for an empath.

An empath could be dragged under so easily by those they loved. They felt emotions and absorbed them. It would destroy her spirit to be surrounded by a life of death. An empath was emphatically a being that relied upon positive energy. A glowing and resonant force that brought calm and unity to all the Other races. It was one of the things that had made them so valuable.

Her hands gripped his wrist, pulling him closer, deeper into her mouth and he kept his body from hers by a thread.

He needed to fuck her.

The dress could be gone in an instant, her legs open in less. He could be in her right now, this very moment, his cock lodged to the hilt in her hot depths.

Her eyes were open and looking at him without knowledge of who he was or what she was doing.

She will know it's me. It would be his body over hers, his hips wedged in the cradle of her thighs and she'd cry out him name, over and over again. He stumbled away from her.

The wound on her chest was gone, her skin whole and unblemished under her torn and bloody dress.

A wave of vertigo washed over him as he righted himself. Val made a sound of distress. Lucas walked away from her, waiting for her to come to herself, trying to think of something else besides his cock in her heat.

Physically he was wrecked, weaker than he'd been in centuries from the blood Marion and Valerie had taken, the poison in the arrows and the wounds inflicted upon him and the amount of energy it had taken to return to her apartment safely.

He looked out her window, leaning against the wall, arms crossed in front of him, the wound on his wrist still dripping blood. He needed to bind it. He was so weak it wouldn't heal on its own.

"Lucas?" Val said, knowing she sounded fragile.

He turned towards her but didn't move closer, staying on the other side of the room. What the hell had happened?

Val's hand was wiping at her mouth, his dark blood upon her fingers, the blood staining her lips. She looked at her hand, examined the blood and sat up, her dress gaping in the process. She looked shocked, her eyes unnaturally wide. Her gaze was locked on his face, the dress ignored. He did his best to ignore it as well.

"What happened?"

"There was a brawl." His tone was self-deprecating but weary. At this moment, he seemed near human.

His shoulders were slightly slumped, his features soft and mortal. "And so they tried to contain me. Your Hunters came at an opportune moment and we fled." Here there was a lengthy pause as though he was done talking, but something about the way he stood, a tension maybe, made her think he had more to say. "You would have died, so I fed you."

She nodded jerkily, suspicions confirmed. "What does that mean?"

He stood still and the moment dragged. When he answered her she knew it wasn't the whole truth. "Nothing. It means you are healed, that is all."

He's lying.

"I won't be a vampire, will I?"

He shook his head slowly in negation, the corners of his full lips turned down slightly as he stared at the carpet, like he was unwilling to look at her.

So she looked at him instead, trying to understand his strange, almost vulnerable mood.

He looked awful, his movements jerky and hesitant. His clothes were covered in blood and torn. He was still imposing and strong but she could almost feel the effort it took for him to stand there and stay animated.

He is so hungry.

She could *feel* it.

Lucas watched her watching him. All he wanted to do was to drink her down. Drink her until it killed her and set him on fire, an ecstasy of emotion that would carry him away like a tide. Perhaps her blood would kill him. He wanted it anyway.

A stranger thought came to him, crowding out the last. What if she were just a normal human he could drink from? He could take her across his lap and drink from her gently, give them both pleasure and keep the mental distance he had with anyone else. He wished for the discipline to enjoy the taste of her blood in a quiet way, instead of the cacophony of emotion, pain, and pleasure that would no doubt accompany even the smallest taste of her blood. Lucas shook his head; it was foolish to be distracted.

He was sixteen hundred years old and had been in an emotional half state of existence for hundreds of years. If he drank from her, his reaction would be extreme. Her blood was too intense for someone as old as him. Like a starved person being offered a steak, their body rejected it, needed plain water and time to adjust to food again.

Lucas could smell her empathic blood. Knew she wasn't merely mortal. Every time he was with her he felt almost intoxicated by her scent alone. And she desired him. That changed the call of her blood and her scent so that she wasn't just alluring but nearly impossible to resist.

She wasn't trained to control her blood, like empaths had been centuries ago. He was fairly certain that if he drank from her she would only give him desire since it was what she felt. Feed him desire for her until it consumed them both.

What pleasure might that bring? She was like opium. He blinked, suddenly aware that he was staring at her neck, watching the steady beat of her pulse push lightly against her skin.

Val watched him in his stillness. He'd disappeared into himself, a gorgeous and bloody automaton standing in her bedroom. There were no blinking or nervous gestures.

He is really dead.

She could forget that sometimes, like when he looked at her like he was just a man desiring a woman or when he told her the history of vampires and Others. She'd thought he'd been robotic before, but this was scary.

It made her want to flee, make a dash for her bathroom even though the door was no protection against him. Was he thinking about eating her?

He blinked and made a little half bow towards her before leaving out the front door and she knew he was too weak to dematerialize.

Valerie went to her kitchen and found a box of cookies. Shortbread. The fat content was insane but she had just survived a stabbing, attack, and near shooting, calories were the least of her problems. *It would be nice to live long enough to gain ten pounds.* She finished off the cookies with a glass of milk and hobbled back to bed, sore all over.

What did it mean that she'd drunk from Lucas? Would he have a hold over her? Her eyes closed and she fell asleep, the feel of Lucas as he'd held her close and tried to disappear with her like a ghostly embrace.

CHAPTER 12

LONDON, ENGLAND

The phone rang and Valerie reached for it, enjoying the happy realization that nothing hurt when she stretched. She was healed from Lucas' blood. It had worked. Saved her life and she wasn't a vampire. She didn't want to dwell on it too much.

"Hello?"

"Val." Jack's voice sounded gravelly and tired. Jack didn't speak, the moment dragging out until she heard him say her name in a devastated way.

This is the call.

She just knew it. Something about the silence, the pain in his voice. She spoke in a whisper, "Is he alive?"

"He's not gonna make it Val. The damage is too severe. I know he wants to see you before it's too late." His voice trembled at the end and she knew he was just as upset as she was. Maybe more since Nate had been a father to Jack in earnest, whereas she'd been a reminder of his lost love and a liability that needed to be honed and cajoled.

She'd been work whereas Jack had been his hope. She got out of bed, already at the closet grabbing her suitcase.

"Where are you?" She asked trying to think about practical things.

"Italy. Rome."

She almost screamed, furious that she'd even have to ask. *Of course* it was Rome. Where she'd been last night. Where she had almost died. Did he know? Had he seen her?

"What's the hospital?"

"Sant'Andrea. I'll see you soon, Val." He hung up and she hurled the phone at the wall, overcome by rage and sadness.

Hastily, she got ready and went downstairs to the street. She found a cab easily and had him take her to Stansted Airport where the next flight left in three hours.

Lucas could get her there instantly. She called him and left a message. *Where the hell is he?*

She felt betrayed. He'd *promised* her that he'd take care of Jack and her father and he hadn't. Part of her knew that was unreasonable, he was in the middle of a coup, with potentially no allies and fighting for his own life but she was still angry.

The next few hours passed in a haze. She tried to read a few magazines on the plane but it was pointless. Images of her father, conversations had, moments where he'd been disappointed ran through her mind.

His voice.

His expressions.

Gone forever.

The way he used to tuck her in at night when she was little, or the way he hunched his shoulders when he was mad or irritated with her.

Most of her memories were conflicted. They'd let each other down, but that didn't mean she didn't love him. Maybe she should have made more effort, tried harder to let him know how much she cared, that even though she kept apart from him she did love him.

Would have, could have, should have.

The airport outside of Rome was busy, everyone seeming to be in just as much of a hurry as she was. She waited for her taxi and tried to focus on the drive instead of her grief. The taxi driver had a death wish, smoking and swearing at the radio in Italian as he careened down the streets like they were a ball in a pinball machine.

She knew some of the words he muttered because of Jack. Like when he'd cut his finger preparing dinner and had to get three stitches, or when she'd tried to sneak out and go to parties. All the memories of her life seemed to wash through her, and by the time she arrived at the hospital she was a trembling mess. She got out of the taxi at the hospital and walked to the front entrance.

There was a bench outside and she recognized Jack sitting there, hands clasped and head down as the world went on around him. She called to him and he looked up, brushing a hand over his cheek to wipe away tears. He came towards her and opened his arms, gripping her tightly.

She finally pulled away from him and met his eyes. They were so dark they were almost black. He looked haggard and she realized he'd lost weight since she'd seen him last. She could see the definition of his cheekbones, his features more severe in their beauty than they had been, any softness sloughed away.

"He's gone Val."

She licked her lips, her throat dry and her body oddly numb. "Did he say anything?"

Jack shook his head slowly. "No. He never woke up. Last night we attacked some vampires. A lot of vampires actually, and your father was hit, knocked out. He didn't wake up."

"What should I do?"

His hands went to her arms and squeezed her gently. "I don't know. We can leave or you can see him. He's still in the hospital room. I guess it depends on whether or not you need to see him one last time. If you have things to say...."

The vampires had killed him. She did want to see it, needed to know how it was done. She wondered which vampire had killed her father. Jack took her suitcase, pulling it behind them as they walked to the elevator. He led her past a bustling nurses' station to a closed door. He gestured to it but stepped back.

"You don't want to go in?" she asked.

"No, I've seen him. I know." He nodded and she realized he was angry at her. He'd been there and she hadn't.

Great. This would be *another* argument they could have for the rest of their lives.

She went into the room and closed the door behind her. The curtain was pulled closed and she didn't want to open it, like it would be too noisy or rude somehow. She looked for the separation of material instead and stepped through quietly. *Stupid.*

Her father was gray. There were no tubes or monitors in the room. Just silence. He was dead. What would they put in him? Nate's hand was above the bed spread and she touched it lightly. She didn't have anything to say. But she sat down anyway and waited to cry.

Nothing happened. She'd cried on the plane, in the airport, even in the taxi. Now she was here and she had nothing left. She stood and looked at him. A bruise on the side of his face disappeared into the bandages wrapped around his head.

There were no bite marks. Her father would have hated that.

She left and found Jack sitting in a chair, arms crossed and head tilted back as he stared at nothing.

"Who did it?" she asked, her voice sharp.

Jack looked bewildered for a moment. "I don't know. The whole thing was a blur." He shrugged, watching her carefully.

"Do you know what the vampire looked like? Male or female?"

He frowned. "I don't have any idea. The whole place was chaos."

She had nothing to say. She needed to find Lucas. Jack stood before her and his hand rose like he was going to touch her arm, but then he stopped and folded them instead. A nurse called her name, waving a phone receiver at her.

Jack went with her, reaching the nurse first and taking the phone, voice curious. She didn't mind that he took the call, he'd want to do all the funeral arrangements anyway. He was a control freak. "Buono Sera?" The vowels were smooth and liquid.

Jack's gaze flicked to Val, "Who is this?" he asked in English.

Val grabbed the phone from him and he let her, leaning against the nurse's station in a lazy motion that made Valerie's heart beat faster in fear.

"Hello?" She wanted her voice to be blank.

"Valerie," Lucas said tonelessly.

Her voice shook with emotion. "Where are you?"

"I am in Rome. Shall I send a driver?"

"No." Jack was still looking at her suspiciously.

Fuck it. She hung up the phone and threw up her hands, turning to walk away. Jack grabbed her arm, stopping her, his grip too firm to be comfortable.

"Who was that?" Each word was punctuated and slow. He moved closer to her, crowding her space and she wanted to back up. She stayed still, her head going back to look at him since he was so tall. He held a finger in front of her face, and spoke in a venomously quiet tone. "Don't lie to me Val. Don't put us on that road. Do you understand me?"

She pulled free of his grip. He let her go as though she burned him, watching as she rubbed her arm to get the circulation going again. "I'm not your sister. I'm not your girlfriend and I'm not your responsibility. Do you get it, Jack? I'm not." Each word felt vicious and hard, like she was punching every statement into his body.

He nodded and looked away from her. "I have to fill out paperwork. Wait for me and I'll take you to the hotel."

"No. I want to go now. I'll meet you later. I can find somewhere to stay."

He gave a bitter laugh. "The *hell* you will. I know you—I know you and...."

She could see him thinking, deciding what to say and what not to say, his posture implacable and set. "Nate's gone, Val. Just go to the hotel. We've been on the edge for too long. If you're not there when I get there things will change."

Val didn't know what she heard in his voice, anger and lust, defiance and despair. He'd let her go, that's what he was telling her. If she wasn't there, he wouldn't come find her. She gave a jerky nod and he handed her a card. The hotel and its address. He let her leave and she felt him watching her the whole way.

CHAPTER 13

ROME, ITALY

She went to her hotel room and opened the door. The lights were already on and the window was open, sounds of the palazzo below drifting in with the breeze.

Lucas was sitting in a chair next to the window, looking as though he belonged there. "I just got here and checked in? How did you get here first?"

He smiled at her benignly, ignoring the question.

The anger came back in a rush, scorching her grief into ash. No more being good and frightened. She wanted answers and by god she was going to get them. She'd push and provoke until he told her or killed her. He wouldn't fucking manipulate her anymore.

Val closed the door and set the deadbolt. When she turned back towards Lucas he was watching her, a faintly questioning expression on his face.

"Shall I be frightened then?" he asked mockingly.

"You *promised* me! If I helped you, you would keep them safe. All that crap about how your word of honor meant something to you. I even believed you! What a fucking *idiot*, I am. Why should I have believed you?"

She'd been stalking towards him, her anger making her brave and reckless. She wanted to hit him, punish him for Nate and Jack, for taking her life away, for making her want him, punish him for every shitty thing that had ever happened to her.

He let her approach, uncrossing his legs and leaning forward—*waiting*. Because he was in control. That's what he was telling her with his mocking voice and patient tone.

The hell he is.

The chair looked small; the whole room was small with him in it.

She took a deep breath, trying to calm her rage.

"What will you have of me?" he murmured.

Val walked up to him and he settled back in the chair, letting her crowd his space and come between his thighs. "Did you know the Hunters would be there?" Her eyes searched his face, looking for signs of deception.

"I did not. There were too many vampires in that room last night. It was not safe for Hunters there." She believed him and she wondered if that was foolish.

"Then who told them? How did they know?"

"I do not know."

"Guess." she said, voice filled with rage.

There was a tension in his shoulders, the sense that he was holding himself very still, like she was an animal in the jungle and he was waiting to see if she'd pounce. Or maybe he was just trying not to laugh at her. "There is no point. I do not know."

Her hands fisted at her sides. "I called you. My father was hurt and I needed to be here." The unspoken accusation was there. *Where were you that you couldn't get me here before he died?*

He inclined his head but said nothing.

"Did you know my father was there last night?"

"What does this serve? You seek to hold me accountable for actions I could neither control nor foresee."

He *knew*. She was certain of it. "That's not true. I think you could have done something. All this time you have asked for my trust, pretended that you are omnipotent and that you would be able to protect me and my family, but that was a lie."

His hand reached up to her and he took her chin in his hand. "Did you expect the truth from me?"

Val felt stupid but nodded, tears in her eyes. "I did." Why? Because he'd saved her? Because he was beautiful and she wanted him?

She looked away from his cold blue eyes and tried to watch his mouth, his full lips and even teeth. She'd never even seen a hint of fang. He must have them.

"Valerie, it was not foolish to trust me." She jerked her face away from his grip and he released her easily, the light touch broken.

Wasn't it? She thought of all the things he didn't tell her. What was his interest in her? Any Hunter, any *person* would have done his bidding if he'd threatened their family, so why her? She'd been too trusting or too afraid to push for answers but that time was over.

"Why won't you drink my blood?" It was the question at the forefront of her mind, spoken before she had time to think about asking anything else.

He smiled at her, a genuine smile that held a hint of something male or chauvinistic. "I would have avoided giving you my blood if I could have. Blood holds power. By drinking my blood you are bound to me. Only lightly. It would grow stronger if it was repeated frequently. And," he paused, "you may know my feelings as well. They might be clear to you or you might find yourself guessing and be correct. I do not know how strong the bond is."

He raked his hand through his hair. She watched him do it.

Nervous.

"As for my restraint in taking your blood, your blood would have untold consequences. It would bring me to my knees, and as tempting as that is, my answer is no." He said it calmly, almost jokingly, but there was a hardness at the end of his words that got her attention.

He turned his face from her. She didn't like that, her hand reaching out to his jaw, fingers sliding down his skin. *Granite.* He closed his eyes and almost flinched away from her touch, she felt his jaw clench under her fingers and then his skin was warm, and she could feel stubble under her fingers.

She moved her hands into his hair. He didn't need thick, golden, shiny hair.

Something dark shifted inside of her and she wanted to tug it, use the weight of his hair to pull his head back, make *him* look at her. Instead of her constant fascination.

"It hurts you to play human for me, doesn't it?"

He turned back towards her and their gazes locked. "Do you know it or guess it?" His voice was deep.

She thought about the question. "I know it."

His hands rose, resting on her waist keeping her between his legs.

That small touch made her breath hitch. Maybe because it was possessive, or maybe it was the look in his eyes that went with it—hot and dominant.

Untamed. That was it. The look in his eyes, the tension in his body, he was different tonight because he wasn't in control of himself. Not like before, where he was only as close as he wanted to be. Right now he was here, present and in *this*. Right now, he'd give her anything she wanted.

She decided to ask him again, "Did you know the Hunters would show up last night?"

"I did not."

Her hand fisted lightly in his hair, tugging his head back so that he looked up at her. He could kill her in a moment but he was pretending to be pliant for her. She liked the way he closed his eyes as his head went back, the furrow of his brow and the way his fingers were tightening on her hips.

What did he hope to accomplish? What did he really need from her that he couldn't get from someone else?

"Do you *want* to drink my blood?" Almost the same question but not.

She felt something from him, an eagerness and a restraint, like he tamped down his first response. But his expression didn't change from polite interest. His voice, when he answered, was deep and caressing, sliding over her body like it was his hands and lips instead. "More than anything I have ever wanted."

Truth.

She became lightheaded with fear and a pleasure so heavy she didn't want to acknowledge it. Her nipples pebbled and she wanted him in her. Immediately. Now. Hard. Fast.

A rush of desire pulsed through her and he closed his eyes, taking a breath that flared his nostrils, his hands gripping her hips tightly.

His eyes were sapphire blue when he opened them, his smile rueful and human. He gentled his hold on her hips and said thickly, "I will not drink your blood. As much as I want to, I won't." He didn't say the words like a man afraid, or at least not like he was confessing a guilty secret.

As though he read her mind, he said, "There is no shame in not wanting your blood. If anything, there is shame in wanting it, for your blood is a weakness, a mirror of emotion and feeling which vampires spend centuries disposing of."

"Why? What is it about my blood?" He looked down briefly. Was he thinking or hiding his expression?

With a sigh and a noise so slight she might have imagined it, he leaned forward, resting his head against her stomach as though gathering himself. Then he straightened, leaned back into the chair and stopped touching her. The cool mask back in place.

"You are an empath. Your blood restores feeling and emotion for a vampire, can settle a werewolf. Your kind were delegates between the vampires, the shape shifters and the Fey."

Empath. The revelation cut through the fog of lust and anger that was wrapped around her. Finally, an answer. What he wanted from her and why. His fascination with her. Did it explain her fascination with him too?

"Are empaths human?" She was scared of the answer.

"Yes. For all practical purposes, an empath is human."

"Why practical, what does that mean?"

"The Others are gone. You would have no one to use your powers on, assuming you had power. You are not a full empath, your abilities would most likely be limited. It's dangerous to be an empath, even part empath. Vampires are all that remain, the only species you could affect, and they would not thank you for it."

"Except you?"

His voice was oh-so-neutral when he said, "Except for me."

"Why?" she touched his face and his hair, stroked his neck, couldn't stop touching him as she listened to him talk to her quietly. He held eye contact with her, like he wouldn't look away if she wouldn't, forging a bond of some sort, maybe wanting her to know that he was telling the truth.

"Because I feel very few things. My attraction to you and your response to me...I have been existing for a very long time. Marion was right when she said my existence has become a curse of sorts. I stand on the outside looking in and there, just over the threshold is you. There is much I would give to cross that space."

"What happened to the empaths?"

He paused and she tried to feel what he was feeling, straining as though listening for music played far away.

He's keeping himself from me.

"I did nothing to protect your kind. The wolves did. They revered empaths, whereas the vampires feared them like a vengeful God. And the Fey—they had their own issues with empaths. The wolves were decimated and the vampires turned their backs...."

"Why don't I feel your answer now?"

"Restraint comes with age child," he said flippantly.

No, she needed to know these things, what he felt about the destruction of... her kind. Yeah, that little nugget was gonna come out of the vault for examination later. She was an empath? Did WTF suffice as a response?

"I can't tell when you're lying anymore or what you're feeling. I want to know."

"If I relax my shields so that you can feel the bond, we shall both regret it." He spoke to her like she was a child.

"Who are you to make that decision? I need to *know*. Not just be a pawn."

"I will answer your questions and then I must go. Ask." His voice was implacable and cold.

What was the point in asking questions when she wouldn't know if he was lying to her or keeping things from her? Fuck that.

The anger was overwhelming. She wanted to kill him, stab him, destroy him. Her hand flew, slapping his cheek hard, but he moved and her nails scraped his neck, creating deep red marks on his still soft flesh. He hissed in a breath and looked back at her, a light in his eyes that made her shiver.

"Will you protect me?" Gasped and husky words.

His brows drew together as though confused, and he reached a hand up to the scratches, touching them lightly as though they actually hurt.

"How could I not?" The words were ironic but his emotions came from him, a fierce sincerity followed by desire. "Be careful with that." His defenses were lowered again, his words almost having an emotional echo that slid through her veins and made her feel weighted.

Be careful with what? Her nails? Provoking him? His shields went up, the weight went away, that feeling of rightness gone again.

Her hand went to his jaw then scratched her fingers down his neck, scoring the same place as before. Desire slapped her back, making her gasp at what he felt, like she'd been floating without gravity and was now being squashed under its heavy weight.

His hands were on her hips, jerking her forward so that she fell towards him, legs spread over him as he settled her on top of him, his eyes level with her own, every long lash delineated, blue eyes so close that she could see his pupils contract slightly.

"It's very bad for your longevity to try and make a vampire lose control."

Someone's heart was pounding, so loudly that it ricocheted around the room and between them like a live thing. Was his heart beating? Was it hers? Hers as he heard it?

And then he kissed her, gentle at first, almost hesitant and tender, no response she'd ever attribute to him. His hand came up, cradling her head in his large palm before tilting his head and plunging his tongue into her mouth with desperate urgency.

Yes.

Her whole body relaxed, her core settling against him more firmly so that he moaned lightly and twitched her even closer, rocking his hardness deeply against her.

She gave a small cry of surprise and delight, winding her arms around his neck.

This was what she needed. Too much was happening: her father, Jack, empath bullshit. But this immediate fulfillment was something she could lose herself in. She could deal with consequences later.

Abandoning herself to the pleasure she leaned forward, pushing her breasts flat against his chest as his arms clasped behind her then stroked her back and sides. His hands roamed to her thighs, resting on the inside, along the juncture where her thighs met her pelvis. He rubbed this thumbs along that slope in a firm caress that made her wriggle closer to him, showing her what he would do to her when he moved his fingers to the very center of her.

Still he kissed her, gentle kisses turning into deep hungry strokes of his tongue, but once she started moving against him more urgently, her body restlessly wanting his, the kisses changed, his head tilted again so that he could taste more of her, claim her, mimicking what it would be like when he sank his cock deep into her body. They were both breathing harshly and his hands lifted to her face, cupping her tenderly even as his tongue devoured her.

His hands swept down her neck, then her chest, grazing her nipples so lightly that she made a noise of frustration. Despite her protest his hands skated lower until they were resting beneath her breasts but not touching them.

She arched farther into him, trying to put her breasts into his hands, the motion pressing her damp heat against him hard. If he'd been human it would have hurt but he groaned, a sound more animal than man and he did as she wished, his hands cupping her breasts in his palms, his fingers finding her nipples through her sweater and bra.

Pleasure coursed from her nipples to her center as though he was toying with her there instead. A great sigh of pleasure came from her and he inhaled, taking her breath deep into his body.

Breaking the kiss, she moved her lips to his jaw and down his neck to where his pulse was beating steadily. She ran her tongue over it and he shuddered beneath her, his hands splayed over her ass, shoving her closer, deeper as he met her from below.

His breathing mirrored hers, a fine tremor in his hands as they roamed her body restlessly. Her body was tight, swollen and on edge.

And there was that duality again, that desire was everything but she didn't know who it belonged to. Hers or his or the both of them together.

Her mouth hovered over his neck, most of his body frozen as he waited, still pressing himself against her, almost despite himself. And then she struck, letting her teeth close lightly against the marks on his flesh, before licking him soothingly.

She sucked on his flesh as though the skin was directly linked to his cock. And *fuck*, maybe it was.

His breath had turned ragged, but he groaned and stopped her, making her stand although her legs were shaky and she wasn't done yet. She felt the loss of his cock against her core like a phantom limb, something she'd never forget and needed to have back.

She almost fell, gripping his hard bicep as he tucked his thumbs in her underwear and pulled them down her legs, fingers trailing downwards. She stepped out of them and his head was so close to her core that she began to tremble.

Very slowly, he looked up at her, his eyes meeting hers, maybe reading the desperation on her face. He smiled so cockily, so surely that she didn't know if she wanted to hit him or kiss him. "Don't I get to see what fifteen hundred years of experience gets a girl these days?"

He laughed thickly and stood up, hands on her legs again, caressing firmly up her body until his hands were back on her ass, under her skirt while he stepped backwards to the chair, pulling her forward again so she straddled him. Her skirt was like a stage curtain between them.

His heated gaze was focused between her legs like he could will the fabric away, hands roving from her hips to her thighs and her ass, the skirt moving and shifting, almost exposing her but never quite.

Voice thick with desire, gaze still focused between her legs, hands moving, confidence purring from him, he responded, "What does fifteen hundred years get you?"

His gaze climbed her body, stroked her breasts, her neck and lips before reaching her eyes. She bit her lip, the teasing, his voice and everything they had already done putting her close to orgasm.

He made a noise like a growl before answering, "Knowledge, stamina, control. The right touch and the right time, in the right place." And then his fingers were touching her, stroking so that she writhed on his hand and began to tremble, the orgasm *close*. The match to her spark. The pressure and stroke of his fingers as perfect as he'd promised.

She could only half hear him, she was so close to coming.

"But that's not the question you should be asking." His breath teased her ear, voice close and intimate as he kept her on the edge. He knew how close she was, her body writhing, begging him unashamedly, to finish her. "The question is how much passion, lust and desire can a woman stand when a man hasn't been this...*hard*...hungry...and desperate, for *centuries*." He flicked his index finger across her gently and she came.

His fingers slid along her slick flesh, coaxing aftershocks from her, making her feel limp...but hungry. Hungry for him to fill her and take her, hungry for his flesh and his blood, even for his gasps of passion. She wanted to devour him. *Is that what I want or does he want it?*

She bit his neck and his fingers hesitated for the barest second before he made a noise deep in his throat.

Her mouth went back to his, letting his tongue fuck her as she knew his cock wanted to. His fingers were still on her, stroking her, rubbing—he was going to make her come again. She began to tremble, feeling the moment of pleasure gathering within her, impossibly soon. He stroked her a little harder, a little faster and she came, the shock of it reverberating throughout her body. She hadn't known she was one of *those* women. A multiple orgasm woman.

She collapsed against him and he eased his hand away from her body.

He kissed her lips, his whole body taut with arousal. Val kissed his neck again and his hand went to the back of her head, urging her mouth harder against the scratches she had made until she was sucking him harshly, harder than a hicky but not enough to draw blood.

He was trying to distract himself from what he really wanted, she could feel his desire clearly, as though he was saying the words aloud: *I need to be in you. Fuck you. Claim you. Make you* mine.

She reached down and grabbed his hand that was still wet from her body, pulling it between them. His eyes opened and their gazes locked.

"No." His voice was rough and strong. Purposeful. She shook her head at him like he was a naughty child trying to deceive her. She brought his fingers closer to his mouth and he didn't stop her.

He'd stopped breathing. He was holding himself in check, no longer willing to push himself with her. Too close to losing control. He wouldn't breathe her in, taste her or feel her anymore. He was going to leave. Sanity. That was what he fucking needed. Her fingers were hot on his hand as she brought his wet fingers to his lips.

"Is this my desire, to have you lick me off your own hand? Or yours?" Please, let it be his, she thought.

"Mine." He said, burning frustration making his words ragged.

She should have been embarrassed by what she was doing and was sure a large part of her would be utterly mortified when this was over but that was a distant buzz in her mind, crowded out by this haze of desire, his urges overwhelming her.

"Do it. Lick me off of you."

"No." But he licked his lips even as he tried to pull back from her a little. She did it instead, licked his index finger that was still wet with her come then leaned forward and kissed him, her tongue sliding into his mouth, transferring the taste of herself to him.

She pulled away from him and his eyes were closed, brow furrowed as though in pain or deep concentration. "It's a hold on me. This binds me to you. It's not a game. Your essence, body and blood, all of it will link us together." The words were slow and pulled from him, weak sounding.

Despite the words, his emotions and desire urged her on, negated them, overwhelming her with his need to have her and absorb her. He was worried about being bound to her, but lured to it as well.

She couldn't think beyond his desire. She felt like a devil and enjoyed it. "You want to be bound to me," she whispered. "That's your secret, isn't it, Lucas? This is what you want more than anything in the entire world. My taste, in you, tying *you* to *me*."

She still held his hand between them but he pulled it away easily and rubbed his hand along his pants furiously, wiping her off of him.

His voice was harsh and tightly leashed. "Do not play with me."

She felt his desire disappear like swiping an eraser across a chalkboard. Gone.

"I must go, this is reckless." He stalked towards the door, the hard bulge of his erection in his slacks drawing her attention.

It probably wouldn't have fit anyway.

"Valerie. This is the peril of an empath, getting swept away by another's emotions. You must guard yourself against everyone." He shook his head, staring at the floor and pacing.

Lucas paced?

"My...want of you is too strong; it could overwhelm you and rebound back to me if we are not careful Valerie. Do you understand what that means? You could act not because *you* desire something but because another does. You might commit any number of sins only to recoil in horror when the emotion has passed."

Was he saying her feelings for him were not real? "So you took advantage of me?" She felt the rise of some sharp emotion in him, it stabbed at her and then was gone, shut down again.

"If I were a different man you'd be lying under me and screaming my name. Do *not* underestimate your own desire. It is a testament to my strength that we are conversing at all."

"This is why I react to you so strongly, because I'm an empath and you are—what —powerful?"

He took a moment to answer. "The lust is your own but your reaction to my own desires has grown since I fed you."

"For how long?"

Again he paused as though considering his answer carefully. She wanted to kill him for taking so long. "I am not fully healed from yesterday. In a day or two I will be whole and that should be enough for me to prevent," he threw her an irritated glance, "*this*, from happening again.

Bad Valerie, no more orgasms for you. That's good, right? Val frowned. "So you think you can block it from me?"

"I do."

She thought of something important, "Does being an empath affect my humanity in anyway? Am I even human?" She felt sick just asking the question. He took a breath and she wondered if he could feel the pain the question caused.

"You are human. Being an empath has never made a noticeable impact upon humans. They have no susceptibilities to empaths nor empaths to them as far as I am aware. You get no extra strength or powers, no longevity or protection.

"What do I get? Sounds like a bum gig so far. How do you know for sure that I even am one?"

"If this were five hundred years ago it would give you safe passage among the Fey, vampires and wolves. You would be sought after and involved in our...politics. But the wolves and Fey are probably gone so your only appeal is to vampires. Young vampires still have emotions thus your impact is limited. The older and more powerful a vampire is the more...interesting you become. Your kind was a moral compass. I've seen an empath kill a vampire from emotions, drive them to suicide. Or inspire them, give them joy and passion. It can be a wondrous thing."

"Can I do that? Is that why you don't want my blood?"

He made a dismissive gesture as though it were irrelevant. "Do not get ahead of yourself. I need to tell you what is occurring before I leave. A Challenge has been called. Any vampire who seeks to take my place must answer and be victorious."

"There is going to be a fight for control of the vampires?"

He agreed with a slight movement of his head.

"When?"

"Tonight."

Her mouth dropped open. "Why so soon? Why not wait until you have your power back?"

"That is not possible. Marion attacked me in the open. My supporters fled. It is too tenuous to wait."

"What happens if you lose?"

He actually smiled at her. Like a parent to a child, a reassuring smile. It was sincere and she could see little lines appear at the corners of his eyes, laugh lines bracketing his mouth, as though he'd smiled a lot as a human. "A fair contest is impossible for me to lose. That is why Marion attacked me as she did."

"Why would she go along with a Challenge if she cannot win?"

"I suspect she believes she can." He looked mildly disgusted with himself. "Vampires are very hierarchical, they do not respond well to chaos and change. Things are unsettled. The Challenge is designed to settle leadership disputes quickly."

"What am I supposed to do?" she asked worriedly.

"Nothing. This has nothing to do with you. I only wanted you to know that when we next meet your safety will be assured. This situation will be resolved. I will be unavailable for a few days."

He turned and walked to the door, unlocking it. "Why are you leaving that way? Shouldn't you just poof on out of here."

He paused, one large hand on the door handle. "I shall try to conserve as much strength as possible for the Challenge."

"You *said* it was nothing to worry about. I didn't realize dematerializing took that much strength."

"I do not know how many Challengers there will be and who is still loyal to me, if any of the vampires are. It could be a long contest. Why tempt fate?" He said, closing the door behind him.

She wanted to tell him to wait, to stay and explain more but part of that was the lust talking and the other part of it was because she was afraid for him. And *that* was stupid.

She'd watched him talk and could barely listen she was so desperate to let him take her. All the kissing and fondling had only made the craving for him worse. It was like giving a hungry person a bowl of soup, really good soup, but then not having a main course.

She *really* wanted the main course.

But maybe she didn't. Maybe it was just him who wanted her and his feelings made her feel lustily psycho.

She shivered at the memory of how much he'd desired her. How she'd been able to feel him holding himself back. The strength of his control had been an aphrodisiac. She'd wanted to know what was under that, see what he would do if he decided to simply give in and do what he wanted.

Val took a shower, instantly feeling half of her energy go down the drain. She was exhausted mentally and physically. Her father was gone. She was an empath. Lucas might die. She had almost slept with him. Jack knew something was going on.

How many of those things could she actually control? She laughed weakly, struggling to turn off the water she was so wiped out. None of it. She had no control over her those things. Everything happened to her. That was her life. She needed to make her own decisions. Be her own person. *Maybe there is a book for that.*

Maybe things would be better when she was stronger. Perhaps she could resist better when she was healed. If she could just stay away from Lucas for a little while she'd have a chance to regroup and see what was real, and what was the blood.

She crawled under the stiff sheets and closed her eyes, sleep instantly there to drag her under.

Her body jerked, as though she'd been about to fall and reacted involuntarily.

What if Lucas died? All because of Marion, whom he seemed to hate. But if he did hate her, then why had he allowed Marion to live for so long? She'd spoken of him like they'd been lovers for centuries. What was she to him? She wanted to know. Then she was dreaming about walking on a bridge.

This isn't my dream.

It was nighttime and cold. She could see a woman coming towards her. Tall, thin and hard, long dark hair cascading around her shoulders, a child in her arms.

Marion.

Not a dream, a memory.

She was on a bridge in London, watching Marion through Lucas' eyes.

CHAPTER 14

LONDON, ENGLAND

1927

Marion walked quickly, heels echoing on the cement. To all the world she appeared a mortal woman, carrying a sleeping child home after a long day.

Lucas watched her, as emotionally engaged in the scene before him as he would be if he was watching a badly acted play. Actually, that summed up Marion nicely: a bad play that never ended.

She shifted the girl's form closer to her, trying to lift her higher, so her face would be tucked against Marion's neck. The heavy red cloak slipped down to show a pale cheek and Marion took the time to stop, cover the girl's fair hair back up and settle her exactly how she wanted.

There was never logic to anything Marion did. She acted in the moment.

Her 'children' learned or they died. There was to be no crying and no complaining. No whining and certainly no running away. Marion liked the idea of dissent, that her children were individuals and would love her despite her sadistic coddling, but they could never give her what she really needed.

A foil. Someone to smack her down and keep her in line.

The wind rose as Marion stepped out onto the bridge that overlooked the Thames. Her hair lashed at her face and swirled about her like a mad ghost, the curls being pulled and loosened haphazardly. Again the cloak slipped and Marion left it, focusing on the wind and the shimmering water below her.

It was a full moon and the water was inky black and reflective, choppy because of the current and breeze. She looked over the ledge then laughed at something. The woman was mad.

She put the bundle down on the ground. The arms and legs instantly splaying open in a way Marion undoubtedly disapproved of. She made a stern tsking noise and wrapped the girl tightly in the cloak, swaddling her in the dense fabric.

Mothers did that to soothe their babies and so she did it for her children too. Of course, the girl was twelve so it looked a bit odd, but Marion wouldn't notice.

She sat back on her heels, the knot complete, a velvet mummy with only her face exposed to the night. Marion put her hands on the cold concrete and leaned down to give the girl a gentle kiss on the lips.

For pity's sake.

Sighing, she picked her up, walking confidently back to the rail. With an effortless heave she threw the girl over the bridge, like a woman dumping a chamber pot out the window.

Lucas moved out of the shadows and Marion whirled around, a kid caught with a sweet after daddy had told her no.

With a smile on her face she walked to him, hands clasped in front of her.

"What happened, Marion?"

"Nothing." Still smiling, she shrugged. Her breath fogged the air, her body still warm from the girl's blood.

"How many is that this year?"

Marion licked her lips nervously. "Two. She was the second this year, just two. And her death was a mistake. She became sick."

The lies were just insulting. "Marion, it's March. And I know she was neither ill nor a runaway."

Marion looked genuinely frightened for a moment then gave another careless shrug. "What would you have me do Lucas? I see a pretty girl, she reminds me of Margaret and I try—I do *try* to take only the girls you allow, but sometimes I am overcome. It's the mother in me. I love too deeply, Lucas." She sounded so pitiably sad.

Lucas looked into her eyes, rich brown eyes that were beseeching him so prettily and frowned. This would end. One way or another. "Marion, there can be no more mistakes. You are to make a companion."

She gasped in horror and her hand flew to her mouth in shock, her little fangs flashing like diamonds. "Non!"

"There have been too many accidents and you are too restless. It's dangerous for you and work for me. I won't spend my time policing you. You will make someone to be your equal. I want to meet the person you choose as consort. I will be there for the change, ensure that a sufficient amount of your life-force goes into their making. I want them to be more powerful than you. You will become Second to whomever you choose. Do you understand me?"

Lucas saw fury flash in her eyes. But she was too powerful to be wandering around murdering at will. Too unpredictable. She needed someone to tame her, and that wouldn't happen if her chosen wasn't powerful enough to contain her.

She gave a laugh that pierced him like shards of glass. "You want me to be better behaved? You think to chain me like a *dog*? How dare you! I am six hundred years old. I *try* to live as you bid me but you ask too much. It is unnatural and perverse, Lucas. I *did* love that girl. I love them all!" Huge tears welled in her eyes and cascaded down her cheeks.

If he killed her now, he could go.

Marion decided to try a different tactic, "Please Lucas, for what we had, the love you bore *us*, do not take this from me. I know it must be hard for you, alone for so long and to see what I have with my children, that special bond that only a mother can have... but hurting me won't make you less alone or happier." She waited, gaging the effect she might have had on him.

And there it was. The reason she lived. 'don't kill me because of the love you bore *us*.' How many deaths did he allow because he'd once loved?

"Marion, I do not kill you in sufferance of the past we share, but the world is changing and little girls cannot disappear the way they have these last hundreds of years. The humans have come too far, it risks exposing us all. None of these girls are Margaret and they never shall be. You must change. Find someone to care for you. Bring him or her to me and I shall oversee the transformation. You have a year. Find someone.

"A year!" she screamed, "You want me to choose a partner for *eternity* in one year? You want me to be miserable. Admit it, you only wish to curb me because my power is a threat to you. Everyone else is gone, except for me. Don't pretend that I am so stupid to not see it! That you force the second most powerful vampire in the world to give up power on pain of death, only so that there is no risk to your throne."

"Treasonous words, Marion."

"True words," she mocked him, "The world is changing, Lucas. You cannot rule with absolute power as before. These humans have evolved, there is *democracy* now," she said democracy like it contained letters she had never heard before.

"That has nothing to do with our race. I do not fear you Marion. We know the outcome of a contest." He moved before she could react, invading her personal space and cupping his hand against her face gently: a parody of tenderness. His hand moved downwards, touching the lean lines of her neck and he knew she understood the threat; he'd rip her head off before she could do a thing to defend herself.

He knew his power burned her. Marion held herself still, pushing all of her energy into her flesh, forcing herself to be just as hard as him. He gave her a sad little smile, his power running over her, forcing her flesh to softness. Then his fingers squeezed her throat.

"I will rip your head off of your swanlike neck, if you do not come to me with a consort within the year." He released her and stepped away, vanishing before she could tell him what an utter bastard he was.

For the next two months Marion was in a fury, leaving a bloodbath behind her, killing anyone who would go with her, savagely tearing their throats out to display her frustration with Lucas. She was like a dog who peed in the house when her owner left her alone for too long.

He had done enough to spare her. Last chance and if she didn't fall into line he'd break his word and kill her. He waited for her in her apartment.

He saw her wrinkle her nose at the smell. She walked into the dining room, where the smell worsened, seeing chairs filled with corpses. Flies buzzed around their heads, resting on their eyes and mouths.

Lucas strode into the room and grabbed her quickly. She tried to react, managing to hit him with one fist before he picked her up and threw her onto the dining room table.

She landed on top of a dead sailor with a thud and recoiled away from him, scooting backwards, misjudging the distance so that she plopped off the side of the table and into the lap of a small dead boy with dark hair and dirty clothes. Marion scrambled to her feet.

Lucas came towards her again, slowly and precisely.

"Kneel." His voice was like thunder.

She complied. He saw her comprehend.

Her eyes dropped to the carpet, nipples pebbling against the bodice of her gown. "Lucas", she breathed, the word filled with desire. Even as she feared for her life she desired him.

It was almost irritating.

He grabbed her from the floor and threw her into the wall, her cry of pain sounding suspiciously like pleasure. She sagged but kept her feet and waited for him to come to her.

"You have fouled my home," she said, and it sounded flirtatious.

Marion pulled up her skirts, baring her legs and thighs. She made her stance wider, put her hand between her legs and touched herself.

Now that *was* irritating.

"Lucas, Lucas, come to me." Her hands lifted to her breasts, lifting them as an offering to him and pinching her nipples. He didn't move.

Centuries ago he would have taken her roughly, goaded on her by her frenzied sexuality. She'd had no inhibitions with him, had sunk lower and lower to try and keep him.

"I have rescinded your year."

Her eyes widened. "You won't! Break your word to Margaret? Everyone will know you for a liar. You jeopardize your own throne if you kill me."

"You are wanton and cruel, I give you one last choice to find a master who can contain you. But I will wait for you no longer. Come." He held out his hand and she reached for him, making sure the hand she outstretched was the one that still glistened with her juices.

He ignored it, gathering her bony frame close to him, stretching his will over hers, transporting them from London to San Francisco in less than a minute.

He looked around at the houses and shops, the hills that were overlaid by streets. This city was a symbol of man subduing mother nature.

That never seemed to turn out well.

They stood in front of a building, the acrid scent of cigarettes and cigars, alcohol, human sweat and lust overlaid everything. Raucous calls from both men and women rolled out in greeting.

The door was guarded by a large human male. He nodded curtly at them and opened the door. It was dark inside and they went down a dark hallway lined with closed doors. The sounds of sex and violence drifted out from behind the doors as they made their way to the main theater.

The theater was filled with tables, lots of men and a smattering of women. It was Prohibition and everyone was drinking with abandon, enjoying alcohol while they had access to it. Lucas watched Marian respond to the crowd around her, losing herself to the beat and pulse of the patron's hearts and desires.

He went to a table right before the stage, a reserved sign and an opened bottle of wine set before them. He held out a chair for her and she sat, smoothing her hair and shifting agitatedly in her seat. After 600 years she still responded like a mortal- quick to anger and fuck, always looking to laugh or cry, desperately seeking *more*.

But Lucas knew the truth: eventually there was no more.

He heard a groan from the stage and looked up from the table to see the performance nearing the end. Lucas presumed it was almost over, he'd heard one of the men have a climax and the other one was close, if the amount of grunting and writhing was any indication.

Lucas looked back to the table. Hopefully the wine would be decent.

Marion reached out her hand and touched his, a beseeching look in her eyes. She shook her head a little and he saw tears in her eyes.

He flicked a glance to the stage, where the men had left, a lull before the next act began.

"So wise, Lucas. Knowing everyone's wants but your own. You bring me here and play me like a fiddle. I witnessed something beautiful on that stage. What did you see?"

"I have no interest in making you believe I desire something from you. I want nothing but your compliance."

"What about my happiness?"

He slanted her a narrow glance.

"What about your happiness?" she said.

"My wants. My happiness.... For someone who might not survive the evening you are very philosophical."

She jerked back from him. "If I become as cold as you then I will allow you to kill me in truth!"

"Let us hope I am still around to see it. Look now. Here is your chance."

Marion looked around her like something was about to jump out at her.

A few people shuffled out of the theater. Two men next to her rose and walked out, going towards a door that was held open by a woman wearing only a pair of lacy underwear.

Marion watched the men embrace and he knew she felt loneliness like a stake through the heart.

Then the crowd quieted and a woman came out onto the stage. She was fully dressed but wearing men's clothes, her shirt a crisp white and unbuttoned several buttons down, exposing a shadow of cleavage. She had short dark hair and was so severe with her hard gaze and bright red lips.

Marion stared at her, transfixed.

"Her name is Rachel," Lucas said.

Such presence from a mere human was very unusual. Rachel stood still, waiting, until another woman came out, crawling forward on hands and knees. She was naked, large breasts swaying with each forward motion, blond hair loosed and flowing over her shoulders. She held a riding crop between her teeth, gaze fixed on Rachel.

She stopped at Rachel's feet and sat backwards on her knees, face up tilted so that Rachel could take the crop, her face glazed with adoration and submission.

Rachel reached down a hand and pulled the blond to her feet. She didn't take the crop, but left it clenched between the woman's teeth. Rachel made a shushing noise and Marion reacted to the voice, leaning forward slightly, eyes swaying closed.

One would think he had brought her to a hypnotist she was acting so entranced.

Rachel stroked her hands down the woman's shoulders to her breasts where she pinched the women's nipples cruelly. The blond shivered and made another muffled noise. Rachel snapped her fingers and a young man appeared at her side, carrying a velvet cushion.

Marion rose from her seat a little, trying to see what was on the cushion.

"Nipple clamps and a fleschette," Lucas explained patiently.

She darted a quick glance at him, looking slightly suspicious.

The show passed fairly quickly, small rivulets of blood sliding towards the edge of the stage and dripping to the floor as Rachel lightly cut into the naked, and now clamped, woman.

And now Rachel stood on the stage alone, the bloody woman led off to recover, the audience stunned to silence by the violent performance. She slapped the fleschette against her thigh and waited.

Her posture was casual, her attitude beyond confident as she waited. She glanced at Lucas and he inclined his head slightly. Rachel's gaze turned to Marion, locked on her and for a moment their roles were reversed. Marion was the frightened human and Rachel was the Hunter who had captured her prey with her gaze.

Marion stood and walked to the stage, extended her hand and it was grasped loosely as the cruel woman jumped to the floor gracefully. She inclined her head, "I'm Rachel."

Marion smiled and blushed, "Rachel. I'm Marion."

Rachel cocked her head to the side and slid her hands into her pants pockets, watching expectantly.

They stood that way for a moment, silent and assessing and then Marion laughed, a sound so fresh and happy, that for the barest moment Lucas thought he felt a tiny twinge of envy.

Rachel smiled back and gestured towards the rooms where they could be alone. Marion dropped her hand and began to walk out of the main room, sashaying her hips in a bold invitation.

Rachel glanced at him again before nodding—a bargain struck. Then she followed Marion into one of the rooms.

Lucas glanced at his wine, decided to leave it and disappeared.

CHAPTER 15

ROME, ITALY
PRESENT DAY

The rustling sound of satin woke Valerie up. Her body tensed and she lay there like a surprised rabbit. She was sure she'd heard a noise, but it was dark, still the middle of the night and the door was locked. *Oh right, locked doors kept out no one truly dangerous.*

Was it Jack? What time was it? She was too afraid for it to be Jack.

Had Lucas come back? An inappropriate and poorly timed image of him prowling up the bed to finish what they had started—

Someone was pacing in her room, not even attempting to be quiet. *Not Lucas.*

The smell of iron and rotting flowers was so strong she could taste it in the back of her throat, had to resist the urge to gag. *Vampire.*

If she could get her hand under her pillow and find her gun without the vampire knowing, she *might* get out of this. She moved slowly, hand steady, eyes closed, breath even. This was a do or die moment. Either she was calm and got shit done or she was going to die.

A tinkling laugh came from the dark. Was Doris Day a vampire?

"Just get up sleepy head, I know you're awake. I've been making enough noise…" she paused theatrically and continued in a whisper, "to wake the dead!" She laughed at her own joke and Valerie felt her stomach cramp painfully in terror. *Marion*.

"Let me put you at ease. Your little gun is gone and if you scream I'll kill anyone who comes to help you."

The light switched on and Valerie saw a vision of crimson before her. Marion's auburn hair was piled on top of her head, the red gown long and made with yards and yards of satin as though she were going to a 19th century opera performance instead of some crappy little hotel room in Italy.

Hysterically, she wondered if there was a height requirement for being a vampire. Marion, Lucas and Rachel, they were all so tall.

Marion smoothed her skirts demurely and settled herself into the same chair Lucas had occupied a few hours ago. She leaned back and paused, like a cat seeing a ghost. Her delicate nostrils flared. A peculiar look flashed across her face and then was gone. Rage? Jealousy?

Her expression settled on content happiness, which did nothing to ease the knot of fear in Val's stomach. Marion ran her finger along the arm of the chair slowly, then wiped her hands against each other as though trying to brush off something distasteful. "Well, I see you have been a busy girl. Jack is here for you, Lucas has been…*right here* for you and now you have me. We are going on a little trip. Kind of like a girl's weekend, but with more blood." She laughed again and Valerie pulled the covers tighter around her.

Marion waved a finger at Valerie as though she were talking to a naughty puppy, "Now you listen to me dearie, so long as you don't muck about you *should* come out of this alive. Though, Lord knows, you don't seem worth it. So hop out of bed and get dressed. Wouldn't it be dreadful if Jack showed up and I was *here*? What would he *do*? Can you imagine? He's got quite the death wish....I like that in a man." She finished decisively.

Val stood up, her legs fairly steady as she went to the closet to find something to wear. "It's going to be bloody freezing so wear something warm. If you have something of Lucas' that would be even better. You don't want a hungry vampire to forget that you are marked property. His scent will keep them away."

Val grabbed her jeans and sat down to put them on. "No, I don't have anything of his. I think you misunderstand. He really has no interest in me. It's a business relationship."

Marion's voice was lethally quiet. "What business would he have with a Hunter's daughter? You are too stupid to speak. *If* you don't have any value to him then I may as well kill you now. So try again...."

She glided over, her knuckles brushing down Val's cheek and resting against her neck. Fingers dug into her pulse. It hurt and made it hard to breathe. Val began to feel faint.

"Tell me you have value. Tell me he will choose you, and you can come along." The fingers pushed harder and Valerie began to choke.

"Yes!" she gasped out.

Marion released her, clapping her hands in pleasure. "Great! This is going to be fun. Get dressed already." She settled back in the chair and casually flipped through a magazine while Valerie got her breathing back under control.

"So tell me about it."

Val paused. "About what?"

"About Lucas. Isn't he great in bed? So virile. So *forceful*. Although I confess that I am quite surprised. A Hunter's daughter. After all this time, who'd think that would be the switch to flick. *Click?* What does one do with a switch? It's not a branch to whip with anymore, is it?"

Val didn't know what to say and decided the questions were rhetorical. She buttoned her jeans and looked for a shirt.

Marion ripped a page out of the magazine and waved it at Valerie. "Put this in your purse, will you. I want this dress. I should have worn something with a pocket. Funny, isn't it, all this fabric and no pocket."

Hilarious.

Val looked around the room, the moment feeling very surreal. Marion wanted to talk boys and fashion? *I'm fucked.*

"How much of your blood has he had? How often does he drink from you? Has he promised to change you yet?"

That was a lot of questions. "No. He's not offered to change me."

Marion pursed her lips. "That's odd. But he took you to our little dance, and I know how he's watched you. Oh, he was worked up when you almost died on that dance floor."

The whole thing seemed a bit hazy to Valerie, no doubt fatal blood loss would do that to you, but "worked up" didn't seem like an accurate description of Lucas' behavior that night. Calm with moments of irritation seemed more apt.

"Does he drink from you every day? Is it a *quickie* or do you feel faint afterwards?"

It didn't seem like a good idea to tell Marion that Lucas didn't want her blood. He'd told her that a vampire might kill her for being an empath. "It's his choice. We do whatever he wants."

Marion huffed and raised a hand to her chest as though shocked. "Let me give you some advice. Woman to...girl," she said, condescendingly.

Since Marion was cradle robbing anyone under 300 Val didn't take offense.

"*Don't* give him whatever he wants. You will lose him very quickly. Never let him get bored. Although, really, Lucas has been bored for a good two hundred years, nothing you do can keep him for long, I expect. How do you entertain a man whose copy of the Kama Sutra is made of wood cuts?" Marion laughed.

Was that a joke? Was she...serious?

Val finished dressing, put on her coat and went to get her purse. She needed that purse. She didn't know how much the holy water and stake could really help her. If things came down to a hand to hand fight she was toast, but she had to have something!

She put her purse over her, wearing it across her body so that it wouldn't fall off while Marion studied her intently. She threw the magazine to the side lightly, her inhuman strength making the magazine slam into the wall with tremendous force, a little puff of paint and plaster chipping off and settling on the cover.

"Right. You know how to do this. Put your arms around me, sweetheart." Marion said suggestively.

Val blinked and looked away. Not wanting to see Marion come towards her but afraid to look away as well. She felt Marion's bony arms clasp her and pull her forward so that their bodies were flush.

She had to turn her face to keep from being pushed into Marion's small chest. The cold began at her feet, whipped around her, spreading upwards like she was a plant caught in winter's first frost.

The journey was terrible, painful and disorienting. When they materialized in a dark, basement-type room, little bits of ice clung to her fingers.

Val wiped her icy hands on her clothes and Marion shrugged, a frown tugging her lips. "Damn that man, he's so good at everything. He makes me look like an amateur. Next time bring a hat."

Val spoke and noticed her breath fogged in front of her, "Why, damn him?"

Marion shook her head lightly and looked around, as though trying to get her bearings. "Well, first of all, because he deserves it. He's been impossible for the last few hundred years. You know he used to be incredible—fabulous in the sack, and if you were going to rape and pillage, he was the man you wanted at your back."

She shook her head in disgust. "But now? The worst conversation! No parties. He doesn't even *try* to amuse us or keep us happy. Lucas used to get things done!" She paused, her head cocked birdlike to the left as she listened intently.

Valerie didn't hear anything.

"I can feel him here somewhere. Come on then."

Marion rushed off and Val hurried to keep up, almost jogging. Her joints ached from the cold trip and she couldn't help but wonder why it had been so different from travelling with Lucas. Was it raw power or did he shelter her in some way?

They came to a staircase and Marion rushed up them, already at the top when Val had only taken a few steps. She turned the corner and kept going while Val tried to move faster. She didn't think it would be a good idea to get lost.

She needed to get to Lucas. He'd keep her safe. Even if she tried to make a break for it, she wouldn't get very far since Marion was so fast. She heard Marion call out a friendly greeting and then she backed up and looked down the stairs at Val, a wide smile on her face as though Val was in for a treat.

Oh shit.

Marion held a finger to her lips, signaling for Valerie to be quiet before moving out of sight again.

What should she do? Should she be quiet? What if it was Lucas? She strained to listen but Marion's voice was low. Marion came back and gestured for Val to come up the stairs. "Surprise! What do you think? They didn't have any in blond."

Rachel stood before her, wearing a tailored black dress shirt with lace along the edges and a high collar. Her slacks were black wool, ending with a pair of insanely high heels that made her look like a runway model. Her blood red lips were arranged in a frown. Rachel looked Val over very carefully like she was an alien, maybe a unicorn.

Rachel's voice was light and feminine. "What the hell are you going to do with her?"

Marion clucked at Rachel, as though that were a stupid question, then leaned in to give her a quick peck on the lips. Rachel kissed her back absently, eyes never leaving Val.

"She's insurance. She'll force Lucas to keep Primogeniture for the challenge."

Rachel finally looked away from Valerie, confusion on her face. "What's Primogeniture?"

Marion giggled like a school girl, her skeletal hand raising to her lips in a parody of femininity. "Oh you Americans! No culture! No sense of tradition."

Rachel shot a look at Val that seemed to say, 'can you believe I put up with this every day?' Rachel had almost killed her yesterday. They were not buddy buddy.

"Well, Primogeniture used to apply to estates. It meant that the first born son got all the land and house and money, the kids born later got squat. If I lose tonight, Lucas could kill you too. Not just because you plotted with me but because my whole line commits treason with me. But

"Want to make a swap. You for her.

"Oh darling, I forgot. Why would you know? It's been six hundred years since there was a Challenge." She stood straight up and adopted a lecturing posture, her hands folded together in front of her, her voice that of a teacher who liked a good flogging, "The Challenged—in this case Lucas—has the right to invoke Primogeniture. If he loses, his whole bloodline won't get wiped out. He can choose *one* to survive. But it doesn't have to be the first born. Vampires try so *very* hard to stay alive that the threat of a whole bloodline being wiped out is enough to keep supporters on the side. Stick with the current king and they're safe. But Primogeniture means that some of these pussies who are dithering about might support us." She looked very pleased as she watched Rachel thinking over the information.

Rachel frowned. "But she's not a vampire. Wouldn't he choose Dmitri or someone directly of his making?"

Marion's little girl voice was back. "You need to pay attention to these things. I'm sure we have gone over this before. Haven't I? Anyway, Dmitri is head of his own line now. Lucas hasn't made a vampire in over two hundred years. I can't think of anyone he would want to walk out of that room alive." A huge grin split her face. "Except her. He won't let her die! He'll have to choose her to keep her safe. It's a swap darling. You will be safe if I lose. She will be safe if he loses. It's a win-win for us! Kiss me for doing something wonderful." She closed her eyes and leaned forward, lips puckered.

Rachel ignored the upturned face. "You really think she's that important to him?"

Marion kept her eyes closed, still waiting for a kiss. "Yes. Ahem."

A smile tugged at Rachel's lips as she leaned forward to kiss Marion. The kiss was tentative, no more than a quick brush of lips. Marion trembled and leaned forward so that Rachel supported her weight. She took Marion's lip into her mouth and bit down hard, Marion squealing in surprise or pain. She pulled Marion into her arms, kissing her in earnest until blood slid down Marion's chin.

Val felt queasy and looked at the floor.

The pair broke apart and Rachel wiped up the stray trail of blood on Marion's chin with her thumb, sucking it into her mouth as Marion watched her avidly.

Thank god she hadn't eaten before coming here.

She liked gay people, she could care less what they got up to, but murderous lesbians who drank each other's blood was a bit more tolerance than Val could muster. One had to draw the line somewhere, right?

Marion snapped her fingers and a long black cloak appeared. She draped it around Val, hiding her face. "Now, you are to be quiet and helpful. You will do everything I say, exactly as I tell you to, or I will break something of yours, like an arm or a neck. Do you understand?"

Val nodded jerkily.

"Great. I hate misunderstandings."

Rachel extended her arm and Marion grasped it as they led the way.

"Tell me what to expect," Rachel said.

Marion sighed theatrically. "Oh, well. Let's see. Everyone will get there, have a chat and catch up—time passes so quickly sometimes. I remember the last time we had a meeting, Genevieve was still making that ridiculous joke about not seeing me since Pompeii went to hell. You see what's so ridiculous about that, right? It was 79 AD for crying out loud. Even Lucas wasn't around! Anyway, so you have to gab a little, then we'll sit down and Lucas will demand that everyone swear fealty to him. First up is Bruce, big mountain of a man with a deliciously wicked scar on his face. It took out his eye, poor brute. Anyway, he's a swordsman."

"Does he stand a chance of killing Lucas?"

"Good god, no! This is a question of attrition. We throw men at him until the job is done. We are going to peck him apart like a bird. And what a pecker Bruce has. Oh poo, don't be jealous. If he can get in a good thrust or two—no, I'm not trying to antagonize you—then that should be sufficient."

"Lucas is almost invincible. I worry that—"

"No, darling, hush. Lucas *was* near invincible, but after last night he's quite weakened. Even if he'd gobbled down a few werewolves since last night, he wouldn't be up to his full strength. Between the poison, blood loss and power transfers, he's weak. Look at dead girl walking here. It took a hell of a lot to fix her." Marion threw a glance at Val, "Bruce will stab him at least once or twice and so will the others. One after the other, all night long. Have faith. Lucas will be dead before sunrise. And I will get a tiara."

Valerie tried to keep quiet, straining to catch every word. Was it true that Lucas was in such bad shape? She thought of him leaving by the door, not even willing to dematerialize last night.

She put her hand in her purse, hoping the cloak would hide any movement. She found the stake, but left it there. The bottle of holy water was small but much easier to hide in her hand. Even if it didn't help, she needed something to help her feel more confident.

They walked down a wide hallway. The ground was covered in flagstone and she could hear water dripping, like they were in a cave. Torches were lit periodically, shadowy pools of darkness gaping between each one.

They reached a set of doors where two guards stood impassively. They wore swords and had their heads covered in helmets, like knights from long ago. Marion stopped and rapped her knuckles on the helmet, the sound echoing in the hallway. "The first thing I will do is get rid of these damned suits of armor! He refuses to modernize!"

The guards opened the doors and Marion took a deep breath, patting her hair. "Let's go get me a throne!" she said happily.

CHAPTER 16

PRAGUE, CZECH REPUBLIC

Marion told Val to stay close as they entered. The room was filled with rows of chairs and crowded. At least a hundred vampires filled the hall. She looked around slowly at the male and female vampires who were chatting and laughing, as though this were a fashion show, not a contest to the death.

The group was decidedly odd, not just their PC appearance (Pigmentally Challenged as Val liked to say). But it was like a conference collision, with half the attendees dressed in business wear and the other half dressed like they were going to an adult Halloween Party. A party where inhibitions and life expectancies were left at the door.

Lucas was seated in a massive throne that was covered in red velvet. He'd cut his hair and all those silken strands that she'd been unable to resist touching were gone. His hair was wavy. Some of it fell forward onto his forehead while the back was barely long enough to graze his collar. He looked modern, the haircut exposing his cheekbones, making him look more alive.

His clothes were different too. He was no longer in a modern suit, but wearing what she could only describe as gentleman's clothing from three hundred years ago. He wore breeches and even hose. Hose! How could a man make tights look so sexy? His shirt was ivory and unbuttoned at the throat, he looked like a romantic hero come to life.

Val realized that she hadn't really understood that Lucas had lived through civilizations, discarding centuries and customs like clothing, until now. But now, he looked like a warrior. A man who had survived for over a millennia, because he was stronger, fiercer, and more beautiful than any other man.

He was deceptively relaxed, his chin resting on one large hand as he watched the vampires below him. His gaze moved to Marion and Rachel, then beyond, settling on Val. She wondered if he could sense her through the cloak. She felt her heartbeat slow as he watched her. A wave of energy enveloped her and she felt herself answering an unvoiced question.

'Yes, it's me. I'm here.' The response was almost intangible, but she felt it well from her and radiate outwards towards him. He didn't change expression and she wondered if she'd imagined the odd connection. Was it real? A reaction to having his blood inside of her?

Lucas looked away from her as though bored. He drummed his fingers on the arm of the throne.

Marion hissed something at her and pushed her into a chair, her back slamming against the wood. She made a slight noise and found

Lucas' gaze back upon her. He shook his head slightly, his gaze leaving her and continuing around the room.

She tried to reach him again, still wondering if the connection from a moment ago had been real or imagined. His shoulders tensed and felt the connection she hadn't really recognized, shut down.

She clenched the holy water tight.

There was nothing to do but wait.

With a hush, the vampires stilled and Val got goose bumps. A guard behind Lucas moved forward, a silver staff in his hands. He stopped at the edge of the steps and struck the ground with his staff three times, the sound crashing through the room in a heavy beat.

Then he stepped back to his place behind the dais and Marion stood. Murmurs rose around the room.

Marion stood before him and waited. Lucas was patient, letting the moment drag out until the excitement in the crowd swelled, then began to subside. Valerie realized Lucas was a showman, playing the crowd. Seconds passed as Lucas and Marion stared at each other.

Marion broke the stare, head jerking up haughtily. As far as a dominance contest went, Lucas won. He looked around the room, all the other vampires looking away or at their feet as his gaze touched them.

He spoke, voice deep and flowing with almost no accent, "My child, will you not bow before your maker?" he said, chidingly.

Marion's voice rang out in response, "No, my liege. My path is no longer with yours. We are *via fracta* and I offer you Challenge." Valerie heard the formality in the words and translated the Latin to 'a break in the road'.

Lucas inclined his head and Marion arranged her skirts, preparing to sit back down in her seat.

"I decline Primogeniture. If I am victorious I will claim the blood of your house, and consign the memory of your name to those of the Forgotten before you. If you lose, Rachel dies. Every vampire created by one who Challenges me will die. Are there any who support my child, Marion?"

The silence lengthened as Valerie nervously waited to see who the Challengers were.

Marion stood again and gestured for Valerie to stand. Valerie stayed seated and Marion yanked her upwards, the cloak pulled away from her and thrown to the floor in a flashy move.

Some of the vampires leaned forward as though to see her better, while others nodded and a few froze. Lucas turned his gaze to Marion. "I understand your eagerness for death, but you must respect the sanctity of ritual. I assume you have something to say before we continue?"

Marion seemed vaguely nonplussed by Lucas' lack of reaction at Val's reveal. "If I am victorious, I claim *your* house, Lucas, son of Tiberius Junius. Do you wish to offer Primogeniture and save one of your own?" Her voice was smug, her grip biting.

Lucas smiled again, a wicked smile that made Valerie shiver. "I do not."

Her heart froze in her chest, coldness and terror slamming into her so that her next breath was a stutter. If Lucas lost she would die too. He wouldn't save her or do anything to spare her. And she'd trusted him? Talk about bad taste in men.

She felt Rachel startle beside her and Marion's grip loosened briefly. "Do you know how I will kill her?" Her voice was lethal.

"I'm more interested in how I will kill you. You guessed wrong Marion. I will not protect her."

Marion snarled and turned to Valerie, shaking her like a ragdoll, venting her frustration. One hand was on her shoulder, twisting for leverage, the other on Val's chin, like she was going to pull the head off a toy doll.

Frantically, she pulled the cork out of the bottle of holy water, throwing it in Marion's face. Marion let go of her, recoiling backwards in pain, her skin sizzling, the smell of burning meat filling the room. Marion screamed and reached for Valerie with a snarl. Val threw herself backwards, desperate to escape.

Lucas' booming voice made Marion freeze. "You cannot touch her until after you win, Marion! Kill her and Rachel dies in exchange."

Val fell, tripping over the leg of a chair, but someone caught her before she hit the ground. It was Lucas, at her side before she could hit the ground.

He righted her gently, holding out his arm to her. Her hand shook as she placed it around his bicep, letting him tuck her close to him.

Lucas led her up the steps of the dais, walking her to a chair that sat against the wall, next to one of the guards, before gesturing for her to sit down. She sat, back to the wall, facing the crowd, but obscured from Lucas' view by the back of his throne.

Her breathing was ragged, adrenaline and fear twisting through her stomach. All the vampires in the audience were staring at her.

Incongruously, she thought about how ordinary she must appear next to Lucas: her boring jeans and rumpled shirt, compared to his bright splendor. He knelt down before her, his eyes looking into hers for a moment. Quickly, he caressed a hand down her cheek before standing and walking away from her.

What did that mean? Was it an apology for denying to save her? Marion had brought her here expecting Lucas to keep her safe. If he lost, she'd still walk out of here alive and he'd said no. If he died tonight, so did she. Did he really think a friendly gesture, like patting a dog on the head was going to make her forgive that? Fat fucking chance.

Here was another example of how stupid she'd been to believe him. And then to let him do those things to her last night. Let him? Okay, the truth was, she'd wanted him—*bad*. She'd not only been an active participant but the aggressor.

To think she'd spent so long loving Jack from a distance, never having the cajones to do anything about it. And now she might die, and what had she accomplished? Nothing. All the time she'd spent running away from her destiny and she was still ass deep in vampires.

Full circle. Back where I started.

She made a vow, if she got out of here alive she was going to make a change, Tina Turner style: kick the vampire to the curb and hound Jack until he gave their relationship a chance.

She'd wound up with nothing because she'd been so guarded. Lesson learned.

Her deep contemplations were interrupted by a burly vampire with curly hair and a scar down the side of his face. The first several vampires had sworn featly to Lucas. They'd approached the dais, given a little bow, said a few words about how great he was and how they'd follow him to the death, but this one was different—Bruce. It had to be.

The room became still and the weight of the vampires' collective gaze was like a shimmer before her eyes. The heavily muscled vampire walked up to the throne and didn't bow. She saw Lucas' shoulders straighten as he leaned slightly forward. A quick strain of thoughts and images came to her, muffled like someone was playing music but then they shut the window, cutting off the sound. *He won that fight in Verona...not in a fair fight.*

What 'not in a fair fight', Val wondered desperately? Had Lucas lost to Bruce before? Was he so weak he thought Bruce could kill him?

Shit! Val hadn't really thought he could lose. Since the day she'd met him, he'd been larger than life. Bigger, stronger—invincible. When he'd said he was unkillable she'd believed him, assumed it was true and never questioned it.

But Marion and Rachel didn't seem to think he was invincible. Bruce was willing to fight Lucas to the death. He must think he had a chance. And with Lucas injured, maybe he had a good one.

Marion had said Bruce was a renowned fighter. His goal was to win, but failing that, to harm. They'd overwhelm Lucas with numbers, each contestant pecking at him, tearing him down so that by the time Marion had to fight him he'd be too weak to win.

"My liege." His voice was gravelly. Lucas inclined his head for him to continue. "We have walked this earth together for three hundred and fifty years. You were always reasonable. We all know how you have put the vampires first. Secured our place in the world, but the rumors—" his gaze flicked to Marion, "say that you seek to bring back the wolves and the Fey. That you would create chaos, even jeopardize everything we fought for." He lowered his head, deferential as he waited for Lucas to respond.

"You were not present when the Fey and the wolves roamed this world. You do not know, as I do, how our people have changed and lost because of their absence. Either you believe in me, as your Lord and Maker, or you Challenge me. If I am victorious I will do as I see fit. You must either fall in line or die."

The man shook his head, still unwilling to look at Lucas but disturbed. His words were stilted, as though he wasn't usually prone to talking and wanted to make sure he had the words precise, nothing extra tossed into the world. "My Lord. Always you have had our interests at the forefront of your heart, but you are not the same as you were even a hundred years ago. We are not unaware of your weariness."

Bruce looked at Valerie from under his lashes, "Happy I am that you think of creating a companion, but I fear it is not enough. Do you wish to kill us all?"

Valerie felt the uneasiness in the room encroaching upon her, constricting her chest like a snake. The crowd shifted uneasily while waiting for Lucas to respond.

None of the vampires seemed shocked by the question. Maybe his hold on the vampires was shaky. Lucas gestured for Bruce to be at ease and the man raised his head, staring intently at Lucas as he waited for his king to respond.

Lucas stood, descending the steps with inhuman swiftness. Bruce stepped backwards, trying to keep Lucas away from him. But Lucas moved forward in a small rush, slashing inhumanly fast, blood suddenly pouring from Bruce's neck in heavy pulses. Bruce grabbed his throat, eyes wild, trying to keep his blood in his body.

Lucas reached for Bruce's arm and pulled until the limb came away with a sloppy, aching sound. It was wet and deep, the pop of the bone resonating through Val unpleasantly, like she could feel the vibration of it in her body.

Lucas tossed the arm to Marion, who batted it away from her and tried to keep her composure while ensuring the arm didn't land in her lap.

Blood spattered Lucas, dripping from his short hair as he lunged at Bruce again. The other arm came free, Bruce falling to the ground, totally shocked by the swiftness of the attack.

Shouldn't someone have said "go"? Had she blinked and missed it?

Bruce was choking, saying something while Lucas stood over him, waiting for Bruce to die. He was like a little boy with an insect, taking him apart piece by piece.

Finally, when Val was one wet sound away from dry heaving, Lucas grabbed Bruce's hair, raised his foot, rigid thigh muscles braced against the man's torso, and popped Bruce's head off, tossing it onto the pile of limbs at his side.

As soon as his head came off, everything was silent.

No one moved or breathed. Bruce stopped moaning. His eyes were wide and then Valerie saw something terrible, something she knew she'd never forget.

Bruce blinked.

He was still alive.

Lucas snapped his fingers and a guard came forward holding a long wooden staff out to Lucas' waiting hand. With a casual move, like a gentleman tapping his cane against the sidewalk, he skewered Bruce through the heart, every piece of him turning to ash in a moment.

Lucas walked back to his throne and sat back down, as though nothing untoward had happened.

He settled himself, running a hand through his hair, pushing it off of his face, blood smearing in his golden locks. He looked at his bloody hand with mild distaste, wiping the blood onto his breeches.

"No. I do not want everyone dead," he paused, "Come now, who will stand with Marion and Challenge me?" he said it in a happy voice, like he wanted dissent.

Some of the vampires let out shaky sighs. Moving again like a paused movie returned to play.

Marion leaned forward eagerly when the question was asked, waiting to see who would stand beside her, clearly hoping that no one had changed their minds about challenging Lucas.

Several men looked to Marion furtively before quickly glancing away. Val guessed that they had been the undecided ones, and after

Lucas' little display, they were not going to Challenge him. She wouldn't. As far as torture went, he'd put the evil back in medieval.

Marion was furious, near vibrating in her chair as she stood and began to shout. "Non! It was not a fair fight. The Challenge had not yet begun. You killed him in cold blood!"

Lucas stood, turning to Marion, smile feral. "I don't see how that can be fixed now. As powerful as I am, you expect me to wait? To play your petty games? This is *mine*. Everyone here is *mine*! I killed the Fey and the wolves! I brought us out of the dark ages and made us prosper. No one takes from *me*." The final words were furious and guttural.

They leaned forward to make sure they caught every syllable, most of the vampires falling out of their chairs to the ground, abasing themselves before him.

He's a scary bastard and I almost slept with him! Mortified, didn't begin to cover it.

Marion shouted back at him, "You kill him because you are weak! Admit it, you may not win a fair fight and so you seek to evade the rules, clutching at the throne like a petty tyrant." Her tone was bitter, but changed to placating and wise, "You are above this Lucas. Let your memory remain untainted. The greatest king who ever ruled does not go out as a *cheater*, as a shadow of the man you once were. Take your death with honor."

Lucas chuckled darkly. "Your time will come, my dear. Pray you are right, that I cheat out of weakness rather than disgust at being bound by rules. Or else it will be your ashes in that fireplace."

Lucas turned from her and hesitantly, another Challenger moved forward.

He was bald, with huge muscles and dark skin. He looked like a genie and Valerie became afraid. This man was just as deadly as Bruce except Lucas wouldn't have the element of surprise, would have to fight him fairly.

Could he win?

The man was soulless, evil coming off of him in dark currents that polluted the air around him. He was a killer, a figure to inspire children to stay in bed, the threat that lurked in the dark.

"I challenge you because you deserve the final death. You took her from me and I'll kill you for it."

Lucas was still for a bare moment then gave an ugly laugh.

"*Lucretia*? You Challenge me because of that bitch? Good god! You are a fool. She could wipe out a village in a night and still want more. She was never satisfied...and she certainly wasn't satisfied by *you*."

The bald man clenched his fists in rage, long white fangs extended as he hissed at Lucas angrily.

Lucas regarded him calmly, voice chill and flat. "She asked me to do it. She'd been your companion for only twenty, thirty years? But she welcomed me into her body and before she died, she thanked me."

The bald man lunged forward, a beefy fist flying towards Lucas' face.

Lucas grabbed the man's arm and threw him forward, using the man's momentum against him. The fight happened so quickly Valerie could barely see the individual movements, the two of them moving in flash choreography, like the fast flicker of a camera lens, each still a violent instant as they pummeled each other.

The man stumbled and Lucas kicked him in the back of the head before he could stand, neck snapping at an unnatural angel. The bald man shook it off, the terrible sound of bones grating against each other as they were forced back into place was like popcorn popping in the cavernous room.

He gave a cry of rage and turned, fury driving him on. Lucas gave ground, let the man push him backwards.

"You know, she wasn't a real red head." Lucas taunted casually.

His opponent yelled in rage, swinging harder and faster until his punches and lunges became sloppy.

Val had never seen him like this: playful and murderous. Was this the real Lucas?

Lucas grabbed the man's arm and threw him to the ground, pulling until the man's arm broke and hung at an odd angle. His foot was on the back of the man's head, and another sickening crunch reverberated off the walls, as his neck re-broke. And then Lucas flipped him over, his hand in a fist as he slammed it into the man's chest, punching through his ribcage.

Everyone seemed to draw a breath at once, one woman clutching her chest sympathetically. Then they exhaled and the action resumed, the audience rustling like disturbed snakes, honing in on the death before them. Lucas pulled his hand out of the vampire's body, the heart clenched tight in his fist. Then it was all ash, and it spilled from Lucas' fingers like confetti.

Val stared at Lucas. His face was haggard, harsh lines bracketing his mouth as he dusted his hands. He was half turned from the crowd and she could see his profile, the intensity and determination of him but also, a growing black stain at his side.

It was the wound from the night before and it was seeping, expanding as she watched, like an oil slick in the ocean. Was there something she could do to interrupt the Challenge? Some way to take a break and bandage his wound in hopes that no one else would notice?

As though he knew what she was thinking, he turned to her and shook his head once.

No.

There was no stopping. He turned and faced the crowd. Marion grabbed Rachel's hand excitedly and whispered in her ear loudly, a stage whisper that carried throughout the room, "Look, he's hurt. Didn't I tell you he was weak?"

Lucas ignored them and another man shuffled out of the crowd. He was a thin man of medium build who was so nondescript that as soon as Valerie looked away from him she could barely remember what he looked like. She imagined he'd been a tailor or an accountant in a previous life. He certainly didn't seem like a threat to Lucas.

"Edgar." Lucas put a hand on his shoulder. "You Challenge me of your own free will? A contest to the death?"

Edgar flushed and opened his hands nervously. "Yes. Yes I do. The Fey, the wolves. It's lunacy, Lucas. I stood by you as we cut them down. One after the other, all that time ago."

His voice was wistful, as though lost in remembrance of the battles they had fought together. "Remember, the moon guiding our blades to victory...and you... when the Black Witch took my son, you were there. You cried with me. But now you are not the warrior you were. To seek out that which we destroyed, make them prosper again—*why*?"

Surprisingly, Lucas bowed to him. "My friend, I ask you to rescind your Challenge."

The man gave a rueful smile. "My Lord, for the love I bear you, I *beg* you to not pursue the Fey nor the wolves. Life is still exciting enough without creating danger."

Lucas shook his head in soft denial. "There you are wrong, my friend. We have become like petulant children, destroying the world and humans for a pleasure without boundaries. If anyone is to understand my motives, it should be you." The man gritted his teeth and looked away from Lucas, the conversation at an end.

Lucas stepped back, no longer the friend, but the king. "How would you Challenge me?"

The man gave a little nod and called for his weapon. A guard came forward, offering a sword. He took it, raised it to his lips and kissed the blade, the silver metal smoking as it made contact with his flesh.

Another guard came forward, handing Lucas a huge broadsword. It was so large and heavy that Valerie knew she wouldn't be able to lift it, let alone wield the thing.

Not that anyone wanted her to fight.

Lucas swung the sword in a lazy arc, testing the heft of it in a practiced move before meeting Edgar in the middle of the room. The people in the front row, closest to the action, looked a little nervous about the two men fighting right in front of them. A guard thumped the ground with his staff, signaling the start of their fight.

Lucas smiled grimly and assumed a fighting stance, giving no indication that he felt the wound in his side, which was now dripping onto the floor. With a harsh clang Edgar's sword crashed into Lucas'.

Lucas braced himself and turned, twisting his weapon so that Edgar's blade was deflected to the side. He thrust forward, but Edgar danced back, blocking the thrust and twisting into an attack that pushed Lucas backwards, his sword flashing through the air like lightning.

Lucas was graceful, his body well balanced, the moves and steps more like a ballet than a fight. With each lunge his back was straight and rigid, his thigh muscles bunching with each step.

Valerie was disheartened to realize that she was fixating on Lucas' hotness instead of the battle to the death that was going on in front of her. She closed her eyes, wanting to block him out: like looking away from the sun.

Edgar was good. Even if he did look like a harried businessman. He was stealthy and fast. But Lucas was a force, unstoppable and inexorable, parrying the blows easily, toying with Edgar until Edgar put a foot wrong, allowing Lucas to lunge in for the kill.

But the smaller man feinted to the side, dropping to the ground heavily while thrusting his sword into the side of Lucas' already bleeding body. With a roar Lucas recoiled, Edgar's blade glinting with blood.

Lucas gave a snarl of rage, like a wounded animal, as Edgar rolled to his feet and tried to press his advantage, rushing forward and aiming for Lucas' heart.

Lucas stumbled to the side, tilting away from the killing blow so that it ripped his shirt and grazed his chest but didn't enter his body. The force of Edgar's missed thrust carried him forward, into the emptied chairs. Lucas whirled, his sword sinking into Edgar's torso, just above his belly button, before exiting out near his shoulder.

Lucas didn't draw his blade free, but stood close to his friend, almost like he was shielding him from the crowd. A look of sad surprise crossed Edgar's face as his features dulled and then dried, falling towards Lucas who, discarding his sword, attempted to catch him before he turned to dust. But it was too late. Edgar was gone, ash raining down on Lucas' arms and feet.

He wiped the ash across his chest, over his heart, smearing the bloody scrape Edgar had made with the man's ashes, as though making Edgar a part of him.

Valerie felt Lucas' pain crash into her as his mental shields lowered for a moment. His side blazed with pain, but it was nothing compared to the grief that overcame him for having to kill his friend.

A dozen images passed through her mind, like rocks skipping over the still surface of a cold lake: Lucas and Edgar on horseback talking, them both drinking blood from the same woman, Lucas pressed to her front as Edgar was pressed to her back, Edgar kneeling over a body and weeping while Lucas watched and stood guard, protecting his grieving friend. Then the memories were zipped away from her and she felt like a voyeur.

Lucas walked back to the dais, his sword held loosely in one hand. His gaze caught hers, held her so that she was unable to look away as he advanced towards her in a graceful, predatory walk.

He's going to drink me now.

His brows lifted in a slight look of amusement and disdain that was undermined by the copious amounts of blood that trailed from him and dripped to the floor.

She wondered how severe his injury was, but his gaze said something different: *look how easy this is.*

He handed the sword back to the guard before heading back to the center of the room and making a low bow to Marion. Lucas extended his hand to her, "My love?" His voice was dark and seductive, a quiet ruthlessness underlying his tone.

Marion jerked out of her chair and stalked towards him in a fury. Things had obviously gone much worse that she'd expected.

She'd been a fool for doing this and her expression said that she knew it.

As Marion neared Lucas he closed his eyes, his brows pulled together in a frown. She stopped and seemed to shrink back for a moment before forcing herself to move forward again. He made a disappointed noise in his throat and spoke in a clear voice. "Who helped you? I smell the power and know you are no longer second to Rachel in power. Tell me who."

Marion gasped, her gaze jerking back to Rachel and around the room, seeking out those who'd donated blood and power to her cause.

Frozen in place, she didn't speak.

"Why don't you whisper it to me?" he said.

She gave a little nod and he leaned in listening while she said something to him. He nodded and looked around the room.

The audience was still, like wax figurines. Marion licked her lips in a nervous gesture, "What about me?"

"What about you?" he said with obvious disgust. The accent was back, his words having an odd cadence.

"You would not spare me also?" Her voice was hesitant.

"You are the organizer of this treason. How could I spare you after this? With all these witnesses. Have a care for your memory, Marion. Where is your *conviction*?" he mocked.

Marion blinked rapidly, her chest rising and falling as she breathed quickly. Her voice was breathy and distant, "Me, Margaret, my little girl...all those years, all our time together. You couldn't. You couldn't be so cruel to me."

Valerie wondered if Marion was that crazy, that it hadn't really occurred to her that Lucas would kill her for trying to take his throne?

"Shall I assume you don't wish to fight?"

She nodded tightly and flushed, her shoulders hunching in like a beaten dog.

Was that it, Valerie wondered? Was Marion really giving up now?

Lucas seemed impatient. "Kneel."

Marion looked back, frantically trying to catch sight of Rachel who was leaning forward in her chair as though ready to spring forward and rescue Marion if she had to. Val could see Marion's will deflating before her eyes, like melting snow in the bright sunshine.

Trembling, Marion fell to her knees, head bowed, cowering slightly away from him as though to protect herself from a blow.

Rachel moved from her chair, coming forward and standing behind Marion, her hand on Marion's head to protect her.

He looked to Rachel, "I expected more from you. You were supposed to keep her under control."

Rachel spoke calmly and angrily, "It was the Fey, they killed her daughter and now you want to bring them back to the world. She snapped."

Lucas huffed, "The plague killed Margaret, the Fey had nothing to do with it."

Rachel's voice held conviction, "She was convinced it was the Fey that brought the plague. She told me the story of her village, how they had been protected for decades and then, after the summer solstice, when they didn't offer a virgin, the Fey punished them, letting the plague cover the town like ivy."

Lucas ran a weary hand through his hair. "Bring in the coffins."

Guards moved to the doors and opened them, moving aside for the guards who brought the coffins in to the middle of the room. Three humans came in at the end, clanking silver chains piled high in their arms. They threw them into a pile that glinted like jewels in the torch light.

Valerie felt herself relaxing now that she thought she might live to get out of this. Her thighs and arms throbbed, blood rushing back into the clenched muscles.

He looked to Rachel, features hard. "Who was it? Who was stupid enough to give her more power?"

"She already told you."

Lucas waited and Rachel looked like she was going to refuse to answer but Lucas raised his hand, pointing a blood covered finger towards her.

She dropped her eyes and gave a quick nod, rattling off some names before the crowd began talking and moving, pushing some vampires forward to take their punishment.

Lucas beckoned to the coffins and those from the crowd shuffled forwards. There were five of them, two women and three men, and they all climbed into the coffins and laid down without protest.

Two of them beseeched Lucas to be kind to their companion's or kin. Lucas said nothing, watching disinterestedly as the guards nailed the coffins shut and wrapped them in chains.

The heavy coffins were lifted and taken from the room but at the door someone started screaming and a coffin lurched sideways as the woman inside thrashed, trying to get out.

Lucas looked at several people in the audience, the kin and companions of those who'd been taken away. "A century. I will review their punishment then."

The room burst into noise, a woman in the front who was wearing jeans and looked vaguely like a has-been pop star wailed and cried in anguish that the punishment was too harsh, while a few others clasped hands as though relieved that the sentence was not worse.

After a few noisy moments Lucas silenced the audience with a glare and turned back to Rachel and Marion. Rachel had sunk to the floor and was holding Marion against her, letting her cry, Marion's brown curls pressed tight under her chin. Lucas knelt down beside them, his larger form eclipsing theirs.

He held out his hand and Rachel took Marion's limp arm and passed it to Lucas. His head descended and he pierced Marion's wrist, drinking from her in huge draughts. Marion seemed to collapse in on herself, her flesh becoming paler as he drank the power from her.

A great deal of time seemed to pass before he dropped her hand and went back to his throne. He sat down and waited while Marion and Rachel huddled together on the floor.

Marion's hair was dull, her cheeks hollow, the veins in her hands and arms bulging like a famine victim.

"Rachel," Lucas said, deceptively mild.

It took Rachel a few tries to speak. "My Liege."

"Drink from her." Rachel's head snapped up, her gaze finding his. Her brows furrowed together as though confused. Why would Lucas make Rachel stronger if he was going to kill her?

"How much?"

"I will tell you when to cease."

Rachel studied him for a moment before speaking to Marion quietly, "Will you let me, my love?" She petted her face gently.

Marion tilted her head in agreement, exposing her neck. Slowly, she bit down on Marion's jugular, wrapping her arms around the frail body. Marion became more brittle, older, caving in on herself. Her flesh becoming coarser, more wrinkled, she was no longer human. Tears were streaming down Rachel's face and it looked like Marion was dead. How could there be any life left in her? Her skin was already ashy.

"Now, crawl to me," Lucas said in a tone to make the devil proud.

Valerie shivered at the command and bit her lip to try and distract herself. The room waited, looking between the two of them as Rachel slunk forward on hands and knees, all feline grace, her moves almost seductive. She tried not to feel too jealous. Hello, traitor.

Her moves were sinuous as she crawled up the steps. Rachel stared fixedly at Lucas, waiting for him to tell her when she was close enough, her head now level with his knee.

He was like a statue.

Valerie could see Rachel trembling, tears on her lashes as she waited for Lucas to give her some sign of what he expected. She slanted him a quick look under her lashes, but he was still, waiting for her to figure out what she should do next if she wanted to survive.

Hesitantly, she moved forward, her lips going to his shoe. Rachel opened her mouth, her tongue rasping against the soft suede. After a few moments he waved her away and she backed down the stairs, careful to avoid eye contact. Lucas signaled to the guard and another coffin was brought in and placed on the floor.

Rachel flinched but Lucas gestured to Marion, "Put her in it."

Marion looked like a bundle of bones tucked into a dress, half the weight she'd been before. She looked like a bundle of sticks shifting away, too weak to crawl as Rachel approached her.

Rachel reached Marion, touching her lightly on the back, and Marion moaned piteously. Batting at Rachel pathetically. Ignoring her struggles, Rachel leaned down, swung Marion into her arms and subdued her, kissing her face and neck as she walked her to the coffin.

Rachel lowered her down, like putting a child to bed, arranging her arms in the coffin, straightening the crimson skirts. Then she stood, stepping back slightly, tears running down her face. A human moved forward, carrying a hammer and nails.

"No. She will do it," Lucas said.

The human nodded and dropped everything to the floor, backing away with wide eyes. Rachel flinched like she'd been struck and turned a murderous gaze on Lucas.

"Should I just kill her then?"

"No."

Slowly Rachel took the lid to the coffin and placed it on top. She hammered in the nails steadily and when the lid was secure he told her to get the silver chains.

"Wrap the coffin. No gloves," he said, beyond bored.

Rachel went to the chains, looked at them and hesitated. She touched a link, and smoke rose from her hand. Breathing deeply, trembling, she reached out again, grabbing the chain with two hands and rushing to the coffin, throwing it away from her as quickly as she could.

Valerie covered her mouth with her arm, trying to breathe in the smell of her wool coat instead of the stench of burning vampire that was growing stronger each time Rachel touched the chains.

As the minutes passed the vampires became more discomfited, the majority of them not wanting to watch Rachel's flesh sizzle down to the bone. But there was also a sizable minority that watched avidly, absorbing each flicker of Rachel's pain and despair like they were watching a play.

"It doesn't hurt so much when the skin is gone. The bone doesn't burn, don't you find that interesting?" Lucas said to her.

Eyes as wide as saucers, she looked at him, seemingly unable to respond.

Lucas forced her to continue, watching with a dispassionate gaze as she stumbled, trembled and cried.

Finally, the coffin was wrapped.

He stood and Rachel fell to her knees, head bowed to the floor, careful not to let her ruined hands touch anything. "Swear allegiance to me and beg my humble forgiveness."

The words tumbled from her lips, like she wanted to say them before he had a chance to take it back, or before she was sick. Val bet on being sick. *I want to be sick.*

"Marion is alive. Are you pleased?"

Rachel's voice was high and wobbly, "You are a gracious lord and master. I am pleased."

"Do you want to know the conditions for her continued existence?"

Rachel waited, head lowered, unwilling or unable to nod encouragement. "It's you, Rachel. I keep her alive so that I have your loyalty. Fail me and she will never come out of that coffin. It could take her two hundred years to die in there. You don't know the pain and hunger of being trapped in a coffin, young as you are, lenient as I have been. But you see, don't you. That it is a torture?"

Tears splashed onto the floor in front of her. "Yes, my lord. It is a torture."

"Come here so I can tell you how you will please me."

Guards came and grabbed her, hauling her up the steps and dropping her in front of Lucas. Her short hair was tangled and streaked with…everything. Blood, tears, worse. He spoke to her softly but Rachel's face froze in horror at his muffled words.

Straining with all her might, Valerie tried to hear what he said but couldn't. Not completely. The guards came back and picked her up again, dragging her from the hall as Valerie thought about what he might have said. She'd only heard one word clearly: "Roanoke".

CHAPTER 17

PRAGUE, CZECH REPUBLIC

Rachel was carried away and all the vampires filed out of the room, meeting adjourned. The room was empty but for Val and Lucas.

His eyes were closed but he opened them when she approached, looking at her as though surprised she was still in the room. His eyes were sky blue and he seemed tired. That was her guess, anyway.

"You didn't protect me," she said.

"Didn't I?"

"Marion expected you to save me and you didn't. If you had died in this fight, she would have killed me too."

He gave her a condescending smile, "If I had perished you would not have lived. She would have tasted you and known what you were. She'd have used you, bled you over and over again, whoring you out for power and favors until you were dry and broken."

"How flattering. The only reason I'm in danger is because of you."

"Now that is an unusual picture. Jack and your father are just as guilty as I for involving you in our world. Do you not blame them as well?"

Valerie was angry. It was now or never and she was going to be free of him if it killed her. "The difference is that I *love* them. I would die for Jack and he would die for me. I won't do this anymore. You don't really need me anyway. This is some elaborate scheme to get into my... *blood*. It's nothing to do with me as a person, but as a toy for you, the novelty empath."

He raised a finger as though he was going to urge her to be quiet, or make a point and wanted her attention. "Don't pretend to know my motivations. For you or the Others. I want them back. And I want you."

"Whatever. Just let me go. Let me leave and live my life. If you did *actually* care for me then you wouldn't want me involved in this."

"You want me to be unselfish? A vampire is selfishness. We kill so that we can survive, that is the ultimate selfishness."

She changed the subject, looking for more arguments to try to convince him to leave her alone. "I won't be a vampire. I'd rather die. If you changed me I would kill myself at the first opportunity."

Lucas chuckled humorlessly, "It is easy to be righteous when you speak of the unknown. You do not need to persuade me. You may go."

"What's the catch?"

He smiled. A genuine smile that crinkled his eyes and made her think of him as the man he used to be instead of the blood spattered monster sitting on a throne before her.

"I don't need one. Go to Jack. Convince him of your love and the future you will have. When he decides to kill me, come back and beg me for his life. We need discuss nothing until then."

"If he doesn't come after you, will you leave us alone? Let us be together?"

"You are so certain you belong with him? You have been drawn to me from the moment we met. You behave with me as though I am your lover, but that's done with now?"

He was cool and collected, talking to her matter of factly. This was a big deal, a breakup in fact. If he wanted her he should be pleading, shouting, trying to kiss her, geez, *something* to convince her beyond this calm conversation.

She swallowed heavily, not wanting to talk about her relationship with him. "I think you've done a good job putting yourself in my way, don't you? My mom dies from a vampire attack and while you deny it... I think you must have known. You showed up during...formative years. A golden monster who saved my life. Of course I'm drawn to you. But that's not enough. Plus, you wouldn't want anything to do with me if I was a normal girl."

He raised an eyebrow in disagreement but said nothing in his defense. *I need to get out of here.*

"Take me home."

He stood up, looming over her in a way that made her heart pound faster. Frightened and excited at once.

"I've just saved your life."

"Is that what we're calling it? I think you put it in danger—at best it's a wash."

He took a step closer and she backed up.

"I've secured my throne."

"Kudos on that one."

"Would you have missed me had I perished? Did you not think of all the things we might have done together if we had known what fate had in store for us? The sex and passion. Would we have even gone to the ball if we had known we might not have long to live?"

"That's why they say hindsight is twenty-twenty." She could barely get the words out. Focus, desire, the things she'd just said she wanted from him, he was giving her.

"Do you know how many children are born nine months after a victory." It didn't seem like a question. More like a fact, or, big swallow, like a declaration of intent.

I thought vampires couldn't have kids—oh! He wanted to bed her? Now? Here?

By the look on his face, she was thinking the answer was yes. Her breath stuttered in her lungs and she wanted to wrap her legs around him like a monkey.

She wanted to run. She wanted to stay. Her fight or flight response was all fucked up like the compass on a plane, unable to decide which way it's going, right before it crashes into the ocean.

"That's...um...an unusual pick up line, I was not aware of that. It makes sense I suppose." *And even if it sucks you can totally practice on me.*

Because he was a victor and she did feel like he had won. And he was charged after the battle, his body thrumming with lust for her. She could feel it, like an echo of her own.

"What do you feel for me? Is it just lust?"

He looked at her a little oddly, surprised maybe. "Just lust? You say it like lust is a paltry thing, like Cleopatra did not bring down empires because of lust or that fortunes have not been lost over the urgent necessity to make someone their own."

His gaze burned into hers, words quiet and forceful. "You want me to feel more? You want a declaration? Love? I can tell you that I have wanted *nothing* more than you for hundreds upon hundreds of years, that I will kill anyone for you, anyone you can name. In me you have a shield, could have a lover, a friend and a confidant."

His gaze dipped to her neck and it felt like her pulse jumped up to meet him, wanted to feel that hot press of fangs poised at the top of her skin, wanted to dwell in that moment of anticipation just before he would close his mouth, slipping those sharp points into her body.

Would he do it softly? Would it hurt? Or would it be quick and primal? Her nipples pebbled and she actually rubbed her neck, trying to dispel some of the want.

Hundreds upon hundreds of years he said. That would be starring in some of her better fantasies for the rest of her life. But she didn't need fantasies. Here was the real deal. And he was taking her to bed.

He wanted her. Like fiery ants marching across her skin, she could feel how much he wanted her. But, it was like he was waiting for some sign from her.

She crossed her arms, hunching her shoulders, trying to think past the desire for him. She closed her eyes to block him out. *Think.*

"But you wouldn't love me, right?" Man, she'd meant to sound tougher when she said that. Instead of hopeful and desperate. She waited for his answer, like she was standing on a ledge waiting for a small pebble to hit the bottom of the ravine.

It took forever.

She couldn't wait any longer.

He's Lucas. He's a vampire. He doesn't love. He fucks. He kills. He desires.

But she wanted it all. Could he love her? "What if you drank my blood?"

"If I drank your blood would I love you?" He covered his mouth with his hand, fingers pressed to his lips, looking away from her. "I will do what I can to make you happy. Now. Without that." He shook his head. The whole concept seemed so alien to him, like he wasn't even sure he was pronouncing the word 'happy' correctly.

And a tiny part of her was getting angry. Why *wasn't* he just taking her? He'd just conquered! He was a warrior! What was he waiting for? He knew his effect on her. All he had to do was touch her and he could have her.

But he wasn't.

Another man who wants me, but only on their terms.

"Take me back to Jack. To the hotel."

He looked like she'd slapped him.

"To the hotel, I mean." *Smooth, Val.*

He gave her a searching look, like he was trying to read her mind. "I must change first. Come."

Lucas held his hand out to her. It was covered in dried blood. But under it was *him*, and his claim upon her was on such a fundamental level that it was deeper than desire, worse than lust.

Wasn't that the rub? That what she felt for him was...indefinable. And he only felt lust. Was it like lusting after a handbag? A car?

He tried to wrap it up in a pretty package, talking about Cleopatra and what not, but it boiled down to an itch he wanted her to scratch. And he had no interest in loving her, even if it they could have more.

What the fuck was she talking about? What 'more' could they have? The end game wasn't the two of them with 2.5 kids and a dog that barked too much.

He could never give her the simple things that people used to measure a happy life.

A knife twisted in her gut.

His hand was still outstretched and she took it, ignored the fact that it was covered with blood, that by taking his hand the blood of others coated her too, pushed all that aside so she could touch him for just a little bit longer.

I need therapy.

He led her out of the room, down hallways, past people and guards, yet all she could think of was his hand surrounding hers. How he stood close to her, opened the occasional door for her and stood aside so she could enter first.

Guards stood outside his apartments, and he ushered them through.

"I'll need blood." She heard him say quietly and then the door closed behind them.

This was his bedroom.

It was weird. It smelled like him, the faintest hint of his cologne lingering in the air. And there was his bed. It was definitely king size and covered in a heavily embroidered duvet that looked stolen it from a museum.

He groaned and she whirled around. He was lifting his shirt to take it off, the wound open and seeping dark blood.

He really had almost died tonight. That vicious knowledge punched through her, a vision of Lucas disintegrating before her very eyes—she couldn't even think about it.

Val took a step towards him. Screw the consequences or that it was just lust. She needed him in her, imagined her hand clasped around his shaft pressing him deep into her body. He'd pin her to the bed, grab her thigh, wrapping her leg around his waist as he sank home.

The tight breeches clung to his hips, riding low so that she could see the top of his hipbones, the muscles of his stomach and then his chest. The shirt came off and he tossed it aside, watching her.

Waiting for her to make the move.

That froze her. Why wasn't he coming for her? She closed her eyes, straining to pick up on his emotions, trying to sort them out. It was like taking stones out of a bag, examine it then put it back, pick out another one and figure out what it was. She felt his desire, his triumph and the one that was the brightest: his restraint.

He wanted her to come to him. Covered in blood and fresh from murder, showing her just how alien he was, he wanted her to choose him. And he was in control enough to wait for her to do it. She knew his emotions, had his blood, but they were weak, like the last beating flutters of one's heart before death. Any urgency for this moment was hers.

She opened her eyes and his gaze scorched her. His resolve wavered, desire for her so thick and heavy it was like she could touch it, hold it in her hands like hot sand.

Now he's going to drink me.

He shook his head.

Fuck, I'm transparent. She looked down his body again, unable to help herself, knowing he'd see it, maybe even gloat over the fact that she had to look again. She loved the way his arms had bulged as he tossed the shirt away from him, how he'd discarded the piece of material like it was an impediment from reaching her.

His skin could be naked against hers right now.

Step forward.

Close that distance.

She wanted to—why wasn't she?

There was a knock on the door and he turned, going to it, the broad expanse of his back and shoulders more pale perfection. The two little divots on his lower back, perfect for her fingers to press into.

He was at the door, but he didn't open it, just leaned his head against it before inhaling. "At least try to shield. I suppose I asked for this misery"

He opened the door and reached through, keeping his back to her as he took something from outside the door. She saw his head go back a little, very faintly heard him swallow. She stepped to the side to see what he was doing. He handed an empty glass back outside the door. It had been a pint glass and he'd drained it, handing it back empty, bright red blood clinging to the sides of it, looking like stained glass.

He turned back towards her, door closed, not a speck of blood at the corners of his mouth or anything. But at least she didn't want to kiss him anymore. Yuck.

"You don't drink straight from the source?" Pathetic attempt at distraction.

The wound at his side was healing before her eyes, closing up, new skin spreading over him. "Make yourself at ease. I shall shower and return. Then take you to your room."

Take you to Jack was what he hadn't said. It clearly galled him.

He walked towards her purposefully, almost stalking her, both hands undoing the buttons of his breeches slowly, letting her see each shift of his fingers, as he came closer and closer. And he was arrogant; the set of his shoulders, the challenge in his eyes almost telling her that he knew she wouldn't look away. *That she couldn't look away.*

God, she wanted him. And then he walked past her and she heard the water turn on.

She sat down hard and tried to remember what her game plan was. Go home? Some dude, what was his name? Oh, yeah. Jack.

Jack.

She fell backwards and stared at the ceiling, belatedly realizing that she was lying on Lucas' bed. She turned her head, looking at the pillows. Which side did he sleep on? A book was on the side closest to the door and she guessed that was his side. What did a guy like Lucas read?

She climbed across his bed, wanting to see the book. *If it's 'Men Are From Mars and Women Are From Venus, maybe I'll stay. If it's the 'Kama Sutra' made out of wood cuts, I'll stay too.*

'The Tipping Point', by Malcolm Gladwell. There was a match on the front and it said, 'how little things can make a big difference'. Huh. It was like social psychology. What the hell did she make of that?

She touched his pillow, about to bend down and—*oh shit*.

She was actually going to sniff his pillow when she heard the water shut off. *Thank god I avoided that little sign of desperation.*

She dashed over to the fireplace instead, sitting in a chair, looking blankly at his shelves of hard bound books.

Probably not a Kindle kind of guy.

Just a guess.

She heard water again and turned, seeing Lucas wearing only a towel and brushing his teeth. That had to help. And then...mouthwash.

He was going to kiss her.

Big sigh.

And she was going to let him. *I mean, really. Like I could stop him now.* If she had one wish, right now, it would be for a chastity belt. Please, please don't sleep with him.

He came out of the bathroom—hair damp, drops of water clinging to his shoulders and chest. *Jesus.*

She wanted him to come to her, pick her up and lay her down on his bed, loom over her and kiss her, cover her with his body. Electricity and desire pushed through her, making her clothes feel too tight, her body sensitive and open, waiting for his touch.

Then she remembered his hand pulling out a heart before her eyes.

"You're underdressed," she said. *Up here, Val. Look at his face!* Well, at least she knew he wanted her too. She could see his erection under the towel, heavy and huge, pressed flat against his stomach.

"You want me to take you to him?"

"What?" Look. UP.

She bit her lip so she didn't say, 'No I don't want to go to Jack, I want to stay here with you and fuck you until neither one of us can walk out of this room.'

And if he'd just come grab her, she'd do it. Put aside all of her concerns and give in.

She had an awful idea. A way to sleep with him, stay with him and know how much he really cared for her.

Val stood and looked down at her shirt. It was bloody too. *Go figure.* She lifted her hands to the buttons, undoing the top one and advancing towards him slowly. Her breath was overly loud in her ears, the room totally quiet and now she could smell him, soap and shampoo, that faint lovely humidity of warm, clean skin.

His jaw clenched so tight that his cheekbones were in stark relief. Another button undone. Lucas crossed his arms over his chest, stance a little wider. Knuckles white because his fists were clenched so tight.

She unbuttoned another button, becoming flustered and uncertain. Why hadn't he looked at her?

"Tell me, then."

She hesitated, nonplussed.

"You thought of something you want. Yes? It accounts for your sudden change of heart. Your purpose in disrobing."

His words were quiet but intense, like there was anger under there. Or lust. Some hot emotion.

"You said you'd kill anyone for me." Her voice was raspy.

He didn't say anything. All the buttons were undone and there was a slight gap in the material. Her heart pounded from her boldness. She grasped both sides, ready to take it off, panic making her want to pull the shirt tight. She wasn't brave enough for this. Especially as he still wasn't looking!

"Stop. Who? Tell me who *first*." He held out a hand, like he was keeping the bogeyman away.

She swallowed. Pulled the shirt free, let it drop behind her. Her bra was gray silk with white lace, not the most enticing bra around but her cup runneth over, so why wasn't he looking?

Maybe he isn't a breast guy.

Maybe he'd seen so many pairs over the centuries that he was indifferent or she was just too far down the line of nice chests that he couldn't be bothered to take a peek. Her stomach hit the floor and she wanted to puke.

She hadn't been able to look away, could only think of touching him when he undressed before her, and here she was undressing, the situation reversed and he was totally unmoved.

She felt herself blushing.

He closed his eyes. "Give me the name."

"You won't do it. This was stupid."

"Again, you prove how little you know of me. Tell me who," he commanded.

"Marion." She rushed in, speaking before he could. "You said you want me, lust after me, talk about how you'd do anything for me. That's what I want. I want her dead."

His eyes were still closed. One hand fisted at his side, showing each muscle definitively. The other went behind his head, buried in his hair as he hauled in a breath.

"I need her. Choose something else." He looked at the ceiling, opening his eyes but not looking at her.

"No. I want that bitch dead." Just saying it felt right. Like sunshine after rain.

He covered his face with both hands, talking to her through his hands. "I need Rachel to get to the Fey. My hold upon her is Marion. Choose *anything* else."

Her chest hurt. All his words and they meant nothing. Lucas talked a good game, but when she made a demand, he never gave her what she wanted. She'd almost died tonight because of Marion. She'd murdered Jack's parents.

Killing Marion would give her peace. Like he couldn't come up with some other way to ensure Rachel's loyalty. She'd looked pretty damned loyal when her skin was fried off and she licked his foot.

Lucas wasn't good, he was the monster who'd sanctioned Marion's killings for years.

She pushed him hard. He moved backwards and she shoved again, as hard as she could. His head snapped down, staring at her chest, her shoulders, her stomach. *Now he looks*.

His look was so dark and possessive....*Oops. Okay, he does want me.* "No. Marion. Kill her. Rachel doesn't need to know. The threat works whether she's dead or alive."

His hands raised to her bare upper arms, settling on them lightly, thumbs moving slowly over her flesh. He raised gooseflesh on her skin, the tiny contact making her clench her thighs in need. His gaze was fixed on her chest and neck. Then the line of her shoulder where it connected to her neck.

His voice was hoarse, "And what? I say yes, kill her and you...give yourself to me once? For a night? Then go back to *him*?" It was like he couldn't say Jack's name, like jealousy would choke the letters in his lungs.

Good.

She nodded jerkily, a lump in her throat.

His eyes finally met hers. "I'm afraid not."

Her heart plummeted. *He rejected me.*

"That is all, then? I say no to that and now you take away the chance to be in your bed?" He swore in a language she didn't understand and walked away from her, opening a closet door and disappearing inside. Val grabbed her shirt and put it on, buttoning it with shaking fingers.

Why was she even so upset? Because Marion was still alive? Because she'd wanted Marion's death for Jack and hadn't gotten it? Yeah, that worked.

Good reason.

But there were more. It was like every kiss, every caress, every touch had been a lie. She had been fascinated by him from the moment she met him. And he wanted her because she was an empath, a novelty. He wanted sex and he wanted her to initiate it.

She looked up at him as he came out and blinked hard, surprised to find she'd been on the verge of crying. How could she be so conflicted about him? So sure of his desire one moment and then ignorant the next?

He came towards her and she felt exposed and stupid. Like a child who'd tried to play grown up in her mommy's clothes and tripped. His hands cupped her face and he leaned down, kissing her very gently on the lips.

"After the Fey, ask me again. I *swear* to you that you can have her then. Even...Jack can kill her. If that is what you want. But not now."

She jerked away from him. "*Bullshit.* Don't lie to me. Don't give me words. Give me actions. I feel like everything you've told me was a lie. Everything you've done for me has been at your convenience and cost you *nothing.*"

He followed her, stalking her into the wall. Finally, a display of emotion.

We've been here before.

His accent was thick, the words guttural, "I will give you more words and you will listen to them. You heed me well, my Valkyrie, I will take you home now and you *will* come back to me. And when you do *this* changes. You will be mine. You will be in my bed and you will give in to me. Let there be no misunderstandings between us. You talk of cost and say it has cost me nothing." He looked away from her, to the wall and then back, like he'd fortified himself for his next words. He opened his mouth to say something, but then stopped. Swallowed.

Finally at a loss for words?

He pulled her to him and she felt them disappear, the cold wind swirling around her as he took her back to her hotel room in Italy. He was angry at her now, just as ready to be rid of her as she was of him. Then they were in her room.

Lucas straightened, like he was on the alert.

What? Is someone here?

She was going to turn, see what he saw but he cupped her face in his, leaned down to kiss her. "One last kiss until next time. And next time...we make it to the bed."

His words shivered over her, slightly loud in her ears, like he wanted to make sure she really heard him. His lips touched hers. Soft and still warm from the shower opening over her mouth and she leaned into him, stood on tiptoes and wiggled her hips closer to his, felt his erection against her stomach and tried to press closer. Yes, this was what she'd wanted.

His tongue slid against hers, the taste of him, the magic of his touch making every argument and problem fade away. Only desire was left. "I need you," she gasped out and for the briefest moment he paused, his lips sliding down her throat.

"Your timing is horrific," he said, panting the words out as he placed kisses all over the column of her throat.

She moaned, his hands skating down her back, gripping her buttocks and raising her, pressing his cock against her harder. She cried out and he caught the noise in his mouth like he was going to drink it down.

And then he pulled back, coming up for air like a fish out of water, blinking then looking especially pleased with himself.

Smug bastard.

He touched her cheek with the back of his hand then stroked her neck with his index finger, pausing just over her pulse, tapping her jugular lightly. And it felt like a promise, like he was saying without words—*next time I'll bite you here.*

Why the hell was he doing that? And what did he mean about the bed? She was confused, but he vanished before she could ask him what the tap was about.

Her hotel room was just as she had left it. The magazine Marion had thrown at the wall still on the ground.

As soon as he was gone her room felt bigger.

She needed another shower. Val stripped off her coat and turned towards the bathroom, only to stop when she saw a lean figure leaning against the door-jam; arms folded, expression thunderous. His eyes were black, his face gaunt as though he'd been up all night waiting for her.

"Jack."

Made in the USA
San Bernardino, CA
16 December 2015